FELON ATTORNEY

TheArthur A. Duncan II, Esq.

MASCOT® BOOKS

Thanks to:

My wife Tisha, thanks for being my best friend and mother to my kids. Over the years our union has grown stronger and stronger and no matter what we go through, we put god first and we work through it. Thank you for the "house and picket fence" dream too; that I never believed in until it included you. Lastly, thank you for the time and support to go after my dream to become an attorney and now an author. Love you, babe!

My kids Frankie, Joi, Isaiah, Lauren and Kimanie, thanks for letting Daddy realize his dreams so he can be a father you guys can be proud of.

Mom, thanks for the support through all my foolishness. I'm glad that I finally made you proud.

Dad (Brenda), thanks for being there when I needed you and for all your advice, wisdom and support.

Reverend James and Mary Smith (my grandparents), thanks for being the greatest two people I will ever know. I will love y'all to eternity and your memories will forever live on in my heart.

Ray (Sherri), thanks, homey, for being a friend, a mentor, a colleague, and for your inspiration and for being Godparents to my baby, Lauren.

Roy Jr, Uncle Juney (Jean), thanks for being Great Men to look up to and for all the help and all the support. Thanks for expecting more from me and not giving up.

Dr. Grabiner, thanks for all your support and your assistance from the very start; without you I may not have chosen this path.

Gin, Gin, Lavette, Gladys, Rah, Tasha, Grandma Helen, Nana (Deb) and all my family, friends and My First Calvary Missionary Baptist Church family, thanks for the support and love.

Jeanette Ogden, thanks for giving me an opportunity and for all your help and words of wisdom.

Crystal Peoples-Stokes, thanks for the support.

Pastor Jason Drayton (First Lady Janis), thanks for your prayers, your words of encouragement, leadership and friendship.

Shark, what up Big Homie? Thanks for being there for me through it all. See you soon!

Shout out to my UB Law School classmates (especially the class of 2012) and Cleveland Marshall Law School.

One love to my ol' crew, Shumway and Peckham: Dogg, Dune, Mike, Duck, Malik, Wayno, Shark, Bama and Dap.

Rest in Peace:

My grandparents Mr. and Mrs. Reverend James V. Smith and Mary Jane Smith, Timothy Thompson (Dogg), Lawan Jenkins (Dap), Patrick Bush (Petey), Leon White, Regina Mimms (Mama Gina), Dexter McDuffie (Lil Dex), Andre Thompson (Flip), Vinny Thaddison, Jamel January, Cornel Williams (Cephas), Marco McCarley, Willie Anderson (Poppa Willie), Tiffany Wilhite, Lolo, Danyell Mackin and Jimmy Prude.

www.mascotbooks.com

FELON-ATTORNEY

TheArthur A. Duncan II, Esq.

Foreword

Tone—TheArthur, Esq. (the author)—is an extraordinary individual! Hence, I really enjoyed this book which contains one of the most interesting life stories ever known. After reading the first word of Chapter 1, you will not want to stop until reading the last word of Chapter 20. Be prepared to wipe your eyes quite often while experiencing the full spectrum of emotions. For example, due to the Author's keen sense of humor, portions of this book should trigger intense laughter resulting in your eyes watering uncontrollably. On the other hand, more serious accounts in this book should prompt you to shed tears of joy as well as tears of sorrow. Furthermore, the suspense element of this book will undoubtedly capture your attention. Accordingly, you will be eagerly interested to read more and more in order to learn how the Author somehow managed to survive situation after situation during his incredible journey from the block (as a thug on the rough streets of Buffalo, New York) to the courtroom (as a litigation attorney).

It is noteworthy to explain the significance of the punctuation mark I have strategically placed between the Author's nickname and his given name. The hyphen (-), which can be used generally to connect the bad and the good in all of us, is applied here as the transitional character that signifies how far he has come in life.

About 12 years prior to the triggering event discussed below, I had escaped my hometown of Buffalo, New York to eventually land in the Washington, DC area. While driving to a social gathering one evening, my cousin Chris stated from the passenger seat that the Author was home from federal prison and needed to speak with me about law school. Déjà vu was the initial thought, due to my intimate familiarity with this scenario (i.e., a man survives every imaginable ill of inner-city living to turn his life completely around). So, of course the matter captured my attention.

Over the years, several people sought me out for advice after their release from jail or prison. I have always been willing to listen. However, as an attorney, time is my stock-in-trade (money). In keeping it real (being direct and honest), I don't have any of either to waste. Unfortunately, the majority of those types of conversations were relatively short because they did not quickly prove to be fruitful. With that in mind, at my request, Chris called the Author for what I thought would be a short conversation. I was wrong. We had arrived at our destination around 15 minutes after the call started. We then sat in my car for another 45 minutes or so for me to finish the call. Hence, that initial telephone conversation lasted about an hour!

The Author and I spent the first few minutes of the call laughing and reminiscing. However, the conversation soon turned serious with a focus on his future. He started telling me about all of the progress made in the relatively short time since his release (e.g., reconnected with God, got married, extended their family). After learning that he had also re-enrolled in college and was in his last semester, I asked: "Why did you wait so long before contacting me about law school?" I cannot remember the exact words, but the gist of his response was: I know how you get down (operate), and realized that I had to bring something to the table for you to take me serious. His comment sent a chill down my spine. I then let out my customary chuckle, while thinking to myself: Perhaps he is telling the truth! But, that was just the beginning of my analysis.

I socialize with many, yet bond with few. Hence, my circle has always been tight. In other words, I am particular about my affiliates, which is a very small group of carefully selected individuals. Accordingly, before starting what would become a very close friendship with the Author, I initiated the screening process (i.e., an internal thought-discussion involving a series of questions and answers):

Who is he? I don't really know him. However, Chris co-signed for (endorsed) him and he is Black's childhood friend. Black and I were acquainted through the respective Rap record labels we had launched around the same time.

When, where and how did we meet and interact? We don't have any meaningful history. During our adolescent years, we occasionally played basketball together at various recreational centers and parks. As young men, our paths crossed sparingly in the streets. In the night clubs, for example, we would rhetorically ask each other "what up?" in a friendly tone or exchange head-nods coupled with a chuckle from across the room, then keep it moving (walk or look away). Those customary gestures are simple, yet effective, displays of mutual respect utilized by unfamiliar individuals who don't have much to discuss.

What kind of person is he? All indicators suggest that he manned-up (took full responsibility for his illegal actions) and did his bid (served his federal prison sentence). In other words, I have NEVER heard any rumors of him assuming the risk of illegitimate activities only to transfer the consequences for others to pay the price after he got knocked/caught (i.e., snitching)! This is of the utmost importance to me and would have been a deal-breaker (the deciding factor) because, otherwise, I simply would not be able to trust him. Furthermore, he seems to be a good and God-fearing man as well as a great father, husband and friend.

Why should I help him? I am now convinced that: i) if the tables were turned so that instead I was seeking his assistance, then he would do the same for me; and ii) once established, he will do the same good deed for others in need (i.e., "give back").

After serious thought and careful consideration, I decided to go all-in by doing everything in my power to help the Author realize his dream of becoming a successful attorney. Over the past 8+ years, I have spent countless hours on his project (e.g., LSAT preparation, law school applications, law school exams, Bar application, Bar exam, character and fitness requirements, career advice, New York State Certificate of Relief process, Presidential Pardon research). Unlike many others, I never wavered in my belief that he would succeed. In exchange, every step along the way, I have routinely received sincere expressions of gratitude and appreciation. Those small, yet considerate, gestures speak volumes about the Author's good nature, which confirms that I came to the correct conclusion about him.

Please note that I have also benefited tremendously from the

Author's project:

Company. At the outset, I told him: "I need company!" The point is that I now have the companionship of someone who can also relate to the dichotomy of being situated between two contrasting, yet relative, worlds (i.e., the streets and the legal profession).

a-Tone-ment. In an effort to save my soul, about 20 years ago, my girlfriend (now wife) and I left our hometown of Buffalo, New York to explore options. Since becoming an attorney, I had been burdened by the guilt associated with not returning home permanently. The Author's project provided me with the perfect opportunity to "give back" to that community.

Best Friends for Life. It was inevitable for two good men cut from the same cloth (have a lot in common), after spending so much time together, to become the best of friends. Additionally, our spouses and children have also become life-long friends. Not to mention that my wife and I even got a beautiful Goddaughter (Lea) out of the deal.

In closing, as I have, my prediction is that you will learn a lot from this interesting book. Enjoy!

Boo-Ray, Esq.
May 2015

Preface

Upon hearing about my life, family members, friends, and acquaintances all tell me I've got a story to tell. Well, here it is! And you don't know the half of it. This book is based on my life story, evolving events, and people I came in contact with along the way. Please keep in mind that I am giving my opinions and perceptions of events back when they happened. As my story unfolds, you will see my maturation and the changes in my way of thinking.

I reveal a lot of negative things about myself. I am in no way proud of the things I did but I hope that my past serves as a testimony to much of what I overcame. Most of the things that happened to me were self-inflicted by the bad choices I made, so I cannot blame anybody but myself. Having grown up in a pastor's house, I should've known better. Also, I want to apologize to anyone I unintentionally offend in this book by revisiting bad or hurtful memories. Remember, that past was part of my reality, too.

It took me about three years to complete this book. I had started to convey my personal journal and when my dad discovered it, he encouraged me to finish. I would like to give a special thanks to him for his time and help on this project.

I am so blessed to have the opportunity to write my story. It is my hope that many will learn from my mistakes and be inspired by what I eventually accomplished. It is only by God's grace that I am still alive. I had several chances to turn my life around, and I eventually succeeded. Thank God! He never left my side through the gang violence in South Central Los Angeles or back in Buffalo, New York selling drugs. He kept a watchful eye over me through the fighting, drug transactions, unfaithfulness, family turmoil, loss of friends, impending incarceration, time in a halfway home, death, love, learning, and so much more. I am truly blessed in spite of it all!

Introduction

As we pulled up to a bar around nine o'clock at night, I knew something very bad was about to happen. I was going to jail, about to get robbed, about to get shot, or get killed--or all the above. My man Black, whom I always got my product from, was in jail, so I was on my own. I had been without any crack to sell for two weeks and I was losing a lot of money and customers. *Something gotta give*, I thought to myself. I ran into my god brother Mitch and told him my dilemma. He told me that his man "Q" had connections that could help. I had no idea of what I had to go through to get it. Here I was unarmed with Q and Mitch outside of a bar notorious for drug trafficking with $10,000 and a scale trying to buy some drugs. The bar was also situated right across the street from some crime-infested housing projects, which added to my uneasiness. At the time, the Lower Westside of Buffalo was like New York City for hustlers trying to buy big quantities of drugs. There were a lot of Puerto Ricans,

Dominicans, Columbians, and even some Cubans there hustling and the bar was where a lot of them hung out.

We parked the car and Q went in the bar to see if he could find his connect. It was a hot summer night, so a lot of people were outside hanging out. Cars were pulling up and stopping in the middle of the street. I could hear loud salsa music coming from inside the bar as people were going in and out. The whole scene was out of control.

I could feel my heart beating. My hands were shaking and I began to sweat heavily. I was nervous as hell, but I could not let Mitch know it. After all, I was the street hustler, not him. I knew if I lost my cool, this whole situation could turn bad. As I looked around, I noticed the guys hustling on the corner starting to stare at us. One of them yelled out something in Spanish and pointed towards us. I was ready to go. I knew it was only a matter of time before they would approach us. Mitch and I sat there in the car for about five minutes waiting for Q to come out the bar but it seemed more like an hour.

Finally, Q exited the bar with two guys and came over to the car and said that it would be about 10 minutes. One of the guys he came out with told one of the guys on the corner to come with him. After that, the dudes on the corner stopped looking over at us and left us alone. I kept checking my watch, and after 10 minutes had passed, I turned to Q and nervously said, "Where ya man at? It's been 10 minutes already."

Then seemingly out of nowhere, I noticed the three dudes walking back in our direction. One of the guys shook Q's hand and got into the backseat of the car to hand me a bag. I opened the bag and looked at the product. Inside was a big, clear Ziploc bag containing a hard yellowish substance. I pulled it out the bag and tried to break the product to see how hard it was and then I smelled it. So far, so good. I had been hustling so long that I could tell the quality by the look, hardness, and smell.

I pulled out my little digital scale and put it on the floor of the car. "Yo, I need to break it up into two. My scale only weighs 150 grams at a time," I told the kid.

"Go 'head, Papi it's all there," he responded.

One of the guys he walked up with was standing on the sidewalk near our car making sure everything was alright. He had a hoodie on and kept his hands in the front pouch. He looked like he would murder someone at the drop of a hat. He started talking in Spanish to the guys hustling on the corner. I knew that if anything went wrong, we would all probably be dead. I proceeded to weigh the rest of the crack, put it back in the bag, and then handed the kid the money. He counted it, nodded his head at his man outside, and got out the car to go back into the bar.

Now, I'm ready to go, but Q said he had to go back into the bar. I knew what time it was; he wanted to get a cut. So I said, "Yo, son I got you. I'm going to take care of you."

"Naw, it ain't that," he said. "I'll be right back. I forgot something."

I turned to Mitch. "Yo, ya man is bullshitting. Let's go!"

"Hold on," he responded.

Now we're sitting on this hot ass corner with a scale and damn near a half key of crack. Just then, we heard some commotion coming from the bar and saw Q coming out fighting some dude.

"Oh fuck! Yo, Mitch, pull off!" I hollered. "Leave that muthafucka!"

Mitch said no and jumped out the car to help him. I grabbed my book bag and was about to get out the car, and start walking when Q came running over to the car chased by a crowd. He jumped in and Mitch peeled off.

Damn! I thought, *It's gotta be a better way!*

As I thought about it, I could not believe I had put myself in that type of predicament. Moreover, I could not believe I came back to

Buffalo and had become a drug dealer after everything my family had gone through in Los Angeles because of drugs. After all that misery, hurt, and pain, I dared to sell the same shit that ruined my family's life in LA. Even more so, I could not believe I was living this dangerous street life after narrowly escaping all the gang violence in LA. I begin to ponder it all.

Chapter 1

Los Angeles: A Whole New World

I went back to Cali in 1984, when gang violence in Los Angeles was at its peak, a few years before the movie *Colors* came out. *Colors* gave the nation a small insight on gang violence in LA and how bad it was. I say "back" because I was born in LA but primarily raised in Buffalo, NY.

After I graduated from the eighth grade in Buffalo, I decided to go back to LA and live with my mother, my little brother, and my little brother's father, who also lived in the same household. I also wanted to get to know my father better, whom I had spent time with when I was younger. I had occasionally talked to him on the phone the past four years while living and going to school in Buffalo. My mother left Buffalo and moved to LA and had me when she was 23. Most of the rest of my family on my mother's side all lived in Buffalo. I had established a close relationship with them by going back and forth from LA to Buffalo from ages 5 to 9, until I eventually stayed in Buffalo with my grandparents.

In the LA area, we lived in Inglewood at 97th and Crenshaw. For those unfamiliar with this part of Los Angeles, Inglewood is adjacent to and commonly considered part of South Central LA, which became infamous because of the LA riots. Moving there was a big adjustment for me.

Sadly, I had left all my friends back in Buffalo. Before I left, the Randy Smith basketball league up at Humboldt Park had just started. I had only played one game, which we had lost by two points. I was playing for the JFK Center 8-12 team, although I was really 13. We forged my baptism certificate so I could play. Yep, at the ages of 12 and 13 we had skills! We had a good squad: my man Black, AO, and Ray C. Ray C was nice with the rock and probably would have wound up going pro if he hadn't gotten into trouble later.

For those outside of Buffalo, Rochester, Syracuse, NYC, and probably Cleveland and Erie, Pa., the Randy Smith Summer Basketball League back in the 80s was ranked third in the country behind the Rucker's basketball league in New York City and some other league in Chicago. It had an 8-12 division, 13-15, 16-18, and Unlimited. The Unlimited division was off the hook, to say the least, and full of Buffalo's best players and playground legends with nicknames like Wiggles, Shakes, Dunkin Hines, Ice Black, Stew Beef, Sugar Ray, Saint, Big Woodlard, Hutch, The Beard Brothers, Socks, Chaney, Soup, and Big Ed, just to name a few. Teams that participated were sponsored by local black business like The Peppermint Lounge, The Cotton Club, Love Thang, Pratt Moore Liquor, and Mattie's Texas Hots.

When I went back to LA I didn't know anybody, and everything in LA being so spread out added to my uneasiness. In Buffalo I was from a neighborhood called Sperry Park in the downtown area of

Buffalo where we all knew each other and everybody's parents and families knew your family. Now, I was out here in Cali without a friend in the world. And to make matters worse, I was light in the ass. I was about 5'9" and 130 pounds soakin' wet at the time. In hindsight, there was no way I should have taken my ass back to LA at age 14 to be in the midst of all that Crips and Bloods gang shit, but I was later to find out that the gangs in LA would be the least of my problems.

Out in Cali at age 14 with no friends, I just concentrated on basketball. My father stayed in good shape and jogged every evening after work, so he would come by and get me and sometime his other son, my brother Marcel, so I could play ball and we could all spend time together. My dad lived in West Los Angeles bordering Culver City, so he had to drive all the way to Inglewood to pick me up, which took about 30 minutes depending on the traffic. We would go to Rancho Park on Coliseum near La Brea, right next to Dorsey High and across from the infamous "Jungle" in South Central. The "Jungle" was later made known to people outside of LA by the *Training Day* movie with Denzel.

Originally, I was only going out to LA to visit for the summer, but I wound up staying. Once I was out there around my mom and little brother Ronny and started spending time with my dad, I decided to stay. I did not want to leave my grandparents because I loved them dearly, but there's nothing like your own mom and dad. My mother had always told me how I looked, laughed, and acted like my dad, which piqued my curiosity. After all, my dad was big Tony and I was lil' Tony. Although I missed everyone back in Buffalo and didn't really care for LA that much, I stayed to be around my parents. I had a dad I could talk sports with and go to the park with and a mother here for protection and love. Yeah, it was time for me to stay in Cali. Besides that, I was a Lakers fan and we lived in Inglewood right around the corner from the Forum where they played during the Magic-Worthy-Kareem Championship Era.

For my ninth grade year my father enrolled me in Palms Jr. High School up the street from his apartment in West Los Angeles. Every morning he drove about a half hour to pick me up in Inglewood to take me to school. Three days during the week I walked to his apartment after school and he took me home. Because of my dad's work schedule, the other two days I had to catch the Venice street bus to Crenshaw and then catch the Crenshaw bus home. This trip took about one to two hours venturing through dozens of gang neighborhoods.

If I recall correctly, the intersection of Venice and Crenshaw is probably around 12th Street and Crenshaw Boulevard, and I had to travel to 97th Street and Crenshaw. If you're familiar with gangs in LA, you know that a lot of a gangs' identity are based on the street or number block they are from, e.g., Rollin 20s, 30s, 60s, etc. Well, the 20s were the Bloods, 30s the Crips, I think the 40s were Crips, 50s Bloods, 60s Crips, and so on.

So there I was on the Crenshaw bus by myself going through all these neighborhoods. I know the Lord was with me because even as I write I cannot see how I survived. I saw people get stabbed, thrown off the bus, jumped, and chains snatched. I knew sooner or later someone would mess with me on the bus, and unfortunately the next year my luck ran out.

Now, my life at home with my mother, brother, and my brother's father Jimmy was okay. Plus, my mother's sister and her daughter Val lived across the hall from us and we were constantly going back and forth between apartments. My brother's father, coincidentally, was from Buffalo too. I saw a lot of that. People moved away from home and wound up dating someone from back home. I guess because they have something in common. Anyway, he was cool at first. He thought he was an old school player. He used to rock the Jean

Applejack Hat with mad colors and drove a Mark IV Lincoln back in the day. He had a mean album collection. He mostly collected jazz albums, records like Grover Washington Jr. and Herbie Hancock. He also had an extensive video tape collection of all these old movies like *El Cid* and *The Spartans*. Jimmy was a diehard sports fan and when his teams lost he would be pissed. I mean he would be so pissed you couldn't even talk to him. But when his teams won he was as happy as could be.

Jimmy used to have his co-workers over to drink beer and smoke joints. Even though I was raised by my grandfather, who was a pastor, I knew about weed because my older cousins smoked it. Well, I don't know if marijuana was a gateway drug for Jimmy, who introduced him to it, or whether it was just inevitable, but he decided to take his getting high to the next level.

One day when I came home from playing ball, Jimmy was watching the game with company, or so I thought. I glanced in the room and saw alcohol, cotton swabs, candles, glass pipes, and a white powdery substance on the living room table.

The year was 1983. Cocaine (free-basing) and the drug epidemic it had created was about to tear my life apart in Cali. Many of us have seen the negative effects of cocaine on society; the drug addictions, the job loss, the breaking up of families, incarcerations, violence, and deaths. Later on in life I would experience almost all of it because of cocaine, and that moment was my introduction.

My brother's father had a ritual of drinking a few beers when he got his weekly check from work. He would give my mom money for bills and he would even throw me and my little brother, who was about eight at the time, a couple of bucks for our pockets. He would get drunk on malt liquor and keep everybody up all night talking sports. With his newfound drug he followed the same ritual but added a new step that would become detrimental to our household and well-being. He would drink a few beers on payday, smoke a little weed, and then he would leave and not come back until the middle of the night.

When he did come back, all hell would break loose. "Where's the money?!" he would shout at my mother in their bedroom. The arguing back and forth with my mother would wake me and my little brother. I feared for my mother's safety as I left my room and stood in the hallway. First, he would ask my mom for the money he gave her for bills. If she refused, he would just start going through her purse and take what he could find. Then he'd come and take back the money he gave me and my brother. I remember the glassy-eyed look on his face; he looked like he was possessed by a demon.

Oh, I think I forgot to mention that Jimmy was about 6' 4", and weighed about 260 pounds at the time. He had this big beard that he used to comb with a pick and when he started to get high it would be wild and almost cover his whole face. Well, anyway, he would leave again and come back in another hour or so in a rage and demand more money from my mom. Shortly thereafter, my mother hid her money and told him it was in the bank when he would start these episodes. He started to never go to work the day after payday, and it eventually got him fired. Also, I began to see his album and video collection diminishing down to nothing.

One day I came home from school and the VCR in the living room was gone. This was back in the day when a VCR was big and expensive, costing around a thousand dollars. I felt so angry; I didn't know what to say or do. My brother's father would later apologize. My mother would replace the VCR and he would give her money towards it and the bills when he got paid. But I think you already know where this is going. He would start his payday ritual again and take back all his good deeds and money and eventually steal the VCR again and pawn it for cocaine.

Then when my brother and I were at school and my mother at work, he would start selling his album collection and his videotapes. My brother and I had our own small VCR in our room and I had old videotapes of players such as Jordan, Pearl Washington, James Worthy, Patrick Ewing, Clyde Dressler, and Dominique Wilkins in college. My brother's father told my mom he would never steal from the kids, but eventually that changed too.

Summertime came and my mother took her yearly vacation to Buffalo to visit my grandparents, taking my lil' brother Ronny with her. I was playing in a park basketball league and didn't want to miss the playoffs, so I stayed an extra week at home. I also stayed because I didn't trust my brother's father. In hindsight, and regardless of my noble intention, I could not stop him from stealing our stuff. My dad even got angry at me because I did not stay with him while my mother was vacationing, but I just felt like Jimmy would not take our stuff right in my face. Sadly, he did not care about my presence, and the night after my mother left, he ran in and out of our apartment selling whatever he could get his hands on for cocaine. I told my aunt what was going on and she told me to just stay at her apartment until I left for Buffalo. She also called my mother in Buffalo and told her what was going on. My mother wasn't surprised and probably expected it. What could she do 3,000 miles away?

When my mother, Ronny, and I got back from Buffalo a couple weeks later, our apartment was bare of anything of any value. Ronny was 8 years old at the time and asked a lot of questions.

"Where's the TV and VCR?"

"Where's all my dad's records and videotapes?"

"And where's my dad?" he continued as he began to cry.

My mother was very upset too and went in her room and shut the door. I knew she was in there crying. I didn't want to see her cry, so I left her alone until she came out. I asked her if she was going to put Jimmy out and she said yeah, she didn't have choice.

We didn't see Jimmy until Friday, a couple days later. He called before he came over and my mother agreed to let him back in if he replaced everything he stole. He got paid that day and gave my mother some money for the things he had taken. He apologized to us and swore that he'd never do it again and would stop doing drugs. *Yeah right,* I thought to myself.

When I had elected to stay with Jimmy, I did not intend to get my dad upset and I surely was not choosing my brother's father over my own. I am definitely my father's son without question and was given his namesake for a reason. My dad is from a very small town in Missouri named Poplar Bluff and grew up in a household with 12 brothers and sisters. My grandparents had three sets of twins, and my father and his twin brother were one set. He used to tell me there were times where if you didn't get to the dinner table in time, you did not eat very much. As my father's siblings got older and left home, most of them settled in Chicago while my dad and a couple others went to Cali.

My dad was real cool, laid back, very intelligent, and joked a lot. He talked a little shit too when he interacted with friends. Like I said before, as I describe my dad it's like describing me. I could tell he thought he was a player back in the day. He is a Vietnam vet who got his degree later on in life and worked as a computer analyst. He read a lot and stayed in good shape. I had grown pretty close to my dad, as we spent a lot of time together. He was also very supportive of my basketball dreams. One summer before my sophomore year in high school he got up every weekday morning and drove to Inglewood from West LA to take me to the park to work with me in preparation for tryouts. He stayed in my corner even though my basketball dreams never came true.

As I got older, I started to see more and more of my dad in me, how smart he was and how we had the same sense of humor. Over the years I began to give my kids those long life lesson talks I hated to get from my dad when I was young and have found myself repeating a lot of things to my kids that my dad said to me. I always said that I would not subject my kids to that, but the fact that I remembered so much of what he told me made me see that it works.

Well, anyway, aside from my life at the house, I was going through my own personal growing pains away from home trying to adjust to this new environment. I had graduated again (I had just graduated from the eighth grade back in New York), this time from Palm Jr. High in Cali. My mother enrolled me at Westchester High School, primarily because my cousin Val had just graduated from there.

The school was near the beach in a predominately white section of the city. I came to find out that there were also a few students there in the entertainment business, such as Nia Long, Regina King, and present day movie director Tim Story. Additionally, I wanted to go there because Westchester had played for the basketball city championship the year prior to losing to Crenshaw with Big John (Hotplate) Williams by 40 points. Westchester was still the second best high school basketball team in the city. The drawback of me going to Westchester was that the classmates I had just met at Palms and graduated with were attending Hamilton High and University High. So here I was again all alone and starting over at a new school not knowing a soul.

One day in the gym before actual tryouts I was bragging that I was a good shooter when the varsity coach challenged me to a one-on-one game. He said if I could beat him, I could play varsity, but if I lost, I could not tryout for JV. I was like, "WHAT! Let's do it." I was thinking in my head that can't no old white man beat me in basketball. But everybody on the sideline was saying, "DON'T DO IT!" Luckily, I listened and found out later that this white man could play!

I wound up making JV. Typically my teammates and I had late practices, so we would catch the bus together pretty late. Since the school was near the beach and none of us lived around there, we caught the Manchester bus going back east into the city. This is when I found out firsthand the difference between New York people and California people. Let's just say this gang confrontation wouldn't've happened back in Buff. Somebody would have had my back; be it my friends, classmates, or teammates.

One evening we got on the bus in front of our school coming from basketball practice. As we boarded, we were talking shit like we always did about basketball practice and suddenly everyone got quiet. As I looked toward the back of the bus, I saw why. There were about five or six gangbangers sitting in the back. We normally sat in the back of the bus, but now everybody was spread. I sat down at about the middle. Then I heard a male voice say, "What's up, cuz?" Then he said it again. As I looked up he was like, "Yeah, you!" Then he got up, came over to me, reached in his pocket to pull out this jagged edge pocket knife, put it to my throat, and said, "Give me yo jacket."

I had on a Lakers Starter jacket that was the shit back in the day. He was like, "Yeah, Grape Street Crip, and I need a purple jacket." I felt that my life was on the line. In my short time in LA I had witnessed gang violence committed on other people and watched continuous news reports on TV about gang related crime. Now I was a victim of it. I took the jacket off and gave it to him and everybody laughed and thought it was funny until the other gangbangers with him started messing with everybody else on the bus, taking their money and jewelry.

Now, the reason I made the previous statement about New York people vs. California people is not because I would expect anyone to put his neck on the line for me. I had just met my teammates. My beef was that it became a running joke. Other players on the team would come up to me later and say, "give me yo jacket" and laugh. We didn't do that type of shit on the East Coast. If your teammate or friend got robbed at knife point, you don't laugh. Maybe the players on my team were just immature. The gangbanger could have easily slit my throat, but by the grace of God he didn't. Right then and there I thought of leaving LA and going back to Buffalo, but no. I didn't want to abandon my mom and leave her and my brother with this damn fool at home.

One day I overheard my mother telling my aunt that my brother's father had started hitting her. It made me cry and my stomach hurt. I was only 14 at the time and this really struck a nerve with me. I hated him and just wanted him to go away and die. I used to hope that one of the drug dealers or gangbangers would just kill him.

The next day I was lying in bed when I saw my mother leave and go next door to my aunt's apartment. I got up and went to the bathroom, which was right past my mother's room, and saw that Jimmy was asleep. As I walked back from the bathroom, all I could think of was him hitting my mother. When I went back in my room, I saw my brother's little league baseball bat. I grabbed it and took a few swings and started crying. Somehow I wound up in my mother's room staring at my brother's father. I was still crying when I closed my eyes and yelled, "Why you hit my momma?" I began hitting him with my brother's bat. He woke up after the second or third blow and tried to grab me as he rolled onto the floor. I cried and cried as I thought about all the shit he was putting us through. Then I heard my mother saying, "Tony! Tony! Get up! Take your clothes off and get in the bed. Right now!" I woke up and realized I had been dreaming all along and that asshole ruining our lives was resting peacefully in the other room.

A few weeks later my mother had enough and put him out for good. He had spent his whole check on drugs and took my mother's purse. I guess she genuinely cared for him, and that's why she put up with so much before she did it. My mother was like my grandmother in that she was always the peacemaker and very forgiving to a fault. Even with my brother and I there were times she should have put her foot down for our benefit, but she didn't. My mother was a hardworking black woman who managed to stay at the same job as a social worker for the County of Los Angeles for over 40 years. She was very supportive and wanted the best for my brother and I. She originally moved out to LA when she got married, but the marriage did not last long. A few years later she met my dad and I was born in the summer of 1969. My mother and father were not together, so when I was young my mother primarily raised me by herself. She allowed me to go back and forth to Buffalo until I stayed through the eighth grade and then came back to LA. For the most part, my mother allowed me to make the decision on whether I was going to stay in Buffalo or LA; she just wanted me to be happy.

Well, anyway, when I said she put Jimmy out, I meant the locks were changed. That didn't stop him from coming to our apartment in the middle of the night banging on the windows and doors and waking us up trying to get in. To this day I get a flashback if I'm asleep and someone bangs on a window and wakes me up. I remember one time he came banging on the door at around two in the morning waking us up trying to get in. I told him to go away before my mother got up and came to the door. He got mad and told my mother I disrespected him. What was really disrespectful was the fact that he came over disturbing us in the middle of the night when we all had to get up the next day for work and school.

After she put him out, my mother told me not to let him in for any reason while she was gone. One day, he came knocking on the door while my mom was at work. I told him I couldn't let him in and he said he just wanted to use the phone and would stand by the door.

Trustingly and foolishly, I let him in the apartment to use the phone. He made a call about getting a ride, thanked me, and left. I felt bad that he was a drug addict and my mom had to put him out, because I liked Jimmy in the beginning. So I felt a little better that I was able to help him just a little bit.

As I sat there a moment it dawned on me and I thought to myself, *Jimmy just got me. I bet you the phone is gone.* I went over to the dining room near the door and… yep, he got us. I ran outside to see if I could get it back, but he was nowhere to be found. Damn! Now I had to explain this to my mom. I called my mother at work from the other phone and she was furious. "I told you not to let him in!" she shouted over the phone. I told her I was sorry but she was still upset.

Our apartment building in Inglewood had two apartments downstairs and two up. My family and my aunt had the downstairs apartments. The apartments had a little patio and yard surrounded by a tall wooden fence. The patio/yard was accessible through a large sliding glass door. We kept a broomstick behind the sliding door, so even if it was not locked or if the lock was picked it still wouldn't slide. So, if you wanted to break into our apartments through the patio, there was only one way.

I came home from basketball practice one evening to find shattered glass all over the living room. The VCRs in the living room and my room were gone. The TVs, videotapes, radios, albums, phones, and anything of value was gone. Jimmy had cleaned us out again. My mom called the police, but did not tell them who did it. The landlord put security bars up over the patio doors to match the ones already up on the windows, but I still did not feel safe in the house anymore. I started to have trouble sleeping at night and when I went to school I would hide all my personal stuff just in case he was able to somehow break in again. He left us alone for a spell, and then he began calling and asking my mom to pay his crack debts, telling her that the drug dealers said they would kill him and his whole family if he didn't pay them. My mother called his sister, who had moved out to LA from Buffalo. She paid his crack debt and sent him back to Buffalo to get him away from trouble.

With my brother's father gone, my life at home got a little easier, although my social life didn't. At the time, I had grown in height to about 6' 2" and but I was still skinny at about 165 pounds. I had braces on my teeth, bad acne with blackheads, and dark skin. Dark skin was not in back "in" those days. All the girls wanted the light-skinned Al B. Sure, El De Barge, Christopher Williams-type cats. I didn't stand a chance. My two closest friends at the time were pretty boys and had all the women and didn't let me forget it either. I tried to talk to this one girl and she told me she was into older men. Then I tried to talk to a cheerleader who was a junior, but she was dating one of the 10th graders on the varsity basketball team. I tell you I couldn't win. I felt like I would never get a girlfriend. I didn't take my senior picture and I didn't go to my senior prom. I couldn't wait to get the hell out of high school and eventually LA.

After high school, I got accepted into Cal State LA (CSULA) for the fall of '87. I did not like CSULA either, but that was my fault. I applied blindly and did not do my research into the school. When I got there, I found out that the black population at CSULA was very low. There were mostly Asians and whites, and the only blacks at the school were athletes. I lived about 45 minutes from school and started to go less and less as the year progressed. My biggest downfall was that this girl I liked lived in between my house and school. I had good intentions, but for some reason on my way to class I'd wind up driving down Harvard Place off of Jefferson to visit this brown skin honey with this big butt. The funny part was that she was the same girl from high school who told me she was into older guys and was just being nice to me. I took her kindness and ran with it. Sadly, I even got myself arrested stealing a wallet even though I had the money to pay for it just to fake and tell my family she had bought it for me for Christmas. I remembered the cop called me "TheArthur the thief" and said, "What a fancy name for a crook." After that, I felt so damn stupid I just left her alone.

I eventually dropped out of college altogether and got a job at Ralph's supermarket in Ladera Heights. It was cool, bagging groceries and stuff. It put money in my pocket and I even worked part-time at a corner store on Crenshaw and Century for a couple of days until I found out why the owner really asked me to work there.

The owner was Chinese (not unusual for that area of LA) and saw me come into his store a few times after work in my uniform from Ralph's. He asked me if I could do some stocking and other tasks around his store. At first, I said no, then I said okay and asked him what I would be doing. He said that I would just do some stocking and cleaning up. I was cool with that and came in one night after I got off work at Ralph's. He had me unload a couple of trucks, stock some shelves, sweep, and mop. Well, after I had finished all the work he asked me to do, I asked him what to do next. He said, "Just stand at the door and make sure nobody steals anything." I was cool with that too, thinking he was talking about some little kids coming in stealing candy or some chips or something, but I was soon to find out that that wasn't what he was talking about. Not at all!

I stood around the door for about half an hour when three Bloods came into the store. One of them came over to me and said, "What up, Blood? You supposed to be the muthafuckin' security or something?"

I was like, "Hell naw!"

He said, "Alright then, so you know what time it is?" I nodded my head and started walking towards the back of the store. He and his homies began stealing 40s of beer out of the cooler and grabbing other shit and running out. The one Blood jumped over the counter and mushed the owner in the face and began grabbing cigarettes. They didn't take money and I never saw any weapons, but shit, I wasn't trying to see any either. The funny thing is for some reason the owner thought I was going to or could stop them. Did he really think I was gonna risk my life for his store over some beer and cigarettes?

He started yelling at me, "Stop them! Stop them!"

I faked like I didn't know what was going on and came from the back of the store and said, "What happened?"

He just started pointing at the door yelling, "They robbed me and ran outside!"

I faked like I was running outside to see if I could catch them. I went outside and walked around for a second before coming back in faking like I was out of breath from chasing them. Then I said, "They're gone." The owner closed up the store for the night, paid me, and asked me if I would come back tomorrow. I don't think I even need to answer that question. Yeah, right!

In my spare time I hooped and was getting better and better. Every year in Cali there was a college pro/am where all the best college talent in the area played. The pro/am was a summer league for basketball players finishing college getting ready for the pros and entering and returning college players. I got a chance to play that year, because I knew one of the coaches and did quite well. This gave me hope to play college ball, but by this time I also had a new interest: hip hop.

I had started hanging out and going to clubs like Osco's and Paradise 24 on under 21 nights with two friends who went to Dorsey High. We started dressing up and going out. I was on that NY City Slick Rick/Dana Dane shit, rocking suits with mock necks, my African medallion, and, of course, my suede Bally's. I had also started to rap.

The first rap I ever wrote was, "Youza Sucka." My cousin back in Buffalo had a studio in his house and used to play keyboards for a band and had recently went solo and was now singing and making his own music. I figured I could kill two birds with one stone if I went back to Buffalo. I could play ball at a community college there and make me a demo, before I came back to LA. Plus, I missed Buffalo and all my family and friends. So I bought me a one-way ticket back to Buffalo in September of '88. In hindsight, I never should have left LA, but I did. And I never imagined that when I came back to LA I would have a pocketful of drug money from selling crack, but I did.

Chapter 2

Product of My Environment

I came back to Buffalo and moved back in my grandparent's house down in the basement. Coincidentally, my aunt and cousin who lived next door to me in LA had moved back to Buffalo and into the house next door the prior year because my cousin could not take the LA earthquakes any more. On the street I lived on in Buffalo, my grandfather owned five consecutive houses that were occupied by family members. My grandparents had four children: my mother and aunt, who lived in LA next door to us prior to moving back to Buffalo; an uncle in Nevada; and my oldest aunt, who had three sons. Her sons were seven to ten years older than me and acted like my big brothers. When I was growing up in elementary school living with my grandparents, if I did something wrong, they would never tell on me, just put me on secret punishment. When I left to go out to LA for high school, they were all living with their mom in one of my grandfather's houses two doors over.

When I came back, their mother had moved to Atlanta and her oldest son lived in her old house with his wife and three kids. Her second son, Matt, was the one who had the music studio and lived next door to my grandparents. Her youngest son had moved into one of my grandfather's houses a few blocks away. The last house on the street that my grandfather owned was occupied by my grandmother's niece and her two kids. This type of living arrangement was always fun when I was growing up, which gave me the prerogative to go from house to house. But we grew up and became adults, and now everybody's in each others' business.

School had already started when I got back to Buffalo, and it was too late for me to enroll for the fall term. This gave me more time to work on my game and make my demo. My cousin Matt was in the process of writing songs and preparing to do his own shows. I came around at a good time because I added some hip hop flavor into his songs and performances. Besides rapping, I could dance my ass off. I was doing all the Kid & Play, Scoop and Scrap (Big Daddy Kane's dancers) dancing mixed with a little west coast MC Hammer. I let my hair grow into this crazy high box.

My cousin and I did a few shows. When he did his up tempo songs, I would come out and do all my hip hop dances. Then, he set up a concert-like video shoot. He found another dancer and we put together routines for all his songs. He also found some girl dancers to be in the group. Some of them were fine too. I was mad as hell when I found out they were my cousins. The funny part is that he still has the video to this day and would probably make you a copy for a good laugh.

Besides my music interest, I was back in my hood in the downtown area of Buffalo; we all called it "Down da Way." This area of Buffalo had projects as well as areas with houses. The part of downtown I was from was called Sperry Park, or 31 because that was our neighborhood park and Public School #31 was the school we all went to right across the street.

A lot of things had changed in Buffalo when I came back, and it was partly because of this new spreading drug culture. Before I left, when we did not play ball at the park, we used to hang out and play ball at the YMCA or the PAL. I was mad as hell when I came back and found out that the PAL had been closed. Even the Randy Smith league had ceased to be because it became too dangerous to operate. People started betting big money on the games, the refs were being threatened, players were being kidnapped after games; it got to be too much. That made me upset, because I was looking forward to coming back and playing in the league against all the best talent in the city. They tried to bring it back a couple years later, but it wasn't the same. With that over, I played mostly at Sperry Park and some rec leagues with my cousin Joe. It felt good to be back around all the friends I grew up with. Some of the dudes I had known since kindergarten. We had good runs at the park. My man who lived across the street from the park used to hook up the big speakers and play music while we played ball. And you already know that everybody else was doing their thing too. You had a few dice games going on, people talking shit, ribbing, smoking weed, drinking, and pushing up on the neighborhood chicks. I was comfortable on the court and everybody saw that I was not Lil' TheArthur from elementary school anymore. I had the game to prove it too. But besides basketball, I found out that my friends were into a lot of extracurricular activities.

First, it was the drinking. I drank a few times with my cousin in LA and with my high school basketball team, but not on a regular basis. Now all my friends in Buffalo were drinking 40s of Old English like it was nothing. After we finished hooping, they would ante up and buy about five to six 40s. Crack 'em! Pour some out for the dead homies and get drunk. Some even drank before and while we played. I was not used to that. That malt liquor was no joke and I went home many days buzzing from the park and I had to go sleep it off. To top that off, they were rolling up blunts too. I had smoked weed before in LA, but it was joints not blunts and definitely not in a cipher. The cipher was the group of people you were getting high with, passing the blunt around until it came back to you. After a while I built up enough tolerance to hang with my friends and actually start spearheading some of the sessions at the park.

At night it seemed like all my friends disappeared. I did not know about the "basement" until my man Bird asked me why I never came over there with everybody else. The basement was over my man Juney's house where he lived in the McCarley Gardens with his mom, Mama Gina. Mama Gina, may her soul rest in peace, and Ms. G were like the crew's moms. Mama Gina used to get it in, she kept a blunt of weed burning. The McCarley Gardens was close to downtown too, but it was right across the street from the Fruit Belt neighborhood, so they sort of claimed it. The Fruit Belt was like our brother neighborhood. We used to even hang out in the clubs together. From what I know, we never had a problem with each other when I was out there running the streets. Plus, there were so many people from our hood who moved over there and vice-versa. So, to put it short, it was all love. Well, anyway, I went over there one night and the session was on! Blunts and 40s were everywhere. This was the hangout! From there, we would go to bars and hangouts. I never had to pay for anything. It never dawned on me where they were getting all this money. Nobody had a job.

One day after hooping, instead of going home to shower, I walked down the block with a few of my friends. When we got to the corner of the street where a few of them lived, we just chilled for a minute talking shit. While standing there, this old looking man came up to my man Black and asked him if he had dimes. I was thinking to myself, *Look at this bum ass nigga begging for change. And why does he need dimes so badly?* Shortly afterward, Black ran off behind a house and when he came back he handed the man something and the man gave him a $10 bill.

Sounding like a damn fool, I go, "Y'all be hustling?"

Black goes, "Yeah, Tone. You didn't know? We out here getting it." Black was the man. He was one of the first out the crew to hustle. He was sharp as a tack and seemed like he always had a plan. He was tall and dark-skinned like me and nice on the basketball court. As we began to hustle, we pretty much followed his lead and eventually became known as members of Black's crew.

I did not know what to say when I found out my friends were selling drugs. I acted like it was not a big deal, but all I could think about was what I went through in LA because of drugs. In LA, if it was not for my brother's father, I never would have been exposed to cocaine. But now it was all around me in more ways than one. I swore I would never sell drugs. But as time passed, I found out that money talks and bullshit walks.

I had enrolled in Erie Community College when fall came back around. It was very hard for me to go to class because it was still warm outside and I wanted to hang with my friends at the park. I rarely went to class or did homework, so eventually I stopped going. My grandfather wasn't putting up with me not going to school or working, so I had to find a job. I got a job as a stock clerk at a department store for the holidays, and then I enrolled at Millard Fillmore College for the spring semester. I swear I made an effort to go at first, but the allure of hanging out with my friends was too strong to resist. But this time I was slick by pretending to go to school during the semester. I would get up in the morning and leave home like I was going to school, but I was really going over my friends' houses or just hanging out in the streets. After a while of not having any money or a job, I knew I had to do something to put some money in my pocket. I thought about it and decided I could sell weed.

My friends and I were always riding around trying to find some good weed to smoke. I thought I could be the man, but I had two problems. The first was I didn't have any money to buy a big quantity of weed, and the second was I didn't know who to get the weed from. Luckily being in the hood, finding a weed plug was not a problem. I hooked up with this old head that sold weight quantities of weed, and I borrowed some money from one of my friends and got started. I only borrowed enough to buy an ounce, so after I finished paying back my debt and smoking my share, I had made only enough money to re-up the first time.

After a while, I started making a little money on the block and at the park, but just enough to buy me an outfit here and there and a few drinks when we went out. I especially used to sell all my weed on Thursday's dollar night at the bar on the block called Rhanprn's where everybody was hustling. The crowd used to be crazy, inside and out. Whatever you had that night, you could sell it. Fiends were everywhere, even the casual users who smoked Woos & Cooley's. A "woo" is a crack-laced marijuana blunt and a "Cooley" is a cocaine- or crack-laced cigarette.

The dice games out in the streets were intense. It used to be live as hell! We had a little drinking club in Rhanprn's called the "Ratpack." We used to get drunk as hell. The bar closed at 4am and I rarely made it home on Thursday nights, and when I did, most of the time the sun beat me home. Now, I was not doing anything big with the weed, so I was not drawing any attention to myself, especially at home and on my street with all my relatives, but that would change.

My cousin Val called me one day out of the blue and told me to come next door. I went over and asked her where she had been because I had not seen her in about a week. She said she had just come back from her free trip to Jamaica.

I said, "Free trip? How the hell you get that?"

She told me that not only was it free, she was getting something for going.

"Hold up," I said, "What's the catch?"

She told me she went with this fake scuba diving company that needed people to sign up to go scuba diving in Jamaica. While there, this company filled up the scuba tanks with compressed pounds of weed, so she got a free trip and the company gave her a pound for going. That was where I came in. She gave the pound of weed to me to sell, and we would split the profits down the middle. The good part was that it was all profit and I could start buying a little more weight after this. The bad part was the weed was straight "Buddha," "Censee" from the Mother Earth. I had everybody in the hood looking for me. It was like I was selling crack.

It spread around the hood real fast, that I had the best weed around. People were coming by my grandparents' house looking for me. If I was there, it was an in-and-out transaction. All my relatives on my street were starting to notice, which I didn't mean to happen. I was disrespecting my grandfather as a minister by even having it in his house. Val and I were sharing all the profits, but I was the one catching hell from the family.

Val and I had grown up together for the most part and were more like siblings than cousins. She gave me my first joint and 40 of beer out in LA when I was 14. I remember when we stole my mother's credit card and took my little brother out on a shopping spree at the mall. We figured that since my mother still lived in LA and was in Buffalo visiting, the credit card company wouldn't doubt her if she later reported she'd lost her card out of town on vacation in Buffalo.

We almost got caught when we were in the store and my little brother yelled out her real name, "Val, Val, I want these!" You should have seen the look on her face. Man, if looks could kill! Sadly, the three of us would wind up as co-defendants and all go to federal prison.

Well, anyway, not to get off track, my family started to catch wind of my weed selling. Shit, why wouldn't they? Some of them smoked weed and knew everybody in the hood and you know if you blaze you want the good stuff. They probably had smoked some of my weed and asked where it came from. It probably blew their mind when they found out.

Soon after, I found out I had a one-year-old son named Philip. I had only dealt with his mother briefly and hadn't seen her in over a year. I ran into her one day at a store and she said I needed to come see my son. "Son…what son?" I asked.

"Your son," she replied. I had heard that she had a baby, but I didn't think it was mine. The next day I went over to see him and fell in love with him. I took him home and my mother was here visiting from LA. She took one look at him and said, "Yeah, he's yours."

As a new dad, I wanted to take care of my son and be responsible, so I stopped selling weed and went and got a job at JCPenney's. My job at JCPenney's was only seasonal with a chance I would be hired permanently, but after the holidays I was let go.

Since I was not working, I had a lot of free time, so I started to play a lot of basketball. I met and start hanging around this kid named JR because we were two of the best ball players in our neighborhood around this time. He lived in the Jefferson projects a couple blocks from me. We started to play in all types of rec leagues together all over the city. But more than that, we started getting into a lot of bullshit.

One of his baby mommas had moved on this street on the other side of town that had a lot of crackheads, so JR began hustling out the house. I went over there periodically to pick him up or just chill. He was getting a lot of money over there, and the dudes on the block were jealous. No wonder! He was getting money in their hood and you know dudes weren't going for that. I used to ask him about that, but he said he was cool with them. Yeah, right! I had only sold weed hand-to-hand before and had never worked a gatehouse that sold crack. He had a little system where they would slide the money through the broke lock hole and then he would slide the crack under the door. The fiends were bringing mad shit to him for crack, like watches and jewelry and things that would not fit through the lock hole, so he had to open the door. Unluckily for me, he left to make a run and the money was still coming, so he asked me to stay and hit the licks when they came.

Right after he left, I heard somebody knock on the door. I went to the door and asked them what they needed. A lady answered and said she had some stuff to get rid of. My dumb ass opened the door and two dudes hooded-up busted in. One put the gun on me, hit me on the head with it, and said, "Where the shit at!"

I said, "Man, I don't know!"

Then his man said, "Never mind, I found it!" He came out the other room with some money, packages of crack, and jewelry. The other dude pushed me to the floor and they ran out. JR was walking back when they were running out. I came out after them to see where they were going or what they were riding in. When I saw JR, I yelled out, "Yo! They just robbed me!" The dudes saw him and started running the other way. JR dropped the McDonald's bag in his hand, pulled out his little 25, and started chasing them down the street, shooting at them. They turned the corner, and by the time we got there, they were nowhere to be found. After that, I knew I should've stop hanging with JR, but I didn't.

Later, I heard that he got into it with this kid from his building in the projects up at the JFK Recreation Center. But what I didn't know was how serious it was. We left his apartment to go hoop and I thought the only thing he had in his book bag was his basketball gear. When we got down in the lobby, I heard him say, "There go that nigga right there!" He pulled a sawed-off shotgun out his book bag and start shooting. The kid start shooting too, so I dove on the floor in this pissy-ass lobby. Now the funny part was that JR had an ol' ass two-barrel shotgun that he had only put two shells in. But I swear he must have shot that gun about 10 times. He must have been shooting pellet residue or something. He kept firing as we ran out the other door in the lobby.

The very next night I was on my bike heading to JR's crib in the projects when I saw this chick I was messing with walking with the same dude JR just had the shootout with. I said, "Yo, what up, ma?" She acted like she didn't hear me and kept walking wit' this dude. Then I hollered, "Oh, it's like that now?"

Just then the guy turned around and pulled out his gun and told me to chill. I backed off. Then he said, "Yo, she wit' me."

I was like, "A'ight, cool, you got it!" I got on my bike and rode off. I could not believe that this dude was about shoot me over some hood rat chick. It seemed like I was facing death daily all of a sudden. I realized that I had to change my surroundings if I was going to survive. If not for me, at least for my son. After that, I stop hanging with JR and tried to make up for lost time with Philip.

I was soon to discover that being a father was a big responsibility that I wasn't quite ready for. I wasn't working or hustling, so I couldn't really afford to take care of my son. His mother stayed with her mother on the other side of town. They were on social services, so I had to financially provide for my son. He stayed with me and my family for long periods of time. When I found employment, it would not last for long. Then when I got paid, I'd spend the majority of my money on him, and the shorts I had left over had to last me until I got paid again. Something had to give, but I knew if I went back to hustling, I couldn't stay with my grandparents. I was starting to give up on Buffalo and thought about going back to Cali, but I hadn't accomplished a thing I came here to do. Most importantly, I couldn't leave my son. Then, finally I said "fuck it" and went back to selling weed.

Also around this time my cousin Val had a red Suzuki Sidekick she was tired of and I used to drive it all the time anyway, so she sold it to me. Now I had a son and a car note. There was definitely no turning back now.

I was able to keep my business away from home this time around and kept my family out my business. They knew I was doing something in the streets. I mean, how the hell could I afford a car note and take care of my son without a job? But by then, I had a pager, a stash away from the house, and a stash on the block. My biggest problem at that time was smoking up my profit.

Now the weed game was pretty steady, but the money was very slow to add up. When we would go to the mall, my friends would leave with bags of shit, while I was lucky to have one bag with some Timberlands or something. One by one, my friends started getting in my ear, trying to get me to switch over to selling crack. I swore to myself that I would never do it. I saw what it did to me and my family firsthand back in Cali. To me, selling weed was not really selling drugs, and if I started selling "ready" rock, as we called it in Buffalo, there would be no turning back. But I was tired of counting the same money. Plus, I was now smoking weed on the regular. I think my crew thought I was doing better than I was or had more quantity than I did, because they were always trying to get me to smoke one with them on the block, or they would buy a few bags, if I matched them. Plus, I did not have a steady plug for good weed, so a lot of the time I would run out and then spend re-up money waiting to get more.

One Thursday night on the block, when the bar was poppin', I got involved in this celo game and I lost all my money. Celo is a three dice crap game where one person has the bank and rolls the dice to establish his number point. Then, whoever bets against him gets to roll the dice to try to beat him. It started off with just short money. I called out the bank. "Yo, my bank ten dollars. Who want some?"

"Give me five!"

"And I'll take the other five."

After I had built my bank up to $100, this kid bet against my whole bank and won. After I handed him my money, he shouted out, "Bank one-hundred dollars. Who wants some?" I in turn bet against his whole bank, but lost. His bank then increased to $200. Again I bet against his whole bank. And lost again, making his bank now four-hundred dollars. Foolishly, I bet again. The kid shook the dice in his hand, yelled out some profanity and rolled the dice across the pavement. A lot of people had started to gather around, blocking traffic trying to drive down the street.

The next thing I remember was that I was taking money out my stash spot at home to go back and gamble. I was open and thought to myself, *I can't let this nigga beat me.* I went back and wound up losing it all. I was sick. What was I going to do now?

The next day I went over my man Big Rick's house and asked him if he knew anybody who would front me a pound of weed on consignment. I was too embarrassed to tell him I had lost all my money gambling, but he had to know something was up. He called his cousin and his cousin came by the next day with it. I sold it all, gave his cousin his money, but I was still broke. Plus, Rick was in my ear hard every day trying to get me to switch over. He would scoop me up and we would smoke some weed and then he would tell me how easy and how much money he was getting. I told him I didn't know anything about selling crack. I didn't know how to weigh it, cook it, or bag it, and I didn't have any customers. There were already enough people on the block trying to be the first to hit a lick. He could sense that he was slowly but surely wearing me down. So he goes, "Yo, let's go to my crib and I'll walk you through it".

I had known Big Rick since we were like 10. I used to go on his street and play back in the day because my cousins lived on his street in one of my grandfather's houses that I would eventually move into myself. Big Rick had this truck with rims and crazy loud beats; it seemed like he got it painted a different color every month. In the summer we would pile up in the truck and ride around the city smoking weed and looking for chicks to press up on.

We went to Rick's house and he bagged up an eight ball in powder for me and told me that it weighed 3.5 grams. Then we got in his down low car and he took me to the cook a couple blocks away. It was this old head who smoked crack and whatever else he could get his hands on. I know he did that syrup shit too because he was always slobbering all over the place. Big Rick told him I would be coming to see him and to take care of me. The cook's house was crazy. He had all types of fiends and hookers there, upstairs and down. After the cook finished doing his thing, he let the product cool off and harden.

Big Rick told me how much to give him, which depended on how much you were getting cooked up. So we broke him off a little piece and went back to his house. Then he pulled out a bag of size 20/20 bags and showed me how to bag it. Eight balls were going for 175 back then, and I think we bagged up a little over $300 worth, about 30 dimes, before heading to the block. Rick said he made them kind of big so I could build up my clientele. I walked to the corner thinking, *Damn! What have I gone and got myself into now?*

Chapter 3

No Turning Back

I went up to the block and stashed my dime bags of crack in a Doritos bag and threw it in the field. The corner, which we all called "the block," was on the corner of Shumway and Peckham. On this corner, there was the bar we hustled in front of called the Rhanprn's on one side with residential houses next to it, and there were also a few houses directly across the street. On the other two sides of the corner were vacant fields that we used to stash our drugs. As soon as I hit the block, everybody started asking, "Where the weed at?"

"I ain't got no weed," I replied.

"Stop lying, Tone, I just saw you throw your stash in the field."

Before I could say anything, Big Rick said, "Tone done crossed over. He selling crack now."

Everybody was like, "Word?!"

I said, "Word!"

Then everybody on the corner started giving me five like I had graduated from school or something. I guess now I was really part of the crew because I was at risk in the same way they were.

When I sold my first dime bags of crack, or hit my first lick, as we called it, I felt like I had sold my soul to the devil. An older guy came up on the block and said, "Who got dimes?" Nervously, I got up and went over to the guy and asked him how many he needed. "Can I get three for $25?" he asked.

"Yeah, I got you," I replied. I went to my stash and got the three dimes. I ran back over, made the exchange, counted the money, and sat back down. *Damn, what did I just do?* I thought to myself. I would always be on the corner saying that I would never sell crack, but now I was. I felt like there was no turning back. I was disappointed in myself and felt bad that I had let my surroundings influence me to this point, but that feeling only lasted until the next crackhead came around the corner with some money.

When my man Dogg found out, he laughed and said, "I told you, nigga. I knew you would get tired of counting that short ass weed money and get some real paper." Dogg always had something to say. That was just Dogg being Dogg. We called him Dogg for a reason, and you didn't want to be on his bad side. Dogg was simple and plain, just real and didn't bite his tongue for anybody.

He used to beat everyone to the corner in the morning. Around 8am almost every day, he would be sitting on the step of one of the abandoned houses reading a newspaper and drinking a 40 ounce of beer. You always had to be on point around Dogg, because if he thought you were wrong, he'd call you out in a minute. He had done a tour in Desert Storm and was the wrong dude to mess with.

One time when we were on the block, Dogg was about to hit a lick when the narcs pulled up. Juney yelled out, "5-0!" Dogg turned and saw them, so he ran into the bar to try to flush the packages he had in his hand. When the narcs jumped out, one ran in the bar behind Dogg and the other told us to line up against the wall. A few minutes later, we heard some commotion coming from inside the bar. The narc yelled out to his partner and didn't get a response, so he ran in the bar to check on him. Moments later, they came out the bar with Dogg in handcuffs. The narc who had ran in after Dogg had a bloody nose and looked shook up. Dogg was laughing and said, "I had to give him the business."

As time went by, Rick started frontin' me more and more weight until he began giving me an ounce. This crack shit was crazy to me. Money was coming fast and easy; and I was blowing it just as fast as I was making it. I would pay Rick and spend the rest on clothes, kicks, weed, liquor, and clubbin'. Eventually this caught up to me when I lost my stash with all my drugs. I had spent all my profit and all I had left was enough bagged up crack to sell and pay Rick. I had about $1,500 worth of dimes that I put in a potato chip bag. It was Thursday, so I knew I could sell all my stuff on the block because the bar on the corner would be crowded.

Rick lived down the street from the block and paged me to come smoke some weed and play NBA Live before the bar got to poppin'. He put 35 in my pager, which was our code to buy some cigar blunts so we could smoke some weed. I grabbed my stash, stopped at the store, and then went down to his house.

When I arrived, there were lot of people there and we smoked weed for about an hour or two, passing blunts around the cipher. I left out with my other man, Juney. We rode around town, got some more weed, smoked a little, and looked for some honeys. I did not want to ride with my drugs, so I stashed my shit in Rick's yard.

When I came back about an hour later, I got out of Juney's Blazer and went to the place where I left my stash, but it wasn't there. I couldn't believe it. I was sick! I should have known better. There were always crackheads around trying to steal a stash, and one of them probably saw me hiding my stash and took it. I looked all over the yard, in the garbage, everywhere, but I couldn't find it. I could not tell Rick because he would be mad that I stashed the shit in his yard. Damn! What the fuck was I to do? I walked up to the corner and saw my other man Lee who had weight and I asked him to front me some product. He knew I was getting my stuff from Rick, so I had to make up an excuse. I told him Rick was not around and I ran out and was missing out on a lot of money. He left and came back and gave me a package on consignment.

I ran down the street to this vacant house and bagged up the work and then came back to the block and started hustling. I sold everything I got from Lee, paid him, and he gave me more. After I sold most of that, I gave him his off the top and had enough to pay Rick with the rest. Rick came to the block earlier and asked me if I was done. I lied and said, "Naw, I'm still working on it." Not knowing that he knew about me getting work from Lee already.

The block had a lot of traffic and customers that night, and I was able to make enough to go see Rick with his short. I gave him his money, and then I came clean. I told him what happened, and he said that I should have come to him and that he already knew and was just waiting to see what I was going to do. Lesson learned!

The next day I was at his house playing PlayStation and smoking weed when his cousin came over and said that his grandfather, who lived with him, was at the bar on the corner trying to hustle, selling crack. Rick and I just looked at each other. He said, "Oh shit! My grandfather got yo shit!"

Rick's grandfather was off the hook too. They called him Dude and he used to curse everybody out. I remember one time when we were over Rick's house and this kid knocked on the door. Rick told Bird to get the door. Bird grew up with us and hustled on the corner too. Bird went to the door and said, "Who is it?" And you heard this person outside say his name, but Bird kept fuckin' wit' him saying, "Who?"

Then out of nowhere, Dude yelled from upstairs, "Get the fuck out! That's who the fuck it is!" That shit was so funny. So I already knew if I asked him for my stuff he would have cursed me out for putting it in his yard. There was no way I was going to ask him for my stash because I knew he wouldn't give it to me anyway.

The next day Rick said he asked him about it and he told him that he didn't know what the fuck he was talking about, but gave it to him later on. Rick gave it back to me and since I had paid him back earlier, this was all profit. Which I used to begin buying my own work and getting on my feet.

I didn't want to disrespect my grandparents by bringing that shit in the house with me, so I kept it in the backyard behind the garage. Luckily around this time, my grandfather's tenant in a house down the street from the block and about four or five houses from Rick had moved out. I asked my grandparents if I could rent the house and they let me. I asked my man Juney if he wanted to share the house with me.

Juney was like my brother from another mother. I met Juney back in the seventh grade catching the yellow 'cheese' school bus to PS 72 in South Buffalo. To this day, Juney and I never have gotten into an argument, we were just cool like that. We were together so much that we used to make up these catch phrases and words so that only he and I would know what we were talking about when we were around other people. We would be laughing at something and no one would know why.

Juney moved in and we had officially opened the crew hangout spot. We partied continuously. There were non-stop sessions of celo games, card games, get-togethers, weed, liquor, and women. We would beat up crackheads that came by knocking on the door asking for crack. This was not a gatehouse to sell crack, but sometimes you couldn't blame them. All the hustlers from the corner would be in the house partying and they were fiendin' for drugs. It was hard to leave the party, but money still had to be made.

With so much going on at my house, I had to stay focused and go to the block and get my money. We used to be on the block yelling, "Big Boulders from Bam Bam!" and messing with the fiends asking them, "You smoke crack, don't cha?" from the *Lean on Me* movie.

I found a sweet way to stash my drugs on the block. I bought this hollow rock with a sliding compartment at the bottom. I think it was made to stash a spare key. The only bad part was that it was too good at times. If I got drunk or high on the block and it was dark, sometimes I couldn't find it.

The block was off the hook. We started getting a lot of money and the traffic on the block started getting crazy and the narcs started jumping out on us every day. They'd line us up on the wall or on their car with their guns drawn, take our blunts, step on them, smash them, pour out our 40s, pat us down, and do a bullshit search. The narcs would never find anything unless somebody was just about to make a sale or they caught a fiend right after a purchase. A couple of times I had to swallow some packages when they pulled up. Then when I hit the blunt, everybody would joke and say I was smoking Woos. After they searched us and couldn't find anything, they'd make us leave the corner. We'd jet for a while but then be right back.

The crackheads were mad funny too. I remember one who used to come to the block all the time, thought he was a pimp. He had an old dried up Jerry curl, a cane, and walked with a real limp because one leg was shorter than the other. He used to come to the block with his one and only hoe, they'd buy together at first. Then about an hour later they'd come back solo, trying to cop by themselves and tell you not to tell the other.

There was this other fiend who had a song he'd sing while he was waiting for you to get the crack. He'd be singing, "I'm king of the hypes, I carry a crack pipe," and he had this contraption put together that he used to get high that had about eight lighters taped together.

My man was this old head named Littles who used to come on the block and buy from me. He had much game and was quick with his hands. I had to respect his hustle; he kept me on my toes. For example: he'd come to the block and say, "Yo, Tee, I got this white boy around the corner trying to get high. What can I get for this 50 dollars? And you know I'm trying to make something on the side."

So I'd go, "You know you my man, Littles. I'll give you seven dimes."

Then he'd say, "Cool."

So I'd go to my stash, get seven dimes, and come back and hit him with the crack. When I go to count the money, it's only 41 dollars. So before Littles could leave the block, I'd catch him and say, "Littles, this money ain't right. It's only 41 dollars here!"

He'd say, "Word? Let me see." He'd count the money and be like, "Word, Tee, you right. My bad. This is what the white boy gave me and I didn't even count it. Well, what can I get for this 41 dollars?"

"Just give me one back, you can get six." He'd give me one back along with the money and leave. I'd run to stash the dime I got back and when I counted the money it was only 30 something bucks. I couldn't do anything but laugh.

Littles was slick and I wasn't going to do anything to him because he'd bring me money all night. As a matter of fact, when he'd come back to the block to get some more crack we'd laugh about it. He'd buy some more dimes and say, "Yeah, Tee, I got yo ass good the last time."

Then I'd say, "Yeah, we'll see who's laughing when you go around the corner and smoke that rat poison I just gave yo ass. Now laugh at that!"

As I progressed through this hustling game, I still tried to keep some morals about whom I sold drugs to. I would not sell to people who came on the block with kids, or my relatives. The latter moral principle soon became ineffective. I discovered family members were getting high and would just send other people to the block to purchase for them. As my money got better, I bagged up bigger rocks. I had jumbos! I even used to kill 'em with three and five dollar rocks, which I called "taking their lunch money." Yeah, right! As though these smoked out crackheads cared about eating. I still tried to keep my rule not to sell to relatives, but I had this cousin who was turning tricks to get high and she would come on the block spending crazy loot. She'd always ask to do business with me first and I'd say "Naw, you know I can't do it." Then she'd say okay and then spend about $200 with someone else on the corner. After a while, I started to rationalize. Why not sell to her if she's going to get drugs regardless? So the next time she came on the block, I jogged over to see what she needed and got that money. I thought to myself, *Damn! There goes another 'I will never' out the window.* Then I started to wonder if I had any moral limitation. Was there anything that I would not eventually do?

I felt bad because people I looked up to when I was younger were now buying crack from me. I'd walk off and make a sell to one of them and come back to the crowd on the corner and someone would ask, "Yo, wasn't that so-and-so?"

I'd say, "Word."

He would say "That nigga cracked out; he looks bad!"

"Yeah, I know."

Crack was changing the whole neighborhood. It killed the pickup basketball games at the park because a lot of the old head basketball players were getting high now and all the young cats were too busy hustling and didn't have time to ball. Also, it was crazy when females who used to be fine back in the day would come to the block to buy crack or try to give you head for a couple of dimes. Slowly but surely, the neighborhood started to go down; houses were being neglected, abandoned, and boarded up. You had blocks and blocks of vacant lots and boarded up houses. Sadly, with the drug culture comes violence, but we tried to keep that away from the block. We always said "you can't hustle when you got beef." In our case, we had some beef in the streets but nobody would come down our way looking for us. There were too many of us. There were always at least 5 to 10 of us on the block at a time, sometimes more. So, when there was a problem, it was normally some hood shit. And one time I caught the bad end of it.

I was on the block trying to sell this lady and her friend some dime bags when they tried the old switcheroo with my dope. They asked to see how big my rocks were and then tried to switch it with some bagged up soap or wax, whatever the hell it was. I was hip to it and peeped their game and laughed it off. When she tried to give me the dummy packages back, I said to her, "Stop playing and give me back my shit. It was a good try." But she wouldn't and we got into a heated argument on the block. Now, if she'd been a dude, I would've beaten her down and took my shit back, but this was an older female. Once again I was warring with my morals. Plus, I grew up with two of her nephews and her niece and knew her family well.

Well, anyway, Rick came over to see what was going on and pushed her and told her to get off the block with that bullshit. So she left and I took the little loss. I wasn't worried. I knew she'd be back with some money and I'd just get even with her the next time.

Little did I know she went around the corner to her family's house and told them we beat her up. About 10 minutes later, her father, who was probably around 70 years old at the time, came around the corner walking with a cane with other family members to confront us. We tried to tell them what happened, but they weren't trying to hear it. I think they took this as an opportunity to lash out at us because we were selling crack in the hood and to their family member. Well, anyway, at the time this was happening, there was a block party going on the street and mad people were out.

All of a sudden, one of her nephews pulled up. We all grew up together, so we figured he was just coming to find out what happened, talk, and straighten out this mess. But he jumped out with the Glock, put one in the chamber, and everybody cleared the block running. I could not believe what this had escalated to.

The next day, the kid came on the block, and as usual, we were mad deep. He shook hands and pounded up everybody but me. He told me I had started all this shit and, as Dogg used to say, "threw up his dick beaters," and said, "What's up now?" I was stunned! I peeped how he made sure he was good on the block so he could get a fair one. I wasn't looking for help. Shit, I normally welcomed a fair one.

I squared up with him. Mind you, he was my height, 6' 3", but was mad brolic and outweighed me by about 50 pounds of muscle. Translation: this dude was probably about to whoop my ass. We went in the street and all I could think about was this was all over nothing. I wasn't mad and I didn't want to fight. I grew up idolizing this dude on the basketball court and now we're in the street 'bout to get it in. Then I put my hands down and said, "What are we 'bout to fight over?" I guess he didn't really know either because he could've just snuffed me but he squashed it. We shook hands and he jetted. So we wound up not fighting, but that wasn't the end of it.

The following day I was on the block sitting on some steps when his older brother snuck around the corner and hit me over the head with a pool stick and ran. I jumped up and tried to chase him, but he had opened me up and blood was dripping down my face into my eyes, blinding me. It was in the middle of the summer, so I took off my shirt and put it on my head to stop the bleeding and drove myself to the emergency room. I had to get a few stitches and was discharged. It seemed like the whole family had beef with me and I didn't do anything. But of course, I wasn't innocent and shit happens when you're out there doing wrong.

After that, I didn't see him for about six months, and I am not going to lie, I wasn't looking for him either. I knew if anything happened to the dude they would blame me, and it would bring mad drama to the hood. When I finally saw him, we were in a bar in the hood about eight deep.

He walked in the bar, saw who was in there with me, and came right over to me and said, "Can I talk to you for a minute?" He was about my height, but he was thin like me, so in actuality, this would have been a fair one. Well, that is if I hadn't been there with seven other dudes who were drunk and ready to stomp his ass out.

We went over in the corner and he said, "Yo, I'm sorry about hitting you with the pool stick. I was wrong and I got some money coming from a settlement and I can give you a short for your medical bills." He continued.

I couldn't believe this dude was copping a plea after he had bragged around the whole neighborhood about what he had done to me. I was looking at this muthafucka like, "nigga, please." I knew he was lying and just trying to get out of this situation in the bar. I was getting madder and madder as I stood there listening while he was talking this bullshit to me. I could see that my crew kept glancing my way, ready for me to give the word to jump him.

Then he extended his hand to shake. I just looked at him like he was crazy. He saw that I wasn't trying to shake his hand, so he got loud and said, "So, what's up, we good or what, nigga?"

All these thoughts began to run through my mind about what I should do: *Hit him over the head with the Heineken bottle in my hand; Just swing off and then hit him with a chair; Give the signal for the crew to come over and stomp his ass; or shake his hand and squash the beef.* I shook his hand and ended it, but in my mind it wasn't over. I was gonna see him for what he did one day. But it wasn't gonna to be today. I was too focused on getting money and didn't have time to worry about some bullshit ass hood beef.

As I began to make more money, I also got tired of hustling on the block, which forced me to bear down on the block even harder to get my money right. I'd even pulled some all-nighters. I'd had enough of the narcs fuckin' with me and dealing with the crackheads. The fiends were always trying to hide in the fields and steal ya stash.

I remember one fiend I served pulled out a fake badge and I ran off, but he didn't chase me, he just took my shit. He got a few of us before we realized he was really a crackhead. I tried not to ever do hand-to-hand in the daytime. I'd get the money and then go to the pay phone like I was using it and put the crack in the change return.

Besides dealing with the fiends trying to hit some licks, the block was crazy with celo games. A lot of marijuana blunts were circulating; alcohol and crews of women coming down the way in cars loads four to five deep to see us.

There was always something happening on the corner. My man "Godbody" was part of the 5-percent Nation of Islam originally from Harlem and had everyone on the block studying Muslim 5-percenter lessons. The 5-percent Nation of Islam taught you knowledge of self that the black man was God and descendants from kings and queens in Africa. We gave ourselves attributes; mines was True Wise God Allah and every day when you came on the block you had to recite lessons. We also spoke to each other using terms from the lessons; so you had to study to know what we were talking about.

We took studying our lessons very serious but we also laughed a lot on the block too. One time we hid my man lil' Bird's stash and then give him a lick to hit and laughed while he was in the field frantically looking for his drugs.

I'd say, "Yo, hit this lick, I gotta go bag up." Then, while he was looking in the field for his stash, Godbody would say, "Yo, bring two more!"

Then my man AO would say, "Yo, bring three more!" So he's thinking he's missing out on mad money and would be sick! He'd be in the field looking hard as hell, moving and picking up shit. Yo, I swear that shit used to be funny as hell. You hated to leave the block because you were scared you'd miss some laughs.

I remember once we had cleared off the block because the firemen were running the hydrants when this fiend came on the block saying somebody had bunked her and sold her some bad drugs. The fireman told her to leave because they had to test out the water pressure on the fire hydrant. She said, "I ain't going nowhere until I get my shit!" The fireman told her to move one last time, and when she didn't he just turned the hose on her ass. Yo, that shit was so funny. No disrespect, but it looked like one of the civil rights protest videos. I swear she couldn't have weighed more than 90 pounds, and when he turned the hose on her ass, it lifted her off her feet and blew her across the street. Yo, we laughed so fuckin' hard.

Eventually, I accumulated enough weight licks, stacked my money, and bought my first big eight. A big eight is one eighth of a kilo (125 grams) and sold for about $4,000 at the time. Dogg bought me a bottle of Moet to celebrate my leaving the block. We had an unwritten rule on the block that once you start buying big eights you left the block and let the next person come up. Even though I had stopped hustling on the block, I still caught my first drug arrest on the corner.

I was in the bar one afternoon on the block, chillin', having a few drinks, and waiting for my pager to go off so I could hit a weight lick. I had my usual quarter ounce of weed in my pocket. For smoking purposes, of course. It was summertime and everybody was out deep on the block. I went outside to roll me a blunt when the narcs hit the block hard. I saw them coming, so I just put my blunt in my pocket and went back in the bar, not knowing that everybody on the block had their drugs on them and would run in the bar behind me and go to the bathrooms and start flushing shit. The bar door locked when it closed and you had to be buzzed in. The narcs start banging and kicking the door until the bartender hit the buzzer and let them in.

When they finally got in, they had their guns drawn and made everybody either get against the wall or bar. They found weed on AO and Rick and cuffed them. Then one narc came over to where I was and started searching this kid next to me. I heard him say, "Oh, what's this on the floor?" As I looked on the floor, I could not fuckin' believe what I saw. It was a rolled up brown piece of paper with bags of crack in it. The narc picked it up and unrolled it and said, "Oh, what have we here?" I remember it clearly to this day. Now ain't no fuckin way in the world that shit was there. I had actually looked around when they came in and chose to walk over there and put my hands on the bar and that shit wasn't there.

At first, they were going to arrest this other dude, but then he started blaming people. He yelled out, "That ain't my shit. It must be Bird's." But Bird was already handcuffed on the other side of the room.

Bird said, "Fuck you. That ain't my shit."

Then he turns to me and says, "It must be yours then, Tone!" I swear I fuckin' lost it! I leapt at him, but the narcs rushed me. One hit me in the head with a flashlight he was using to look around the bar and they arrested me.

I sat in my cell all night thinking about whooping the dude's ass who got me thrown in jail. I wound up copping out to a misdemeanor because the DA wanted to send it across the street to the grand jury and try it as a felony. I knew it would be my word against the cops' and I couldn't win. I got sentenced to a year's probation. I just chalked it up to all the dirt I was doing and not getting caught. But you know I had to see that dude when I got out!

We were arraigned the next day in city court. Black had called the crew's lawyer to represent us. The court officer brought us out into the courtroom and sat us down in the front. Our attorney came over and said he would be representing us. Then his hungry ass started asking about his attorney's fee right there in court. When he got to AO, AO just yelled out, "PD! PD! I want a fucking PD!" Everybody in court start laughing, even the court officers.

After we made bail, I went to my building to get some sleep. Coincidently, a little while after I got home the dude who told the police it was my dope on the floor in the bar paged Juney for some work. All the work sold on that block came from us, so he had to cop from one of us to hustle there. Juney got the page and told me the dude I was looking for was on the block waiting for him. I jetted out the building and ran almost a whole city block. When I got close, I slowed down to try to catch my breath and said to him, "You ready to see me for that shit you did?"

He answered, "What shit?" By then I was up on him, so I jawed him! We fought for a few minutes, wrestled, exchanged wild blows, then we both kind of just stopped. I was out of breath and had hurt my fist on his hard ass head. I was done. I'd grown up with the kid, so we were back to being cool a few months later. It was just another day down the way.

Now as my money got better, I started to attract a different level of women. This was both good and bad. While I was on the block selling weed and later switched over to the crack game, I was just dealing with hood chicks or just the ones who frequented the bar. But once I got some money and start dressing the part and pulling out knots at the club and buying rounds, different types of women started to take notice. Not calling them gold diggers, but like Kanye would say, they didn't like being around no broke niggas. We'd see a crew of chicks and hook up, crew on crew. As a matter of fact, it was this one crew that some of the members of my crew were messing with. Since I hadn't seen all of them, I was wondering if there was one for me.

One night in this club I saw them again, but that time I saw a new face and was trying to get to know her. We were at this spot down the way called the Poor Man's Palace. She was a little cutie, so I pushed up. She knew who I was with, so I figured I was already good. She was a little stank acting, but I liked that.

I said, "What's your name, sweetheart?"

"Cindy," she replied.

"I'm Tone," I responded.

We exchanged numbers. When I looked at the number she gave me, I said, "This yo pager number?"

She said, "Yeah".

"Yo, don't page me and put in your pager number," I said.

Then, being a smartass, she says, "Don't page me and put in yours either." We laughed and then we all went outside, my crew and hers.

We were all outside talking shit when I saw Cindy go across the street and get in the car with her uncle. But come to find out it wasn't her uncle, just some old dude she was fuckin' with. I turned to Big Rick and said, "Let me find out this bitch got a sugar daddy." We laughed. Well, anyway, my thoughts exploded. Shit! I didn't give a fuck about his old ass anyway. She was fine and I was going to get that. However, I did wind up having a little trouble with him, later on.

Now, around the time, we were going to all the local night spots like crazy. There was this one spot where everybody hung out called the Club Etcetera. There was always drama there, fights and shootings.

I remember one time when I was there with one of my homies and someone started shooting at the door. You could see people running and screaming. I ran and dove behind the bar and waited for all the ruckus to calm down. When it was cool to come out, I came from behind the bar and looked for my man, but I couldn't find him anywhere. I started to worry and began asking people if they'd seen him. Then all of a sudden, the ladies' bathroom door opened and he comes out laughing with a bunch of fine chicks. I was like, "Damn! I wished I would've hid with y'all!"

Even though some drama was bound to jump off at this bar, we all kept going. We used to go up there about 10 to 15 deep and you already know somebody was bound to get into something; we fought often at the clubs.

One night when we were there, I ran into Cindy. We had stopped talking because we didn't get along and used to argue about nothing, so we just stopped calling each other. We conversed for a minute and exchange numbers again. We talked on the regular for a few weeks or so. She seemed different and then I found out why: she was pregnant. Even though the news was unwelcomed, I had started to like her a lot. So, I was cool with it. She had a son and named him Kenny. His biological father was not around, so I assumed the role. Then later on, I did have a close call with Cindy's old stalking sugar daddy.

He started to drive by her house all the time, and one night he saw my Jeep and started to bang on the door like crazy. He had done it before, so whenever I went to her house I took some protection with me. This time he had about three or four dudes with him. I heard all these other voices and him outside yelling her name. Then he started to bang and kick the downstairs outside door. Cindy lived upstairs, so once you got in the outside door, there were stairs and another door to get into her house. He kept kicking and kicking until he finally kicked the downstairs door in leading to the hallway and stairs. When I heard the bottom door open, I told Cindy to go in the bedroom and close the door; luckily lil' Kenny wasn't there. I turned off all the lights in the house and waited for him. I heard voices in the hallway. It sounded like he was arguing with the guys he was with. Then I heard a car door slam and a car driving away. Fortunately, he had left; only God knows what would have happened if he'd come up the stairs and kicked in the door.

Cindy stayed on the other side of town, so I mainly saw her at night, unless she needed some money or something. I was down the way, all day, ev'ry day doing my thing: getting money, smoking blunts, wil'in' out, and messing with mad honeys. Big Rick's house used to be full of women just sitting around smoking blunts. Dogg used to say he was a rest haven for hos, but we still went there and tried to hook up with one.

I was buying about an ounce of weed a day just to smoke. I smoked when I woke up, then I ate and had to smoke again. I'd ride and go hit a lick and smoke. I'd eat lunch and smoke again. I'd run into a friend and smoke one, then I'd go play NBA Live or Madden and smoke. Then I'd eat again and smoke. We'd drink 40s with lemons or 40s with Guinness stout; we'd call them black balls. After a while, we stopped drinking 40s and graduated to Heinekens, Molson's, or Coronas. Then we'd get some bottles of Hennessy, Remy Martin, or Tanqueray and go out. We'd smoke on the way to the club and then smoke leaving the club. If we could, we'd smoke in the club. Then I'd get up the next day and do it all over again.

The year was 1994 and *Menace to Society* had just come out, so we'd roll up, ride, and go to the movies. I saw *Menace* at the movies like 10 times; me and man Lil Dap. We called him that because he reminded us of 'Lil Dap' from the rap group Group Home. Dap was like 17 at the time, and he was getting money on the block and had all his friends hustling for him. His mom had put him out of the house, because he was hustling, so he stayed with his uncle or grandfather, who lived down the street from me. Eventually he just started to crash on my couch with his man Slew Foot until he got his own place. We called his man Slew Foot because he had bad feet and walked with a crazy limp.

I remember when it rained Dap would stand on the block with a garbage bag on, getting that money. He is the one who started all that 31 hustler shit. We were all at 31 park one day when he came up there mad deep; he had about 15 to 20 young dudes from the hood with him. Since Public School 31 was right across from the park, people called the park 31 too, but it was really named Sperry.

I said, "Dap, how many of y'all are there, like 31? What, y'all the 31 Hustlers or something?"

After that the name just stuck. Dap was the leader and had about 30 young hustlers behind him. Little did I know that this name would spread like wildfire through the whole city and eventually the next generation of 31 Hustlers would be the focus of a federal drug sting and the words '31 Hustlers Bust' would be on the front of the newspaper and the top story on *Eyewitness News*. Go figure.

Everything was good at this time. I was enjoying my little drug dealer lifestyle and my party house. We were always doing something. We even used to block off the street sometimes without a permit and throw a block party. Didn't anybody complain on the street; we'd let everybody know in advance and we'd cookout for the whole street to eat.

One time when we did it, it was Big Rick's birthday, so he flew in DJ Scratch from EPMD to DJ at the block party and then later on at the party at the club. The whole crew was doing its thing and enjoying it. But after doing something wrong for a while, you forget there are eventual consequences. Eventually, there's a price to pay. You forget that karma is a muthafucka and shit happens in the streets. My crew and I were about to experience this firsthand.

Chapter 4

Life of a Hustler

A lot of shit started to happen to me and the crew internally as well as externally. Things all started when we had a cookout at my house. Half the day had passed and nobody had seen or heard from Dap. It kind of dawned on us, suddenly, when he didn't return our pages. We started paging members of his crew and they hadn't seen him either. Not wanting to think the worst, we told ourselves that maybe he was handling some business, had lost his pager, or was just laying up with some chick. But it wasn't like him.

At 11 o'clock that night we were watching the news and found out that the body of a young man was found stabbed to death and wrapped in a carpet around the corner. We all looked at each other in shock and repeated together, "Hell naw!" At the end of the news report, the newsman stated that a neighbor saw a gray car idling in front of his house for about an hour. Dap had just bought a gray

Hyundai Sonata about two months ago. It was his first car, and when he bought it at the auction, he didn't even know how to drive.

I remember riding to the mall with him and he hit two parked cars. He didn't even smoke weed at first, but we corrupted his little ass.

Well, anyway, to top things off, everybody from his crew was coming to my house and nobody had heard from him or could find him. Everybody from his crew was accounted for, except for two dudes who were suspiciously missing and not returning calls.

Someone called up to the Erie County Medical Center where they had taken the body, and from the news report and the description we got, it could be Lil' Dap. We were given permission to come in the next morning to see if we could ID him. I swear I didn't sleep all night. I dozed off and woke up on the couch the next morning with my clothes still on to a knock on the door. Everybody was outside and ready to go to the hospital. That was one of the longest rides I had ever taken in my life.

We went to the coroner's entrance, but the hospital officials only allowed two of us to go in. Lee and Black's big brother went in and came out crying. "It's him," is all I remember hearing after that. I swear, I don't even remember the ride home. I could not stop thinking about his mother. She tried to stop him from selling drugs but he didn't listen, and I partly blamed me and the crew. He looked up to us and we set a bad example. We even encouraged him when we saw he was serious about getting this money. Now he was dead and gone and we had no idea as to how and why. With that thought, my tears began to dry up; anger and revenge started to set in. Now we wanted to know what the fuck happened, who killed Dap, over what, and where the fuck the two other friends were. It was time to load up and put in some work!

We got some info and rode around looking for these two dudes;

they had to know something. And whoever did it took off in Dap's car, which was still missing. But the police beat us to the killer. The kid who did it was this wannabe hustler whose parents had money and lived in the 'burbs. He wanted to be down in the hood where his grandparents lived, trying to get his hustle on. Naturally, he took his ass home after the incident and his parents made him turn himself in.

The way I heard it happened was he paged Dap to come by and hit him with some work. Dap came over and left his car running outside and went in to hit the lick. The other friend was also there and I don't know if he was down with robbing Dap or not, but what it all boiled down to was he was there and didn't help. The wannabe hustling friend tried to strong arm Dap for the drugs and Dap wasn't having it. When Dap turned his back, he stabbed him multiple times, rolled him up in the carpet, and took his car. Then he went out to the 'burbs and had to confess to what happened. His parents called their lawyer and arranged for him to turn himself in, so we never got at him. But we did get a little piece of the other kid.

About a week later we all went to the wake about 10 deep and got in line to view the body for the first time. It was like time just froze; we stopped the viewing line and stood around his casket crying for about 10 minutes. As I looked at him, I wondered if one of us would be next. Then finally, his mother came over and told us we had to let other people see him. We all left out, and as we were coming down the steps of the funeral home, I saw a car pull up and then this dude got out and the car peeled off. I looked and then looked again, and then I heard somebody say his name.

Now the dude was really between a rock and hard place because we were already looking for him to see what he knew. He had been hiding, but not showing up to his man's wake or funeral would make him look even guiltier. He showed up to the wake and it was like someone rang a bell.

I heard someone yell, "There's that bitch ass nigga right there!"

Within seconds, there were about 20 of us on his ass. We were stomping the shit out of him when Dap's mom ran over and draped herself over him, yelling, "Stop! Stop! Please stop! For me!"

The next day we went to his funeral and that even made me angrier. Here we are mourning my man's death and all the preacher was talking about were the consequences of selling drugs and how we were killing each other. I understood the message, but this man didn't even know Dap and couldn't speak on the good things about him and how good-hearted and funny he was.

The next day after the funeral, about five of us went and got tattoos that said "RIP Dap."

Now in addition to Dap passing away, cats in the crew started catching cases. The crew was about 10 deep and now half of us were in the county jail, including Black and Dogg. When Black left, I had to go to Lee to get my weight. I didn't care because we all grew up together and were like family. I had known Lee since kindergarten and used to go over his house all the time growing up and play basketball in his yard. The only problem was that shortly afterward, I got into a disagreement with Lee and he threatened me, saying I wouldn't be able to hustle without him. But I didn't make a big deal out of it; Lee and I have been arguing since we were 5 years old.

Business for me was good around the time. I was re-upping like two to three times a week. I asked Lee for a play to get my next package cheaper, but he said no. That pissed me off because I knew if Black had been around he would've been accommodating. So the next time I copped, I just bought half of what I was normally buying. It didn't make a difference because I was paying the same rate even if I bought more.

About a week later, I heard a rumor that Lee said that I must have been tricking off my bitch and that's why I wasn't buying what I was previously. Now you already know I'm vexed. Fuck that! I didn't need him, so I found me another plug. That's when I found myself at the bar on the lower west side with my god-brother Mitch and his man Q.

About a week after my close call on the west side, Big Rick came down to my house and told me he had a new plug. He called his connect and the dude came through with it. We hustled for a couple of weeks getting our product from him until a little drought came. Then Dogg came home from the county jail and we went to see Black on a visit together. We broke bread and got a chance to get things straight. I found out he thought I was getting work from this crew we had beef with before I started hustling, because I was messing with one dude's little sister. After the misunderstanding was squashed, I was able to get back with the family and the numbers got better. Soon afterward, Black came home.

Around this time, my cousin Val opened up a hip hop clothing store. She had worked for Cross Colors in LA and had met and became cool with Karl Kani. He was from NY, and my cousin was born and partially raised in Buffalo, so they had the east coast in common.

When she first moved back to Buffalo, she noticed a void in hip hop gear. Everybody was driving to NYC to gear up with leathers and outfits. There were a few spots in the malls here, but the selections were limited. Eventually, she found a storefront in Allentown and used some savings to open a spot. At first, she went to LA and bought all her clothes. Then she was able to get accounts to have the clothing delivered. Her boyfriend from LA had moved to Buffalo to be with her. He was an OG Crip from South Central who had done a few bids, but was older now and had settled down.

When it came to the store clothing, of course the crew and I got first dibs on all the new fly shit. Dudes in the streets were upset.

Everybody in the city was rushing to the store, even the haters. Word got out that it was my people's store, which was good and bad. Some people wouldn't go there because they weren't trying to spend any money with my people, because they didn't like me or the crew. Others came because they wanted to spend their money with us as opposed to giving it to the white man. Val asked me to go half with her on the store, but I didn't want to mix business with family.

The store was one of the few in Buffalo with Pelle Pelle Coats. Others small stores that had the merchandise went to NYC and dealt with wholesalers, but my cousin's store had them delivered straight from the company's headquarters.

I used to go with my cousin to Manhattan to look at the new lines and place orders. Over the years, my cousin's store had Cross Colors, Karl Kane, Willie Esco, Fubu, Davoucci leathers, FJ550, Wu Tang's, Avirex leathers, Coretex boots from Vasque, Aku and Dolemite, Columbia gear, Coogi sweaters and dresses, and Maurice Malone gear. Sadly, the store would be the foundation for me, her, and my brother going to federal prison.

With Black home, everything went back to business as usual. Things were good and my girl Cindy was pregnant. We were excited about having a baby together and wanted a girl, since we both had sons already. She had given up her house and her and Kenny was staying with her moms in the Langfield projects. With our baby on the way, I told her to find a spot for us to move in together. She found a nice down low spot on the Upper Westside in a decent area. I think when we moved in we were the only black people on the block. That was cool though; I knew how to play the job role. Coincidently, the apartment she found was near my son Philip's grandmother where he was staying. He was about six or seven at the time, but I still rarely saw him because I was too busy running the streets.

At our new house, I'd get up every morning like I was going to work. I had a down-low car with tinted windows too, so I wasn't making any noise. The only problem with moving in with my girl was she did hair at home. In hindsight, she should've gone to work in a salon and I should've pushed that, but I didn't. Plus, she never pushed the issue either; I think she was comfortable being at home doing hair. The problem was everybody knew where I lived. So if they knew, the dudes they fucked with or were related to knew or could find out. Now the streets knew where I was laying my head and keeping my money and sometimes even my work. Plus, there was never any privacy. I'd come home and there'd be women waiting in the living room and dining room; the kitchen would be full of women, hair everywhere, and loud ass women laughing and gossiping. After a while, I couldn't take it, so I'd stay over my man's house 'til the wee hours.

Sometimes at night I'd fall asleep from all the weed and alcohol and wake up the next morning. I'd look at my pager and see that my girl had paged me a few times before she started putting 304 (hoe) in my pager. Now, I was in no way innocent. Yeah, I cheated; I was a young hustler in the streets getting money. What do you expect? If you think about all the bullshit I was doing in the streets, do you really think I'd give a fuck about cheating on my girlfriend? But I didn't cheat to the extent she thought I did. Nevertheless, over a period of time, our relationship turned sour and Cindy wound up having a miscarriage. I felt bad because I knew that my lifestyle was stressing her out and probably caused it, but I knew we could try again.

Now besides being down the way hitting licks and trying to get paid, I was running the streets and hanging out all night. It really got crazy when they opened up this new club called Jasmine's. This joint was hot; it had two levels, two bars, and a VIP section upstairs overlooking the dance floor. This was the time when Biggie was running shit in hip hop. Everybody was rocking Mauri Gators, Versace Shades, and Coogi's on some dress up shit. Black got real cool with the owner, this Arab cat, and it was on and poppin'. Black started to throw parties at this club and bring rappers from New York City, like Az, Fat Joe, Big Pun, and Smooth the Hustler. To cap that off, he brought in DJs like Kid Capri, Ron G, and DJ Scratch. We ran the club and never paid to get in even when we weren't throwing a party. We had free range to smoke blunts without getting tossed by the bouncers. It was so blatant that cats wanted to smoke their weed with us because they knew they wouldn't get thrown out the club.

I can't lie either, Cindy didn't like to go out no more, so I acted a fool. I knew it was my doing, but she never threatened to leave if I didn't change, so I was like "fuck it, she ain't going nowhere." I rarely came home after going to Jasmine's. I'd be weeded up and drunk and sleep over one of my man's houses if I wasn't swinging an ep' with some random chick. We'd get together after the club closed, smoke some weed, and wait for our pagers to go off if we didn't leave with a chick at the club. Most of the time I woke up on the floor or on one of my homey's couches. As you can imagine, life at the crib wasn't good. I remember one time when I came home after being gone for a couple of days, Cindy had a knife in one of my old basketball pictures stuck in my pillow and a crazy ass note written in lipstick on the mirror. Yeah, I know, that was some movie shit and jive had me shook.

When I arrived, she was gone. I put a little barrier in front of our bedroom door so she couldn't sneak in on me when she came back and try and fuck me up while I was sleep. I know she heard shit about me, but I started to hear shit about her messing around on me. If our shit had been tight and I stayed my ass at home sometimes, I wouldn't believe any of the gossip, but I left the door wide open for doubts. Our relationship was going from bad to worse. The only thing I enjoyed about home was playing and watching TV with lil' Kenny when I came home at a decent hour, which was rare.

Now that everybody was home and getting money, we started to travel on the regular. Buffalo is only a two-hour drive to Toronto, so we started to go up there on a regular basis; clubbin', concerts, and the Caribana in August. We'd get hotel rooms on Yonge Street and party. Then we started to go to Atlanta. Lee used to live down there, so when he started to get some real money, he bought a four-bedroom two-level house in Lithuania outside of Decatur. We were down there all the time. Then Black bought a house two doors down. It was on. We stayed in the strip clubs too; Magic City, Nikki's, Nikki's VIP. We even went to the Blue Flame in the hood. We threw parties during the Freaknik at clubs and at the house. We would stay down there for weeks at a time. When I came back to Buffalo, I had to hustle hard to try to make up all money I had tricked off in Atlanta.

I remember once when we were in Atlanta in the parking lot of Club 112 during the Freaknik. The club was so packed they had stopped letting people in and we had reserved and purchased two tables. Lee went in to get our money back and Juney and I sat outside in Lee's Benz waiting for him to come out while the rest of the crew was waiting with Black in his Land Cruiser. We were trying to holla at some bitches when a group of dudes came walking by singing "New York niggas is the craziest" by Naughty by Nature. The song was the shit at that time, and when it came on everybody would start reppin' where they were from.

Juney says, "Yo, fam, they look familiar. See if they're from Buff."

I go, "Yo, where y'all from?" A couple of the dudes came over, peepin' the NY plates, and said, "Oh, what's good? We from Harlem. Where y'all from, Brooklyn?"

"Naw," I said, "we from Buff!"

The kid says, "Buffalo! And y'all doing it like that?"

"Word! That's my other man behind us in the Land Cruiser."

He looks at Black's NY plates and says, "He from Buff too? Y'all doing it like that in Buffalo? Y'all must be down here getting it too."

"Naw fam, just Buffalo," I replied. By the look on his face, he couldn't believe it. We definitely were reppin' our city in ATL.

Back home, things between me and Cindy continued to get worse. She was unhappy with my lifestyle, so she started to say shit to provoke me and then we'd get into it. I started to plan on moving out but I was still too busy hustling and partying, so I never left. But the day I finally did leave changed my life.

One day Dogg called me about the car he had sold me. He had kept the car and insurance in a female friend's name when he sold it to me, but the insurance was about to expire the next day and I needed to transfer everything over. I went to my house to look for the title and couldn't find it anywhere. For some reason, I started to look through Cindy's things and got the shock of my life.

I went into a bag hanging on the closet doorknob and found pictures of two dudes. That was it. I packed my shit and left. I put my clothes in my trunk and took the safe to a little temporary spot, then went to Juney's house to smoke some weed, play Madden, and plan my next move.

A few hours later, I started getting mad pages from Cindy, but I didn't answer her. I thought to myself, *I ain't fuckin with this bitch. That's it!*

About 30 minutes later, I got a page from my aunt's house. I called back, not thinking that Cindy had gone over there and called. When I called back, my aunt gave her the phone and I'm like, "What? What the fuck do you want?" All I remember hearing after that was "cops" and "kicked in the door."

I left Juney's house and jetted over to my aunt's house. When I go there, Cindy was there with her mom and started to tell me how the police had kicked in the door looking for me, searching the house, and asking her a lot of questions. She said they didn't find anything, so they left and gave her a copy of their search warrant. Mysteriously, the search warrant didn't have my name on it and described me at around 5' 9" and I'm 6'3". Then she started to try to explain about the pictures. She said they were her friend's pictures and that her friend couldn't keep them in the house with her and her boyfriend.

"But you could keep the pictures in the house with your man and risk your relationship, like her shit is more important than yours?" I said. "So let me guess, your pictures are over her house, right?" I asked sarcastically. "If that were true, why didn't you just tell me in the beginning?" But as I thought about it, I should've been thanking her for doing that dumb shit or I would have been in jail. Even if she had been telling the truth and the pictures didn't belong to her, how could I ignore the sign? It was like the writing on the wall, so I was out. Even though I still loved her, I needed to rethink this shit.

To top things off, around this time I had just met this fine ass chick named Erica. She had a rep for messing with a lot of drug dealers, so I guess I was next on the list. I met her the same week my house got raided and I moved out. When I first moved out, I didn't have a place to go. I had gotten rid of my crib down the way that Juney and I had after Cindy got pregnant, so I stored all my stuff at my aunt's house in the basement. At night I had to find a place to lay my head until I found me a new apartment. I split time between hotels, swinging an ep over a chick's house, sleeping on the couch over one of my homies' cribs, and sneaking back home with Cindy every now and then. I started to see Erica more and more; every time I went to the club she was there. She had a whole crew of bitches too, so my crew was always asking me to call her and tell her to bring her girls. Then she fucked around and gave me keys to her house. Cindy had moved back on the eastside and had given me keys to her new house too. So each night, I would go from house to house.

The streets were talking. Everybody knew I was messing around with both of them at the same time. Cindy would call Erica when Erica would page me and they would subsequently get into it over the phone. Then Erica would get angry and ask for her key back. Now, I'm the type of person who doesn't go where he's not wanted, but I didn't give her the key back because I had started stashing my shit in her basement. I had stopped hustling for about three months after the police raided my house. I called my lawyer and he called the police and they said they weren't looking for me. I thought it might be the feds, so I just chilled for a while, which put a big dent in my funds and I would never fully recover. Now, either Erica was in denial or just oblivious to my actions because she saw me coming out of her house a few times with my book bag and never said anything.

One time, she caught me coming out of her house with a big duffle bag and I told her it was just some dirty clothes. She said, "Yeah right" at first, and then I said I would leave the dirty clothes bag if she was going to wash my clothes. After that, she naturally backed off. Eventually, I got a new house and gave her key back. After that, we'd only get up occasionally to swing an episode together. It was what it was, nothing serious. Although she would nearly get somebody killed and almost cost me my freedom later on.

When I got another crib down the way, it was back on! I could cool out, have company, stack my money, and do my thing. But I had to cut down the traffic since I had moved down the street from my grandparents, who habitually stayed on the porch looking down the street being nosey.

My brother moved in with me, which added to the traffic with his friends as well as mine. Although I was enjoying my bachelor life and pad, I never recovered financially from when I stopped hustling after my house got raided and Black started to slow down. He would have his hustle on for a week or two, then he would chill for a week or two. I was loyal, but he could afford to do that, I couldn't. All the profit I made off that little run would go to bills, weed, some gear, and other entertainment. And then I'd be back where I started from, counting the same money. The next thing I knew, it was a drought for about a month or so.

I remember me and Rick making some crack. We added some B12, baking soda, Novocain for the numbing effect, and some other shit. We cooked it and mixed it up. It was mad soft, so we threw it in the freezer where it would harden. We left for a few hours and when we got back, Rick had a big eight lick for 5,000 because of the drought, which weighed 125 grams. He bagged it and went to go hit the lick. Luckily, the kid called Rick on the way there and said never mind because we probably would have started a beef when he found out that he got bunked.

Besides that, I was still hanging out in the club a lot and getting in trouble. One night we went to Beni Hana's for my man Petey's birthday. Petey was my man from Brooklyn. He came to Buffalo originally with some dudes who tried to take over selling drugs in the neighborhood a few years back and decided to stay. He was in jail when the beef started and was never a part of it, so nobody in the crew had a problem with him. He started to buy some weight from me when his connect wasn't around and we became real cool. Then I started to see him in the clubs and we would get drunk and push up on some ladies together. After a while, he just started hanging on the regular with me and the rest of the crew and it was all good. We were at Beni Hana's eating and getting drunk as hell off that sake shit. Then Petey and I went to this bar called Uncle Johnny's and drank double shots of Hennessey. It was then when I discovered that sake and Hennessey don't mix well at all.

After we left there, we decided to go down to this club on the waterfront. We were drunk as hell and weren't there for more than 10 minutes before we got into some shit. I had walked off by myself to the other side of the room when this girl came to me and told me that Petey was outside fighting. I ran outside and saw him chilling and talking with one of the bouncers. I said, "Son, I heard you were out here fighting."

"Naw, I was breaking up this fight between these chicks and they threw me out too."

"Oh, alright, cool. Fuck this spot. Let's jet!" I stated. But Petey and the bouncer dude had started to exchange words and it got heated.

We started to go hard at the bouncer dude because he was acting like he was so tough and we had just seen him at the park jogging with his girl the other day in matching outfits. I said, "Yo, fam, didn't we just see his bitch ass the other day with some tight ass spandex shorts?"

"Word! With his nuts all up in his stomach." We laughed, but we didn't know he had gotten on the radio and called all the bouncers from inside. They came running out deep; it was like 10 brolic muthafuckas running towards us. Petey jawed the first one who ran up, and I was trying to get in my car to get my bat but didn't make it. Two bouncers grabbed me from behind and threw me on the ground in the parking lot. I hit my mouth on the ground and my gold fronts fell out. They held me and Petey down until the police came and we spent the night in jail, but it wasn't over.

The very next weekend I was riding around with Juney drinking beer and he was telling me how his aunt had just gotten arrested at the same spot during a brunch she attended, so we decided to ride by there. We chilled in the parking lot for a minute until I saw the one bouncer who'd had his knee in my back when I got arrested. He was talkin' mad shit too.

Juney said, "Yo, let's pretend like we getting in line to go in and then when we get to the front, set it off."

"Word!" I agreed. We had just finished off our Heinekens, so we put the bottles in our pocket.

Juney told his cousin, "Yo, get behind the wheel and pull up when you see us come running out," We got out of the car and stood in line for a few minutes. Then, Juney got impatient and cut in front of everyone and just went up to the front. The bouncer was behind the door, opening and closing it as he was letting people in. So Juney knocked on the door and as soon as the bouncer opened up and popped his head out, Juney busted the Heineken bottle on his skull and opened him up. He managed to grab Juney while he was falling and pulled him inside the door where the other bouncers were. I ran to the front door, opened it, and saw them wrestling. One of the bouncers was holding him by his coat, so I started punching him until he let Juney go and we both took off running out the door.

When we got to the parking lot, we didn't see Juney's cousin and one of the bouncers was on Juney's ass. Then, I remembered I still had my Heineken bottle in my pocket. I ran up behind the bouncer chasing Juney, got real close, and threw the Heineken bottle and hit him in the back of the head. The bottle shattered with glass flying everywhere and the bouncer went down to his knees. When Juney's cousin finally pulled up, we jumped in the car and got the hell out of Dodge.

It wasn't always good with fighting in the streets; we took some loses too. I remember chilling at my house one day when my man Flip came speeding up in my driveway yelling and blowing his horn. I came out yelling, "Yo, what the fuck is wrong with you?" I knew it was him because he had a 5.0; it was real loud and fast.

I ran outside and as I approached his car, I could see glass all over the place. As I got closer, I could see blood everywhere. "What the fuck happened, you a'ight?!"

"Naw!" he replied in desperation, "this punk muthafucka shot me! Yo, I was at a stop sign and this car pulled along beside me and this muthafucka just start shooting!" I told him to move over and drove him to the ER. He had to have reconstructive surgery on his left arm and he never gained full control of his arm and hand again, but that didn't stop him from catching a body a few years later and going on the run.

Chapter 5

Reap What You Sow

I didn't know that one of the females I was messing with around this time would eventually become my wife. I had met her about three years prior at a club called the Squeeze. I was with my man from the Cold Spring area and standing at the bar trying to order a drink when this little slim goody comes over to me and says, "Can you pretend like you're my boyfriend so this guy over there will leave me alone?"

I looked and saw how fine she was and said, "No doubt! As a matter of fact, we can play boyfriend and girlfriend when we get to my house too." She laughed. Then I said, "What you drinking?" I bought her a drink and then asked her name. She told me it was Tasha and we talked for a minute and I couldn't tell if she really liked me or not. We exchanged numbers and I told her I would call her up.

After that, Tasha and I chilled a few times, smoked some weed together, and naturally I was trying to hit it. So one night when we got together, I took her to a hotel but she wouldn't give me none, so I stopped messing with her. I respected the fact that she wasn't easy, but I didn't have time to wine and dine her; there were too many others that I didn't have to do all that to get the panties.

Between that time and this point of my life I had broken up with Cindy, and Tasha had had a baby, so she wasn't so slim anymore. She was already fine from before, but now she had a body to go with it. I hadn't seen her for a few years before I ran into her. When I saw her I was like, "Damn!" We hooked up and it was nothing serious at first; we became real good friends. She was cool as hell and I could talk to her. I loved the way she handled herself and how she was so self-confident, besides being sexy as hell. We even had several run-ins with Cindy and some jealousy from other women I used to mess with, but she didn't care. I think she knew she had me if she wanted me. I was really feeling her, but didn't want to be in a relationship. At the same time I didn't want to lose her. Eventually we got into a relationship down the road, but I didn't give it 100%, so our relationship struggled constantly on and off again. Furthermore, I had something hanging over my head and kept hearing that the Feds was asking about me and my cousin Val. I was hoping it would go away, but I figured that soon I would have to deal with it. Eventually that day came.

To give a brief history: Val befriended a customer who was hustling, a Dominican from the Bronx. He was in Buffalo hustling and saw that my cousin's customer base was a lot of dudes who hustled. He started to chill up at the store a lot and eventually extended an invitation to my cousin that he would look out for her if she knew some people who were looking for some weight in drugs. At this particular time I was struggling with Black's on-again, off-again availability of work and trying to re-coup financially to at least where I was before.

One evening the kid came by Val's house and we got a chance to talk. His prices were lower than what I was paying at the time, but I was apprehensive and told him that I rarely went outside my circle. He understood and said he would just give it to me to give to my workers and I could pay him later. "See how your people like it and then maybe after that we can do big business with your crew."

I told Black what I was doing and that I would keep him posted on the quality. The next day the guy came through with a drop off. I looked at the work and could tell it had a lot of soda on it because it was soft and broke easy, but I still put it out there to my peoples to get some feedback.

I got rid of some of it, and then my people started calling me back complaining. When I went to go see them, they said the fiends were complaining, so they had to give up mad deals. I told them to just try to get rid of it and I would look out for them on the next go 'round.

A couple days later I got a call from the store and Val told me the dude wanted to talk to me. She put him on the phone and he said, "Hey, Tony, how's it going?"

I said, "Not too good, but I got something for you. Come by my house tomorrow." Then we hung up. That's all I said, but that conversation got me indicted by the FBI for conspiracy to possess and distribute a controlled substance. I came to find out later this guy and his crew back in the Bronx were already under surveillance by the FBI. When he started hanging around Val's store, they bugged the store's phone and start watching us also.

He came by my house the next day and I told him about the complaints and gave him back what I didn't get rid of. He said he was going back to the Bronx and when he came back he would have better product and would call me. He left and I never saw him again.

About a couple of months later the FBI came to see my cousin Val. They told her that if she didn't cooperate, her whole family was going to jail. She wouldn't cooperate, so they left. She called her attorney, but he wasn't able to find out anything. At first, I was mad nervous. I cleaned up my building and started being extra careful and leery of new people asking me if I had work to sell whether I knew them or not. After a while, though, I just went back to doing what I was doing and thought they were just trying to scare us. I always heard that when the feds come, it's a wrap, they already got you, but they didn't come for us; they just threatened her and tried to scare her because she was a female. I thought they were just fishing and didn't have anything. Boy, was I wrong!

It was early 1998 and time for Freaknik down in ATL again. Black was on house arrest, but had put together a concert at the Atrium. So we went down to ATL to do some promotions and have this concert/party. Shit had gotten a little hectic for the crew recently and we didn't have it like we used to. We still went down there pretty deep, though. The concert Black put together featured Bone Thugs 'n' Harmony, Fatal Huseuin (Tupac's man), the Outlaws, and some other country dudes I can't recall. Also, we had DJ Back Spin from Jersey. By this time the Freaknik was winding down in ATL and everybody was starting to go to Daytona Beach during spring break, so it wasn't like it used to be. But we still had fun!

At the hotel, people started dropping off demo tapes and singing for us like we were record producers. We only entertained the females though. Yo! It was crazy. This old head who came down with us almost caught a rape charge and my man "grandson" had to take the girl to the mall and buy her some shit to shut her up. Back in Buffalo, every time we gave parties Juney and I used to walk around with the microphone and get the crowd hyped; so naturally we had to get on the mic in ATL.

After the opening local no-name acts had gone on, I was walking around and heard a familiar voice on the mic. I looked up and saw Juney on the stage with the mic without me hyping up the crowd. I couldn't believe he was up there without me. I ran over there, got up on the stage, and he passed me the mic. I yelled out, "AWWWW YEAH!!!" After we pumped up the crowd for a minute, I heard the remix of the song "Ladies Night" that Queen Latifah had done with Lil' Kim and Left Eye. Just then, this big ass bodyguard bumps me and I turn and see Left Eye coming from the back rapping her part. Oh, shit, I was on the stage with Left Eye! I walked off and got out of the way, but Juney went over to Left Eye and tried to dance all freaky with her while she was rapping. Yo, Juney was so ill. We stayed in ATL for about a week and then drove home to a lot more drama.

Dogg had just bought a motorcycle. I didn't fuck with them because I knew a lot of dudes who got fucked up falling and crashing and had skin graphs and shit. One evening I was at the crib and Black called. "Yo, can you go check on Dogg? He just crashed his bike up on the corner." Black was still under house arrest, so he couldn't go.

I jumped in the whip and by the time I got there, the ambulance had taken him away. I thought he had just crashed like everybody else and skinned himself up until I saw where he had crashed. He ran into a porch and I began to really worry. I got to Buffalo General Hospital and AO, Juney, and Lee were already there gathered in the waiting room. The doctor came out and said, "Where's the immediate family?"

And we were like, "We are his family!"

"Well, I'm sorry to tell you, he didn't make it." NO! This was not happening! Not again! Not Dogg! This time there weren't anybody to go looking for, just sorrow. I hadn't seen him that day, so I wondered if I would've called him or seen him that day if he would still be alive. I was with him the day before and the last thing he said to me was,

"Fam, I'm tired. I'm about to go home." It was surreal. Shit was bad, and about to get worse.

I still remember Dogg's funeral like it was yesterday. The whole day felt like an ongoing nightmare I couldn't wake up from. Like my grandmother used to say, "Like a witch was riding me in my sleep." The funeral was packed; Dogg was loved by many. It was funny, because now all of his lil' chicks started coming out of the woods. Dogg's mom had relocated down South, so she wanted her son buried down there. After the funeral, we all loaded up three cars deep and made a road trip to bury him down there. Little did I know that a couple weeks after we returned my life would be changed. Forever.

One day I was sitting on my front steps eating when a car with dark tinted glass and a lot of antennas pulled up. I stood up to look and was thinking to myself, *Yo, that's them Peoples*--as in the feds. They pulled off about a minute later. I had been hearing about the feds asking questions about me and my cousin Val around town again; they even went to see Val's ex-boyfriend in LA where he had moved back. I should have jetted, but I didn't. If they were coming, let them. I was tired of hearing all those rumors. I should have been more careful of what I asked for.

The next morning at about 6AM I heard someone outside yelling my brother's name. I thought to myself, *Who the fuck out there calling my brother?* I looked outside and it was on! The FBI had my house surrounded with guns out; some of them had on masks to hide their identities. I opened the door and they asked for my brother. I said that he wasn't there.

The agent said, "What's your name?"

"TheArthur Duncan," I said.

"Yeah, you too." He snatched me out the house and threw me on the ground. Then a team went in and searched my house. I heard one yell, "CLEAR!" and then they came back out. They took me back in and let me put some clothes and shoes on. My older cousin, who lived next door to me, had come outside and I told her to call my aunt and Val down the street. After they handcuffed me and walked me to the car, I glanced over and saw they had arrested them too. Now, mind you my grandfather was the pastor of a church, so it wasn't a good look on the street.

They took us downtown to the federal court building. When we arrived, they drove in through a side door and took us underground to this processing center where they took our picture and fingerprinted us. After that, they took us upstairs to a lockup area. A few hours later they brought my brother in too. Then it dawned on me why they were asking for my brother outside my house: the Dominican guy had fronted him some product also.

We all made bail the next day and were put on pre-trial supervision. After we left court, we had to go right over to the federal probation department, meet our probation officers, and get urine tests. So now I had to stop smoking weed. It was bad enough that I got a case, now I had to cope with it sober. Naturally after that I couldn't hustle, but shit, bills still had to be paid and my money was already funny. I chilled for about a month, then tried to get back to it, but you already know wasn't nobody fucking with me since I was hot. When people hear you got a fed case, it's a wrap. People start counting you out; they were even leery about coming by the house, let alone selling or buying some work from me.

For some reason, the summer that followed was crazy; I mean mad fun! We had the neighborhood bar on smash. Almost every night we had it flooded with crews of chicks. Lee had traded in his Benz for a Range Rover and used to park it on the sidewalk next to the bar; it was like a signal. "The Downtown niggas are here!" When they saw the Double R, they knew it was on and poppin' at the bar. I couldn't smoke weed because I was on probation, so I was drinking like a sailor, and after a while my tolerance was crazy. I used to drink mad Hennessy VSOP; double shot after double shot and wouldn't even have a hangover the next day. But anyway, the summer was crazy, and I was messing with mad little freaks, not knowing that one of them would get me put in the hospital, but not before one of my ex-chicks caused us to put somebody else in one, which almost landed us in jail.

It was my birthday at the end of the summer and my pager was blowing up; everybody was asking me what I was doing that night. I told them we would all be at our local bar getting it in. I was single and spreading myself real thin that summer with the ladies. I was really digging Tasha, though, but we weren't officially together yet. Naturally, she was going to be at the bar that night, but unfortunately Erica showed up and got drunk.

We were poppin' bottles of Moet and having a good time when Erica came over and sat on my lap. I pushed her off, but it was too late; Tasha had seen her. Tasha tried to leave, but I stopped her. Then about 10 minutes later, she and Erica walked past each other and bumped into each other. Drinks started to fly and Tasha hit Erica with her keys. It was crazy. We broke up the fight and I told Tasha to go in the back of the bar and chill out while I went outside to talk to Erica.

When I got outside, Erica and her friend were all loud and poppin' mad shit about how I needed to control my bitch. I was calm at first, just trying to settle the situation down, but she went overboard by talking to me like I was some lame or something in my hood and in front of my hangout spot. Naw, that wasn't going to happen. I kept telling her to chill. Then I said, "Just shut the fuck up while I handle this!"

There was this older dude, probably in his 40s, who used to mess with Erica's mom who came outside with Erica after the fight, just standing there. He said to me, "Yo! You need to watch the way you talk to the lady!"

"What? Who the fuck are you?" I replied.

"Don't worry about who I am, just don't talk to the lady like that," he said with a lil' bass in his voice.

I was already hyped up from the whole situation. "Fuck you!" I said before I punched him in the face. He fell to his knees and grabbed my legs, so I fell on top of him. Then people started running out the bar and we all started whooping him out. Some guy who was with him tried to run back into the bar, but the door was locked. We started kicking his ass too. Lee went to the Range Rover and got his bat and started Babe Ruthin' his ass. We heard sirens, so I ran back in the spot, got Tasha, and we all jetted.

When I got to the house, Erica was blowing up my pager and house phone. I finally answered and she said, "Was all that necessary? Y'all done fucked around and killed somebody!"

I was sick. I said, "What? Where you at?" She said she was at the hospital with her mom and they were trying to resuscitate the dude we beat up. I told her to find out what was going on and to call me back. I kept calling her all night, but she didn't answer. I couldn't sleep that night, so I went to see Black, who was still on house arrest, and told him what happened.

The next day, I called Erica's house and she still didn't answer. I was already out on bail and pretrial, so I knew I would sit forever when the shit hit the fan.

Luckily, when I went to the park I ran into Lee talking to his cousin, who was a fireman. His cousin said that he had responded to the scene last night and that they took the dude to the hospital. He had some broken ribs and a collapsed lung, but he didn't die. Man! I was relieved. Now I was thinking that Erica left me thinking I had a murder beef. It would be years before I even spoke to her again.

As fall began to set in, my hustle slowed and slowly but surely people stopped coming by my crib. I was on pretrial, so I had to go to a drug program and submit urine samples on the regular. I had finally gotten all of the weed out my system after not smoking for about three to four months, so my probation officer started letting me come in to report once a month. In the beginning, I had to check in with him once a week.

I had stopped hustling for about six months after I got arrested until things cooled down, so when I started back up, I was working with shorts and had lost all my licks. I knew how to grind though, so it was no problem. I started to build back up, but then someone broke in my house and stole my shit. I tell you, I couldn't win. Then to top things off, karma was about to set in. Big time!

I had started straddling the fence by going to church, but I was still clubbing and trying to hustle. One Sunday in church the minister prophesized she saw some people trying to kill me by stabbing me with knives. I really didn't take her message seriously because she said it like it had already happened. I didn't know this was a prediction, so I continued to go out since Black had resumed throwing frequent club parties at the time.

On this particular night it was my man CS's birthday; he was real cool with the crew. He worked in his father's record shop where we used to get all our mixtapes from. We used to go to his house on the regular and smoke weed and chill out. Plus, he used to have these get-togethers at his house with mad food on Super Bowl Sunday or whenever. Black brought in DJ Backspin from Jersey to do the party. Backspin had put Black's rap artist's song on his mixtape and had DJed the last party we had in ATL during Freaknik. The night was progressing nicely and I was walking around with the mic as usual hyping up the party.

Around last call these niggas decided to jump me. One dude ran up on me from behind and hit me in the head with a pool stick. It dazed me, but I was okay. I turned to see who hit me and I swear this was so unexpected I thought when I turned and the dude saw my face he would say, "Oh, shit, my bad! I thought you were somebody else." But naw, it was on and I was the intended target. This other kid ran up and punched me in the mouth. I just remember grabbing this dude and trying to see his face because I didn't know who the fuck he was. Later on I found out he had just come home and I was supposedly messing with his girl while he was away.

Anyway, I did not recognize him. I threw him against the bar and had his shirt balled up in my left hand while I started punching with the other. Then I got hit in the head again with a pool stick. That second blow brought me to my knees and opened me up. Blood was everywhere and I remember everything going in slow motion; I was in a daze. I thought I was about to die. I couldn't see because of all the blood and then I got hit again around my eyes and fell to the floor. I heard that Juney came out of nowhere, pulled out his blade, and started stabbing them. He poked like three of them before the rest of them started to jump him.

After security came, Juney helped me to his truck and took me to the ER. I got stitches in my face and some staples in my head and the doctor made me spend the night for further testing. I woke up the next morning in the hospital looking like the fucking elephant man. One of my eyes had swollen shut. I started to get visitors and everybody was ready to go to war. I had been in wars before, but it was never my beef. Oddly, I really didn't want any of my friends to shed blood because of me or get killed over my beef. That was crazy, now that I think about it, that I would go to war with my man over his beef but didn't want anything to happen to a friend because of me.

I thought about the prophecy from the minister about someone trying to stab me and then thought about when Juney stabbed the dudes who were jumping me. Is that what she saw? I started to think about all this shit while laid up in the hospital. I was thinking God had a hand in this to allow it to happen. This was my wakeup call! With this revelation, how could I retaliate? But if I didn't, everybody was going to think I was soft. I didn't know what to do, so I wound up doing nothing. I turned to God and let him fight my battles. Eventually my wounds healed, but I was about to go through something that to this day I still feel pain from.

To my grandfather, I was a failure and an embarrassment. Although he still loved me, I was a big disappointment to him. Everybody thought I was going to follow in my uncle's footsteps, who was a corporate executive on the West Coast. But I went to the left. And slowly but surely I went against everything my grandfather believed in, taught me, and raised me to be.

I joined the Nation of Islam and became a Muslim after I heard Minister Farrakhan speak because I loved his pro-black message. I attended the mosque for a couple of months until I lost interest and then I became a 5-percenter for a while. I wasn't working or going to school. I start selling and smoking weed and drinking, then eventually I started to sell crack. My grandfather used to always ask me, "Son, you ever think you going to 'mount to anything?"

I'd say, "I'm gonna try, granddaddy." Sadly, he never lived to see that day. My grandfather was from the old school. He worked 40 hours a week on his regular job at the plant, worked a part-time job at a car lot, and was the pastor of his own small church. He also paid all the church's bills, which is different from these new churches where the pastor gets a salary. Granddad could fix anything from cars to houses. He owned the church building, his home, and about six other houses. He did all his repairs, painting, plowing, and more. He once told me when I was little I used to always say, "I can't wait 'til

I get older so I can help you granddaddy."

Then he'd say, "You grew up and ain't lifted a finger." I remember another time when he had me, my brother, and cousin lined up against the house about to whoop us with a water hose because we had walked all over his new Cadillac picking berries off the tree in the yard. Thank god for my grandmother; she used to save my butt all the time.

Every summer he'd take us down south to Camden, SC where he and my grandmother were from. He had a house and mad land out in the country. The house didn't have running water inside or a bathroom. Luckily, my grandfather's brother made us a shower outside with the water hose. There wasn't a kitchen sink either and we had to warm up water to wash up on one of those old stoves you had to put firewood in. My grandmother used to cook her butt off in that joint, though. My grandfather was convinced there was gold buried on his land, so every year when we went down south he'd bring his metal detector and shovels to search for gold. He'd have my cousin digging for hours and you couldn't talk while they were digging because the ghosts guarding the gold would push it down further. Once when he thought he found something, my grandmother started calling his name looking for us to bring some food. You should have seen the look on his face. He never did find any gold.

My grandfather was the boss of the family and what he said, you did. He had a key and later on used his cross to ask questions. He was convinced that the Lord or an angel was controlling it.

When he asked a question and the cross went around in circles, it meant an angel or the Lord had said yes. If it swung back and forth, it meant no. People used to call him at all hours of the night and he'd be in the kitchen swinging that cross. He used to take baths in all types of concoctions and would be in the tub soaking for hours. When someone had to use the bathroom, he'd just close the shower curtain;

he wasn't about to get out of the tub. You could go in there and he'd be soaking in some red water one night, and then the next night some green stuff.

I remember another time on the 4th of July when everyone was outside shooting off their fireworks. My grandfather said, "Those firecrackers sound just like my 22. I believe that I could shoot it and no one will pay it no mind." So he went and got his pistol, shot it two times into the ground, and then it jammed unexpectedly. Then he started to unintentionally point it at everyone in the backyard trying to unjam it. My cousin Matt and I dove behind the car. One time he even called me a jackass when I lost the hairbrush he told me not to take out the house. Yes indeed, I had a lot of good times growing up with my grandfather. He was the only father I knew until I was 14 and went to Cali and got to know my dad.

Now as my grandfather got older, he was having a harder and harder time with his legs. He was slowly but surely losing the strength in his lower extremities, which killed him. Once we couldn't find him and wound up spotting him under his car. He had gone under there to do some engine work and didn't have the strength to pull himself out. Eventually, he couldn't walk and was too proud to use a wheelchair, so he had to be carried from place to place. At church, he would get the Holy Ghost and roll around in the pulpit. I knew my grandfather couldn't live like that, but he still had his right mind. Soon afterward, he went to the hospital to get a blood transfusion and never came home.

When my grandfather died, I was a failure to him and would've given anything for him to see how I'd turned out. The way I interact with my wife and kids is what I learned watching my grandfather interacting with my grandmother and us. I remember my grandmother turning to me during the funeral and saying, "Tony he left us!" I was speechless. I couldn't say everything would be alright or that I would take care of my grandmother because this happened when I was on pre-trial and about to go to prison in a few months. I wanted to say some words at his funeral but was ashamed at what I had become and had not become. So I just sat there and cried instead.

Chapter 6

Certain Uncertainty

To make matters worse, I had to be around my family who had all gathered at my grandparent's house after the funeral. My successful uncle was there from Nevada, who used to be my favorite uncle but somehow I had developed a disdain for him. He knew I was wasting my life away, so he would say little slick things to me about what I was doing with myself. He'd find a way to get a sarcastic remark in even if I tried to avoid him or avoid having a conversation.

For example, he'd ask how I was. I'd say okay or good and he'd reply that I could be doing a whole lot better. Or he'd ask what was going on and I'd say nothing and he'd say, "Don't you think you need to change that and become a productive citizen?" Man, I couldn't win with him. I just had to stay away until he went back home.

With all the family around, naturally there was lots of talking going on; our arrest was the big elephant in the room. There was also some chatter about me getting jumped in the club and winding up in the hospital. I was told by my cousin Matt, who was like the big brother I never had, had said that I got what I deserved, and what goes around comes around. The sad part is that he was right, but it still hurt me because it felt like it came from the backside. Now that I think about it, I couldn't have been more wrong.

Matt was one of those in your face type of people and didn't fear shit. It probably had something to do with the fact that he was a black belt in karate. But anyway, I saw him outside my grandparent's house after the funeral and he spoke and I didn't. I tried to walk away, but he grabbed me and said, "Yo, we need to talk." This talk changed my life and I will be forever indebted to him for what he said to me man to man.

We sat down in his living room and he told me I was wasting my life and needed to change or I would eventually die in the streets. He talked about how we were all raised and how my grandfather had set a better standard for us to uphold. Matt told me about conversations he'd had with our grandfather before he died and that our grandfather was more than just disappointed in me-- he said my grandfather was scared of me. The thought horrified me. I could hear my grandfather saying to me, "Son, you ain't the same son that left here. What they do to you in California?"

Matt told me that when I used to stash stuff in the yard around the house my grandparents would be looking out the window sometimes and see me. At that point, they didn't know what I was capable of. And the worst part was I was doing all of the things that would make someone fear me. I was selling drugs, carrying weapons, fighting in the streets, smoking weed, and drinking heavily. I had become a monster and didn't even realize it.

The things my cousin said hurt me deeply, I thought to myself, *I was his grandson. I wouldn't hurt him or do anything to cause hurt to him or my grandmother.* But I was doing exactly that, and now I understood. I don't even remember discussing what Matt had said or didn't say about me getting jumped. It wasn't even important anymore. A light in my head had finally been turned on, but I still had a cloud hanging over me that was going to produce rain. I was scheduled for another court date, and I had to deal with my dim prospects before I could look toward the future.

As it got closer and closer to my court date, I began to stress out more and more. It seemed like Tasha and I were breaking up and getting back together every week. I couldn't look forward to or enjoy anything. I would be in a good mood and then think about my case and my mood would turn sour. When I finally went to court, my attorney and the prosecuting Assistant U.S. Attorney (AUSA) would talk and laugh like they grew up together.

One day I got a call from my attorney saying the Dominican guy I had gotten the drugs from was taking a plea and telling everything, so my best bet was to cop out too. I asked him what the government was offering. He said we would know when we went to the Assistant US Attorney's Office the next week. That was one of the longest weeks of my life.

The morning I went down to the AUSA office was sickening. The only thing I could think about was my pending sentence and I also knew I would be encouraged to snitch. The US Attorney had to know about my real crew, and there was no way in hell I was going to tell on them. I prayed and prayed for guidance. I wondered after my awakening if I would get a chance to turn my life around.

I arrived at the AUSA office and was taken to a conference room. It was me against the world, although I was accompanied by my lawyer. At the table were the prosecutor and about six or seven FBI agents. I was thinking, *What are all these agents doing in here? Okay, I get it, they're going to try and scare me using intimidation tactics.*

I sat at the table and recited the Lord's Prayer in my head over and over like my grandmother taught me: *The Lord is my Shepard, I shall not want. The Lord is my Shepard, I shall not want.* Then, the prosecutor started to talk. He said they knew everything already, they just needed my corroboration.

He began by talking about this elaborate Bronx to Buffalo crack pipeline and knew my family was not among the major players. I wondered what they knew and what they thought they knew. He told me he knew I had just gotten a few ounces and that the stuff wasn't any good. Well, he had half of it right: the dope was garbage. I had to give a lot of it back because there was too much soda in it, which made it soft. But he had no idea how much I had gotten from the dude. In the end, I was only looking at 46 to 54 months, according to the sentencing guidelines.

Then the AUSA told me they had a proposition for me. I knew it was coming. One of the agents slid a picture in front of me and said, "Here's your get out of jail free card." I just knew it was going to be a picture of Black, but as I looked down I saw a picture of my man Flip, who was on the run wanted for murder. They figured I would turn him in to avoid going to jail. Then I realized why there were so many people at this meeting--a couple of them were US Marshalls looking for my man. He kept saying they were hot on Flip's trail and would catch him sooner or later. Then what the hell did they need me for?

I lied and said I didn't know where he was and that if I found out, I would let them know. They asked me about a few cities and areas where he could be hiding out, and one of their guesses was accurate. I got word to Flip after I left that he needed to move. The crazy part was they did catch him about two weeks later back in Buffalo and it saved his life. He was a diabetic and couldn't see a doctor since he was on the run. He was forced to take other people's insulin and wound up getting part of his left foot cut off.

About a week later Black called me and told me he needed to talk to me. An hour later he called me and said he was outside. I went outside, jumped in his whip, and we rode. We rode around for 'bout an hour talking about nothing in particular while drinking Hennessey. It started to get dark and we still hadn't talked about anything significant. He parked in the parking lot behind a building. I was thinking this must be some real deep shit. Black always had big plans and schemes, so I figured he had come across something major and wanted to run it by me.

He turned to me, downed his Hennessey, and said, "I'm taking my fed case to trial and need to know what I'm up against." Black was on pre-trial because he got pulled into this major indictment over selling this dude a car. The feds thought his conversation with the kid was really about drugs and they indicted him.

I sat there and thought about what he said to me and it dawned on me what he was implying. I said, "What, you think I'm a fucking snitch?"

"I'm just saying I need to know. You're one of the peoples that can hurt me."

"Naw, man, I ain't no fucking rat. Fam, I wouldn't tell on you." I couldn't believe he was asking me this bullshit. Then he said, "I know they had to ask about me when you took your plea. They know we run together?"

"Fam, I swear they didn't ask me one word about you. I thought they were, but they didn't." I could tell he didn't believe me. He kept asking me, "Is that your word?"

I started to get mad because first, Black was basically asking me if I was a snitch, and now he was calling me a liar. Finally I said, "Yo, I told you they didn't ask about yo bitch ass. Ni--" Just as I got the word "nigga" out my mouth, Black punched me in it. We started to exchange blows in his car with no one around to see or stop us. I knew he kept a gun in the stash, so I was trying to at least daze him enough that I could run and get down the street before he got to his burner. But the burner wasn't in the stash; he had it under the seat. I guess he'd planned on killing me the whole time.

I punched him about two times in the face and saw him reach under the seat. It was dark and all I could see was this dark object in his hand, so I reached for it and grabbed the barrel. As we wrestled, the gun went off two times and shot the steering wheel, making the horn go off. The barrel burned the shit out of my hand when the gun went off. I screamed out in pain, so Black must have thought he shot me and got out the whip and started running. I felt something warm and wet coming down my leg. *Oh shit, this nigga done shot me!* I thought. But I didn't feel any pain. I started to think I must have pissed in my pants when the gun went off.

Then, I heard Black say, "Yo! Yo! You spilling the fuckin' Henny all over yourself!" I woke up still in the car with Black with my cup tipped over in my lap. I couldn't believe how real my dream had been.

Black start laughing and said, "Damn, son, yo ass was over there snoring like a muthafucka!"

I was like, "Yeah, whateva. What did you need to talk to me about anyway?"

He said, "Yo, fam, it's about to go down. I'm about to take my shit to trial. They ain't got shit and I need to know what's against me." I sat there speechless in disbelief that my dream was about to come true in front of my very eyes. I was still a little half asleep and drunk, so I didn't think I was hearing this right.

I said, "So what you trying to say?"

"No disrespect, but I need to know. You're the only person I fuck with who has a fed case that can hurt me, so I had to ask." I was a little heated at first, but I understood at the same time. People were turning on their brothers all over the place. Just like Dogg used to say,

"The game been fucked up ever since Sammy the Bull snitched!"

I said, "Naw, fam. On everything I love, you good." After that, we killed the conversation and went on as if we'd never had it.

After my meeting with the AUSA, I felt better. Now that I knew how much time I was going to get, I started to plan accordingly. I did my research and found out that if I could get boot camp or the drug program in jail, I could almost cut my time in half. Suddenly, four and a half years turned into around three. My court date for sentencing was steadily approaching, so I was kind of hanging in the wind living day by day with no real purpose. My brother, my cousin, and I were all sentenced in a span of about two weeks. My brother got 33 months, I got 46, and they gave my cousin 48. She never sold a pebble, but they were mad at her because she wouldn't snitch. I think I got a few extra months off because I had a speech for the judge I had worked on for about a month. In the speech I talked about my mistakes and going back to school to the point that after my supervised release I was instructed to pursue higher education. Little did the judge or anyone else know that I would take that directive and run with it.

Since we were all first time non-violent felons, the judge gave us a voluntary surrender date. That's when you go and turn yourself into prison. My brother got his destination first: he got a letter in the mail from the U.S. Marshals telling him to turn himself in at Allenwood FPC in Montgomery, PA. FPC stood for Federal Prison Camp and was for non-violent felons, so to speak. I mean, there were stock brokers and others there for white collar crimes, but it was also full of drug dealers and mobsters. The latter two were capable of violence and had probably committed a lot of violent acts but were not presently sentenced for them. And as the saying goes, one's true color eventually will surface. Anyway, I took my brother to jail on his scheduled surrender date. Little did I know that one month later

Black and Juney would be dropping my ass off at the same spot; I got my letter placing me in Allenwood about a week later.

As my surrender date got closer, I began cleaning up the house, packing, and smoking a lot of weed. I started back smoking weed as soon as I left court on the day I was sentenced. I spent the remainder of the summer lifting weights and selling weed to pay the bills, but at the same time I was stressed out smoking most of the money up. My turn in date was October 2nd. I became numb.

The day before I was to leave, I spent some time with my son Philip, who was 10 at the time. I explained to him that daddy had done some bad things and had to answer for his actions and that I loved him. I also asked Cindy to bring Kenny by so I could say goodbye. She brought him and I told him I was going away for a while and to take care of his mother. Kenny was around seven years old and didn't really understand. I tried to hug Cindy goodbye, but she turned the other way, got in her car, and drove off, talking about how she'd be back. I figured she was probably still mad because she asked me to break up with Tasha but I wouldn't do it. Cindy said she was going to be the one who was going to be there for me while I was in jail. However, I never got a piece of mail, visit, or anything from her during the three years I was gone. I would call her to talk to Kenny and she would talk crazy. I even sent Kenny money from jail and never got a thank you or nothing from him or her. I wonder if he ever received it.

Anyway, the night before I went to jail I spent the evening at Tasha's house. Tasha had a one-year-old daughter named Jada when I started dating her. She was three when I went to jail and I had become attached to her. She was always asking me to pick her up, so I carried her around and spoiled her like she was my own. I couldn't say no to her. Now I had to say goodbye.

The next morning we dropped her off at day care and I just sat in the car and cried. Tasha dropped me off at home and we said our goodbyes and she drove away in tears. Petey and my little man Leon came through before I had to leave. Little did I know that would be the last time I would ever see Petey alive.

I had to be at the prison by 1pm and it was a three-hour drive to Allenwood, so we left around 9am to have some cushion. I smoked weed the whole way there. The whole trip was unusually quiet. I just stared out the window most of the time.

We got to Allenwood and Black gave me some money. I got out, shook his and Juney's hands, and checked in. Black yelled out, "Call me when you get situated!"

Chapter 7

From a Name to a Number

Allenwood Federal Prison was in Pennsylvania and situated between the Appalachian Mountains near Williamsport. Everywhere you looked all you could see was a forest full of trees and mountains. The prison camp, where I was designated, was in the front of the complex and there was a long winding road behind it leading to the low, medium, and maximum security prisons.

The prison camp kind of looked like a small community school at first glance; there were about seven or eight one-level buildings situated across the campus. There were sidewalks leading to each building separated by yards of grass.

I went inside the first building I saw near the parking lot and a lady inside told me which building to report to. I went to the R & D building, short for receiving and discharge, and was greeted by this tall, sloppy looking corrections officer (C.O.). He had freckles and a reddish scruffy beard; he looked like a redneck. He asked me my name.

"TheArthur Duncan."

He sarcastically laughed and said, "Yep, we've been expecting you. Strip down to your underwear, put your clothes in this plastic bag, and wait over there." I took my clothes off and waited for him to finish filling out some paperwork before another C.O. came out the back and told me to follow him into this room. I walked in the room, feet cold from standing barefoot on the cement floor.

He looked at me and said, "We gotta make sure you ain't smuggling nothin' up in here," as he began to put on his rubber gloves. I should have expected this, especially coming in straight from the streets, but I hadn't thought about it until I saw him put on the gloves. "Drop 'em and spread 'em!"

When I came out the room, the other C.O. threw me an orange jumpsuit and some blue slippers with a sneaker bottom. He said, "How much time they give you?"

"46 months," I replied.

"Damn," he said. "You must have really pissed somebody off. Get a pillow, a blanket, some soap, toothpaste, a towel, and stand at the door and wait for your escort." About five minutes later an older inmate in khaki pants and a shirt with his name and number on it opened the door and said, "You Duncan?"

"Yeah."

"Follow me." He led me to the other side of the jail grounds, to A unit. I saw other inmates walking around; a few of 'em stared and gave me mean looks. I was hoping I would see my brother, but I didn't and I didn't know when I would.

The inmate walked me into my unit and showed me where my bed was. I had the top bunk over some Italian dude from Long Island.

The units were like dorms. There were dozens of two-man bunks on the sides with locker cabinets to separate each cube. The middle aisle was one-man cubes you only got from seniority or by being a jail trustee. I put my things on the bed and went outside to the smoking area located outside the TV room and just stared at the red sky.

It all started to sink in. I was in jail now and was going to have to spend the next few years of my life here. I felt defeated. But this was the chance I took by my actions in the streets. I guess I didn't think I would ever get caught and face the consequences. Indeed, I had given away my born freedom for a season of illegal prosperity and now I was nothing but a modern day slave subject to the wishes and orders of the Board of Prisons, the Warden, and the C.O.s. My ancestors had risked their lives and died to be free, and I had given my freedom away voluntarily. Was it worth it? The answer was an emphatic no.

All those good times didn't amount to the cost of my freedom. And what did I have to show for all those "good times?" Nothing! Nothing but some pictures and memories. Now I would be a felon for the rest of my life. I had let down my family. Now, when people ask my mom and dad how I'm doing, what are they going to say? And when Philip needed his dad, what was he going to do? Most importantly, I'd let myself down; I deserved better than this. I always told myself I would stop the drug dealer lifestyle after I reached a certain point, but that time never came, and if it did, then something else would pull me back. So now I found myself here, in the middle of nowhere, in a prison camp in Pennsylvania over 200 miles from home, giving away time in my life I can never recapture. I am going to have to learn how to survive here. Or I could die here, mentally as well as physically.

Allenwood FPC was divided into three units (A, B, and C) situated in separate buildings on a small hill relative to the other buildings in the prison camp. A and B were for the general population, and C unit was for the inmates in the nine-month drug program. After inmates finished the program, they were awarded time off their sentences and sent to a halfway house in their hometown for six months before being released. I wanted to get into the program, but you needed under 24 months and a documented drug problem on your jacket to be eligible, then you're put on the waitlist. So I had to do at minimum almost two years of my sentence before I was eligible. I was assigned to A unit, but my brother was in B unit, so we had to go outside our units to see each other.

My assigned bunkie from LI was cool, but he was killing me in other ways. I couldn't sleep because he snored like a wolf and his feet smelled. Every day he and his other Italian friends would hang out in our cube or in front of it talking and acting out mob characters and movies. They even gave me a nickname, "Tony Dunks." It was nothing personal, but I had to get the hell away from those dudes. They were running some bookie shit too. I began to understand very quickly that you could do almost anything in here as you did on the streets if you knew the right people, especially in a prison camp with no fences.

We wore a khaki uniform every day with our inmate number over the shirt pocket. Your inmate number was according to your case number and where you did your crime and got arrested. The code for Buffalo and Rochester prisoners was 055. That's how you could tell where the inmates were from, or at least where they caught their case. They gave everyone black boots and a heavy brown coat for the winter. We were also given a pack of socks, a couple t-shirts, and underwear. Then after that, you had to purchase new socks and underclothes from commissary. Along with food, they also sold sweat suits and sneakers too.

There were second-tier famous people there, like John Gotti's cousin, the lawyer who Lawrence Taylor snitched on, and the man who conned Leonardo DiCaprio and Gwyneth Paltrow out of a lot of money. I came to find out later the kid who started the *Don Diva Magazine* from Harlem was in jail with me too.

A lot of the inmates had been in for a while and started their bids in the medium or maximum level prison and worked their way down to camp status. They originally had received long sentences and now had three or four years left and weren't considered an escape risk. Those were the inmates whom if you were cool with and if they trusted you, they could make your life in jail a whole lot easier. They had and could get stuff nobody else could. Plus, everyone respected them.

Inmates had snuck cell phones, all kinds of drugs, and homemade weapons. There were also individuals who participated in number running, sports betting, and even loan sharking. They even had point spreads and heavy betting on the A league basketball games in rec and softball games. Inmates also snuck off the grounds to go and have sex at a motel about two miles down the road. There was also a lot of homosexual activity in the showers and TV room late night.

One night, this inmate who had wifed this gay inmate named "Lil Kim" was caught having sex in the TV room with another inmate and started fighting the other dude. All the commotion woke everyone up and I could see the dudes fighting in the hallway while "Lil Kim" screamed for them to stop. The C.O.s came in and took both of them away. *This place is wide open*, I thought to myself.

The A and B units had about six dorms each with about 50 to 100 inmates. There were roughly 400 inmates in both A and B units and about 200 inmates in the drug program in Unit C, making it approximately 1,000 inmates from all over the East Coast including: NYC, Philly, D.C., Boston, B-More, and Jersey. There weren't any cells in the camp, so if an inmate wanted to get at you in your sleep, there was nothing to stop him. Allenwood FPC was very dangerous and unpredictable.

I remember when this group of Italians set this guy's bed on fire because they let him in their circle and later found out he was a rat. The hardcore Italians were no joke. The old heads smoked big cigars and played *bocce* and when a new Italian came in, before he could hang with them, he had to show his PSI (presentencing investigation report) so they could determine if he was a snitch. If the report had had 5k1 on it, you were labeled a snitch. If other inmates found out, you might as well have checked yourself into the hole and do your bid there because no one would befriend you.

On my first time going to chow, I saw two people I knew from home; unfortunately one was Tasha's baby daddy. He came to Allenwood from another jail to get into the drug program and was about to go home. He was a cook and when he saw me he said, "Damn, they got you too!" He acted like he cared, but real talk: I knew he was happy as hell I was in jail. He knew I was messing with Tasha and I knew him from the streets through a mutual friend. He sent someone from my unit later that day to get me.

I came outside and he start talking about how Tasha was supposed to be bidding with him when he left and that she wouldn't wait for me either. The funny part was that eventually he proved to be right but not for the reasons he thought. I would come to find out that God had another plan. We were there only about three months together and we stayed our distance, so we never got into it. When he left, he looked out for me and left me his wave cap and a cooking bowl. The commissary didn't stock them, so you had to get them from someone who was leaving who had brought them from another jail.

I put in a slip to get transferred to B unit with my brother and it took about a month before my case manager okayed it and moved me over. When I first got to B unit, I was assigned to bunk with this old head from Philly named Sampson. This dude was funny as hell! We used to go hard with the ribbing; he stuttered when he talked and was missing his two front teeth. He looked like a broke ass Lamont Sanford. I hope he reads this one day. He told me he used to sell crack in church. Sampson wasn't shit!

A few weeks later, a whole cube opened up with an up and down bunk, and my brother and I moved in together. My brother was doing pipe fitting, and I began cleaning in food service and shortly afterward was offered a spot as PM cook. I didn't do any real cooking, it was more like food prepping: opening cans of food, putting the food in pans, serving, and cleaning up afterwards. I got all the leftovers I wanted, like pieces of chicken and vegetables to re-cook back in the unit. The other inmates had to sneak vegetables like onions and broccoli from the salad station out of food service and most of the time the C.O.s would be outside doing a pat down. I remember seeing my man from back home faking a heart attack and falling to the ground so another inmate from Buffalo could avoid a potential pat down and be discovered with a plastic glove full of onions and peppers.

I worked as a PM cook for about six months and got an offer to become one of the food service clerks. My man from Rhode Island, named Benny, was already the clerk and I didn't want to steal his job; he was real cool. He was similar to me, in that, he was smart and had chosen the wrong path. At first we did the work together, but after a while he went to work for Unicor and was getting more money. Unicor was a federal prison industry company that employed inmates. There was a long waiting list and inmates could make a couple hundred dollars a month compared to the 30 and 50 bucks a month the other inmates made at their jobs. In a federal prison camp, everyone is required to work. So my working as a clerk was sweet. I was in charge of the headcount for food services. Since there are no walls or fences in a prison camp, inmates are counted three to four times a day at specific times and the C.O.s also conduct surprise counts to try to catch inmates who wondered away. I remember one time they did a surprise count and caught my man from Niagara Falls coming back from the motel. I think he got six months in the box for that.

My job as the food service clerk was to give an accurate accounting of people on and off the food service premise while the C.O.s were counting the inmates in the units. If I made a mistake and didn't put a person on the list who was present at food service, he had to leave and go back to his unit and get counted there; or if I put him on the food service list and he was up in the unit, then he had to come to food service to be counted. The big issue regarding this count was the fact that it was a 5 o'clock count and the AM cooks had to be counted in food service at that time. If I made a mistake and put one of them on the list on their day off, they would have to get out of bed at 5am and go down to food service just to be counted. I also did the time sheets for pay. The food service consisted of the veggie prep workers, AM and PM cooks, AM and PM dishwashers, bakers, warehouse workers, and all of the cafeteria workers. I think I made about $75 a month. For a regular job in jail outside Unicor, that was good.

After a while, I settled into my little routine with my brother. I remember when I talked to my brother on the phone before I got there he would tell me he was eating canned mackerels. I was like, "Oh hell naw! I ain't eating that shit!" But lo and behold, I found out how to cook the mackerels: a little rice, some Ramen noodles, some Sazon and Adobo seasoning, maybe a beef summer sausage, some broccoli, onions, peppers, and veggies that I snuck out from the salad bar in food service and we were good. Plus, this other kid from Buffalo had left me mad bowls to cook in when he went home.

After work we would go to the gym, lift weights, and then come back to the unit. I'd put some food together, throw it in the microwave, and we'd hit the TV room. We had two TV rooms in each unit with about five TVs and each TV only got certain channels. The TVs in the TV room were not played out loud, you needed to buy a Walkman from commissary and then tune into the TV station to hear it.

On one occasion one of the inmates stole the remote from the C.O.s' office and we were able to watch whatever until somebody snitched.

You had to get used to being in this camp with those scary ass white collar criminals, snitching or dropping slips on you for nothing. You had to be real careful. One time, this inmate asked everyone in the TV room if anyone was watching a TV. Nobody said anything, so he turned the channel and the next day he got written up for intimidation. Somebody dropped a slip on him because they were scared to say they were watching that TV.

The TV rooms were crazy. Inmates had their own chairs with names or some shit on the back of them. When I first got there, I had an old chair with a broken leg, but by the time I left, I had two Cadillacs, a Benz, and a Porsche. I wrote "BuffBABY" on my chairs. When something good was coming on a particular night, everyone would rush to the TV room to put their chair up in front of the TV. We also watched videos, and if you stayed up late, you got ya rocks off on *Uncut* late night on BET. Allenwood banned the new adult magazines from the mail, but you could keep the old ones.

I remember this inmate in my dorm had the Blu Cantrel penthouse joint he paid for with two cases of mackerel. I used to try to stay away from them joints, but every now and then…you know! Inmates used to make fefes and go in the stall with the magazines. A fefe was a heated rubber glove from the microwave with Vaseline in it. Yo, those fefes were like crack!

Watching the games in the TV rooms used to be crazy too. I remember when the Yankees used to play in the playoffs the TV room would be packed. If they lost, people would be throwing chairs and tables. As a matter of fact, if they won, people would still be throwing chairs and tables. The C.O.s would turn on the count light and make everybody go back to their cubicles to be counted. The only thing you'd hear over the loud speaker would be, "Count time! Count time!"

I remember when the Jets were playing the Raiders and everybody in the TV room was mostly from NY and was rooting hard for the Jets. The Raiders scored a TD and everybody got mad. All you could hear was my lil' brother yelling, "YEAH! That's right, that's what I'm talking about!" I swear it was like a commercial. The room got real quiet and it seemed like everybody turned around in unison to see who the hell was rooting for the Raiders in a room full of New Yorkers. Then, this loud mouth Italian guy from Brooklyn said, "Who is this guy? He rooting for the fuckin' Raiders?!"

My brother Ronny went, "You damn right!"

Before I could say anything, my man from Philly went, "Yo, that's Tone's lil' brother; he's good."

By this time, I had a lot of respect in the jail. I even started refereeing the A league basketball games after I hurt my knee and couldn't play anymore and no one ever disrespected me. I learned how to carry myself in jail and stayed away from the foolishness. I developed a lot of camaraderie in the weight room for punishing and going through partners that couldn't hang with my workout routine. Plus, I was very picky about whom I associated with. As I said before, if the inmates who had done a lot of time and had worked their way down to the camp from max or medium fucked with you and gave you respect, you were good. Fortunately, being someone who went straight to the camp, it was almost unheard of how I used to be around those seasoned inmates.

One of them was this kid from Buffalo name Drew who had a pretty big name in the streets. He had already done around 12 years and had about five left. His crew and my peoples were cool in the streets. Drew even told me a few inmates asked him about me and he vouched for me. He was in my unit at first, then he got moved to a different unit but he still used to come through. He didn't care about getting in trouble for some petty shit; he had been down too long. He even used to go in my cube when I wasn't there and make him a sandwich, grab a snack or something, and then leave a little note. I didn't care. Drew and his uncle, who was there too, were the closest thing I had to family in jail at that point and definitely so after Ronny left for boot camp.

Then there was a Christian brother from Harlem named Calvin I hung with who worked in food service with me. He had gotten sentenced to around 20 years and had about four years left. With him and Drew on my team, I was good. I even had some of the seasoned inmates coming up to me and telling me I carried myself well.

This one cat from NY named Eddie Lee was cool as hell. He was about 6' 7", and you could tell he had game at one time, but he had these two big long scars on his knees from operations. He used to come in the weight room and tape pictures of naked women all over the mirrors to give everyone some motivation. He would say, "Ya'll niggas bullshitting in here. Ya'll ain't getting no money, ya'll need some motivation!" Then he would go in his laundry bag and pull out these pictures.

He was in the drug program by the time I had gotten there and had already done a stretch and was about to go home. He told everyone that when he left jail he was going to have a limo full of bitches pick him up. When people went home from R & D, you could stand on the hill and look down to see them leave. Crazy part was that when he left, his man came to get him in a new Benz and arrived before the limo full of women. After he left, about 30 minutes later this dude came back to the jail parking lot in the limo yelling and waving with all these women. I guess he didn't want people thinking he was fronting. A few months later I heard he got killed in Jamaica trying to cop some keys. Eddie Lee was true to his word. He told me one time, "These people in here trying to rehabilitate me, so what the fuck I'm 'pose to do when I get out? I only know how to do one thing, and that's selling coke!" RIP Eddie Lee.

I played A League Basketball when I first got there until my bad knee gave out on me. I was dropping 20 on them cats on one leg. I even played in our little all-star game. There was some real nice ball players there too, and the games were off the hook. As I said before, there was heavy betting with point spreads on the games and inmates would be upset and get in their feelings when they lost.

I remember when these two kids got into a beef during a game and one ran back to his unit and got his lock off his locker, put it in a sock and came back on the court while the other kid was still playing. He ran up behind him and hit him in the head and blood was everywhere. The funny thing was that was the one and only blow he got in because after he hit this kid with the lock, the kid beat the shit out of him! He threw him on the floor and just start pounding him on some straight UFC shit. He might have killed his ass with his bare hands if the C.O.s hadn't come to break it up.

Anyway, after I couldn't play anymore, I started refereeing. Now, you already know this could lead to a volatile situation with people cursing out the refs. I saw it happen a few times when I was playing. My refereeing led me to realize firsthand how much respect I had in the jail as no one ever got out of pocket with me when I was refereeing. The C.O. who ran rec told me if it wasn't for me, there probably wouldn't have been an A league. I don't think he was trying to blow smoke, because he didn't give a fuck if we had a league or not. You should have seen how people would come and get me or look for me when it was game time. And I got whatever prizes the champs of each league or tournament got: sodas, Chex Mix, and whatever else.

I was doing alright in jail, but everything wasn't good for me back home. For the first six months or so, things between me and Tasha were okay. We talked a lot on the phone and she made the three-hour trip to see me a few times, but after a while I could tell the trips weren't going to last. The last time she came to see me in the winter she almost slid off the road driving back. Plus, we were off and on when I was home, so I kind of knew it wasn't going to last while I was gone. But I was going to ride it until the wheels fell off. She rode out the first year with me and then I could hear it in her voice: she told me she wanted to break up. What could I say or do? I was mad as fuck, but at the same time I understood and always felt like I could get her back if I wanted when I got home. I felt bad, so to ease my pain and keep my mind off her, I started calling and writing other females to get some visits. Then I got some more bad news from home: my man Petey had gotten killed over a celo game.

I heard he had knocked the dude out in the middle of the street. But when the dude got up he ran in his building, grabbed his pistol, and shot my man. Even as I write these words, I still can't believe he's gone. My closure stood still. I guess maybe because I didn't see his body in the casket. That was my nigga! Yo, we used to get so many honeys together. Almost every chick I was messing with he was fucking with her friend and vice versa. We were always out together, and if you saw one, someone would ask where the other was. Yeah, I had other real close friends, but for some reason when it was time to hit the clubs or go fuck with some chicks, I was always with my man Petey.

A few months later Juney's moms, Mama Gina, died from an

asthmatic attack. I called Juney and I'll never forget what he said: "Everybody is telling me to be strong, but strong just ain't getting it!" I was sick that I couldn't be there for Juney. We go back over 20 years and I love and miss his mother like she was mine. I just sat in my cube and cried. Outside of that, breaking up with Tasha, not really getting any visits or mail, and my brother leaving me to go to Lewisburg for boot camp, I came to the conclusion I was alone and this was my reality for now and that I couldn't worry about the streets.

Chapter 8

One-on-One with God

There was a little bit of everything going on at Allenwood. I thought about getting some weed and saying fuck it, but by the grace of God I chose a different path. As I look back at this period, I see that God was breaking me down for a one-on-one with him. I was reading my Bible every day, staying out of the streets, going to church and Bible study, and seeking him. When I say I stayed out of the streets in jail, I meant I didn't participate in conversations inmates would have about what they used to do when they were home and all the money and bitches they had. Their reminiscing and bullshitting were mostly lies.

I got a letter and pictures from my cousin Val, who was in a federal prison camp for women in West Virginia. It was good to hear from her and I was glad to know she was doing alright. I was more worried about her mentally than physically because I knew physically she would whoop a bitch's ass. I wasn't glad, but it was good to know my other cousin had violated her supervised release and was down there with her for a while, echoing the saying that 'what the devil meant for bad, God will turn for good.'

Well, that was jail for me. It gave me a chance to break away from what I was doing badly and start anew. More importantly, it gave me a chance to start a relationship with God, and that is what I needed at that juncture in my life. Still on the negative side, I was missing valuable time with my family I could never get back; specifically with my grandmother. She was in her late 70s and alone in her home dealing with the loss of my grandfather. I missed her dearly and called and wrote her often:

9/10/01

Dear Grandma,

How are you doing? The time I had left on the phone cut our talk short, so I decided to write you. I wanted to tell you that I'm doing alright. As a matter of fact, I'm doing better than alright. God works in mysterious ways and like they say, you'll understand bye and bye. Well I understand now why he sent me to jail, it has truly been a blessing for me. My faith has progressed so much and everyday I'm getting stronger in the Lord. I walk around the compound smiling these days, cause it's just so much joy in the Lord. He is so mighty, merciful and caring. I realize now that in order for me to prosper in life I have to put him first and not only that, I want to put him first. He has done so much for me, I was living such a bad life and he spared me. And gave me chance after chance and he has forgiven for my sins. I truly feel blessed because of you and granddaddy that I know him. So many people didn't grow up in the right type of environment, like I did, and they know god and his works and blessings I read the Bible everyday and I go to church every sunday, and I go to Bible study 2 to 3 times a week. And I also fellowship with Christian brothers constantly. One reason why I said it was a blessing I came here it because the brothers that I'm here with can identify with me. They were once in the streets running wild, so they understand, and they are

very powerful in the word and also very encouraging.
If they see me miss a Bible study they get on me
or they come get me. One day when I was reading
the Bible, the Lord told me that every chapter I read,
to read it 3 times for understanding. 1 for the father,
1 for the son and 1 for the Holy Spirit. I still do
the crosses you showed me when I was young,
after I pray. The Lord has showed me that if I
seek him, he will move in my life. Recently I've been
going thru a few things with me and ___ breaking up and
not letting me talk to ___. And it seems
like it all started when I start giving Christ my time.
I know it's not a test. In James chapter 1, 2nd verse
thru the 7th it talks about the trying of your faith.
And I know if I hold fast and put all my trust in him,
I'll want for nothing. In Matthew 6: 25 and 26 It
talks about how the Lord will provide your needs and about
how he provides for the sparrow, saying that we are greater than
a bird, as God's children of course he will take care of us. I
have the faith, so now I must do the work, cause as we
know faith without works is dead. I don't know what plans
the Lord has for me, but it seems as though I'm here in
training for when I come home. I want to give my family
and friends the joy I have in Christ. I also feel like I have
some making up to do to a few people I've disappointed. Going
to jail was someplace I thought I'd never be, but I'm a living
witness and I'm go testify about the wonderful works of God.
Take care of yourself Grandma and I love you God Bless
                                        Love Tony.

My resolve and growing relationship with God would be tested quickly thereafter, so I thought.

One night the entire jail was awakened by a fire in rec. Someone had set the TV in the recreation building on fire and for some reason my unit was supposedly the only one not on lockdown at the time and still had access to rec. So they interviewed everyone in my unit. The C.O.s couldn't come up with any leads, so to set an example they just randomly chose 20 of us: eight blacks, eight Italians, and four Puerto Ricans. I later found out that since the jail had banned PSIs and you couldn't show your paperwork to prove you weren't a snitch, the Italians got mad and one of them put a note under the C.O.s door saying that "he would burn this muthafucka down." And I went and got caught up in this mess, but like I said before, what some meant for evil, God will turn into a blessing.

That evening after they had interviewed everyone, they called my name over the loud speaker while I had my earplugs in reading my Bible. An inmate in the next cube came over and told me that they were calling my name over the loudspeaker to report to the Lieutenant's office. Normally, going to the LT's office was nothing to me because as the clerk in the food service, I had to go to the LT's office to make copies; so I really thought nothing of it. When I got to the LT's office, the C.O.s grabbed me and handcuffed me. I was dumbfounded when I was told I was going to the hole. I didn't know why or for how long. I later found out I was under investigation for the fire and the investigation could last up to six months. I didn't think I would be there for six months and knew they would find out I didn't have anything to do with the fire. Eventually, they found out, but it almost took them a month. I stayed in the hole for over three weeks for nothing. Or so I thought.

There wasn't a hole at the camp, so they had to take us over to the low security prison behind the wall. They gave us orange jumpsuits and took us to a secluded part of the jail that was dark and gloomy. They put me in a cell with some little Italian dude. The cell was very small, with just a metal toilet, a metal sink, a bunk bed, and a small window. It also had a slot in the door for meals, and when you had to use the bathroom, you had to put up a sheet for privacy. We were locked down 23 hours a day, and the only hour we could spend outside the cell was in a cage in the yard in the dead of winter.

The first day I was there, I got a Bible from the chaplain when he came by to check on us. They allowed us to shower twice a week, but you had to put on somebody else's recycled drawers afterwards. I went out for the hour of rec a few times, but to me it was a waste standing out in the cold in a cage. I tried to work out while I was in the hole doing pushups and sit-ups, but I started to feel as though the walls were closing in on me and had to get in the bed and pull the covers over my head. To this day I still feel claustrophobic sometimes.

I was interviewed again about the fire after about two weeks later without a positive outcome, but I was allowed to call home to let my family know I was okay. I called Black because I knew he would answer his phone and he was like, "Yo, fam, how you calling me. I didn't hear no operator?"

I said, "The C.O. called you direct for me. I'm in the hole."

"The hole? What the fuck you do?"

"I didn't do anything. It was a fire and that got me in here for investigation. Can you tell my mom that I'm good?"

He said, "Word, I got you. You alright?"

"Yea, I'm good."

"Where the C.O. at?"

"Shit, he right here. I'm handcuffed talking to you on the speakerphone."

"Oh, so the C.O. can hear us?"

"Yeah."

Then Black said, "Yo, Mr. C.O., if something happens to my man, I'm gonna fuck you up!" The C.O. laughed, hung up the phone, and took me back to my cell. I went back thinking, *Black going to get me fucked up in here!*

I was beginning to feel like I was going to be there for a while. I started to receive my mail from the camp and a couple of days later I had these dreams that would begin to shape my life in a new direction.

In the first dream, I was walking down the street back home and came upon this Catholic church down the way on Hickory Street, St. Columba's. As I walked past the church, I heard singing, so I went up the stairs to go in. I pulled on the door, but it was locked. Then a gust of swirling wind took me up in the air. I start spinning around, worshipping God, and there was a piece of paper with some writing floating over me and I reached for it. Then, I heard a man say, "Yo, you don't want to be up there." He reached out his hand and as I grabbed it, he pulled me down to the ground. Immediately, I grabbed the back of his head and put it on the ground and the ground opened up. I showed him Hell and people down there burning and screaming and I told him if he don't worship God that's where he was going. Suddenly, I woke up. I could not believe how vivid and real that dream was. Initially, I thought maybe I had eaten something bad. It wasn't a nightmare, but I tell you it scared the hell out of me. I knew this was a sign from God. He was about to start directing my path and a few days later I got confirmation.

I had another dream I was riding a bike down another street, and while I was riding past this church, somebody ran out and stopped me and told me to come inside. When I went inside, he said to the pastor, "This is the person I was telling you about." The pastor of the church told me to go and read the 11th chapter of John, and then I woke up. I couldn't wait to read the 11th chapter of John, but it was dark in the hole and we didn't control the lights. Still, I grabbed my Bible and went over to the light coming from the window overlooking the jail yard and read John 11.

Now John 11 is about when Jesus raised Lazarus from the dead and I was wondering, "What does this have to do with me? What is God trying to tell me?" But as I continued to read, I came across the fourth verse where it says, "this was not done unto death, but to glorify God." As I continued to read, the comparison of me being in the hole in a federal prison and Lazarus being laid in a cave grave with a big boulder rock in front dawned on me. Then, in the 43rd verse, Jesus raised Lazarus from the dead and told him to "come forth!" Before I had these dreams, I had started to question why I was in the hole. I truly believed I was doing the right thing in seeking God, reading my Bible, and trying to live holy even though I was in jail. Then, for me to be sent to the hole for something I didn't do made me wonder why. But this was part of my revelation that manifested as my closer walk with Him and my one-on-one with Him. He was breaking me down to build me back up and it all began to become clear that all I was going through was for the glory of God. Just like with Lazarus, I would be a living witness and example of His greatness. I lay back down with a smile on my face and couldn't wait to wake up the next morning to read my Bible.

Ironically, just like Lazarus, I was awakened the next morning by someone yelling my name. "Inmate Duncan!" Then I heard someone say it again. "Inmate Duncan!" I woke up in my bed in the hole. It was a C.O. He said, "Pack yo shit, you going back to the camp." I could not believe how God was revealing things to me and beginning to work in my life; it was almost scary. To me, this was God waking me up from the dead of my past sins and giving me new life like Lazarus.

I went back to the camp. I still had my cube, my bottom bunk, and my job. Most of the time when you go to the hole, you lose your bunk and your job and they make you clean geese shit from off the sidewalks until they find you another job. And that's if they let you come back at all and not transfer you to another jail. I was glad to be back and to get a haircut after more than three weeks…and to get rid of those recycled drawers. But my mood didn't last long.

During my time at Allenwood, there were always some issues with our living conditions. On a few occasions we had dirty brown water for days. The other inmates would still go and workout and not be able to take a shower and have the dorms stinking, or they would take showers in dirty ass brown water. Well, anyway, not more than a couple of days after I had gotten out the hole we had an anthrax scare. One of the C.O.s was giving out the mail in the TV room and found some white powder all over the mail. He freaked out and pulled the alarm. Naturally, once again it had to be in my unit. So now the whole unit had to sleep in the gym overnight. The next day, officials had a hazmat crew come and check out our unit and the white powdery substance the C.O. found. It turned out to be just crumbled up drywall, so they let us go back to our unit.

A few months later, I became eligible for the drug program. I was also eligible for boot camp, but when I found out that boot camp didn't shorten your sentence and I would have to stay in the halfway house for over a year, choosing the drug program was a no-brainer. The drug program was three months longer than the boot camp, but I would get nine to 12 months off my sentence, depending on when I was actually accepted in and my release date. The drug program would limit my stay in the halfway house to six months.

I finally got accepted into a class when I had 26 months left, including good time, which included nine months in the drug program, six months in the halfway house, and 11 months cut off my sentence after successful completion of the drug program. Getting 11 months off my sentence was cool, but later I found out the drug program was no joke. When people knew you had nine months to the door, inmates and C.O.s treated you differently because they knew you were trying to stay out of trouble to go home. They would fuck with you in a way they didn't before. Needless to say, I witnessed quite a few inmates getting kicked out of the program and had to do all their time. I prayed no one would try any shit with me and make me lose my cool. Because of that, I knew those next nine months in jail would probably be my hardest.

Chapter 9

Nine Months to the Door

Now, nine months is nine months. I still had to maintain and do the things I did to survive to get to this point; so I kept a cool head. At the same time, I started to think about all the people who were there for me during my incarceration. Then, I thought about who abandoned me while I was in jail. I understood the world didn't stop while I was in jail, but damn!

With that reality, I seriously considered having my parole transferred to LA and staying with my mother. The only reasons I reconsidered were because I wanted Philip and Kenny to grow up with a father around and because of my grandmother, who was home alone and still living with the pain of my grandfather's passing. Philip was around 12 at the time and needed his dad and I did not know what was going on with Kenny because of my feud with his mother. Plus, Black had expanded his record label and there was a chance it might become big. Black had started a record label before I went to jail and one of his artists opened up for the Cash Money and the Ruff Ryders tour when they were in Buffalo and Rochester. Anyway, not to get ahead of myself, I still had time to decide. In the meantime, I had to survive this drug program.

We met Monday through Friday for about four to five hours a day. We met in big groups and small groups and had one-on-ones with our counselor. We had books to read, homework to do, presentations and projects, and we also had to attend NA/AA meetings. If we got in trouble (a strike), we would be kicked out, so we had to be on our best behavior at all times. Oh, yeah, and we couldn't sleep past 7am.

There were about 20 of us in a class. Since having a drug addiction problem was a prerequisite to get in the program, when we shared stories in groups, a lot of us had to make up shit. For the most part, the inmates in the program were hustlers on the streets and were just trying to go home early, but on the other hand, there were cats you could tell were really fucked up from the streets. There were two young dudes from DC in the program who talked real slow because they used to mess with that "boat" before they got locked up. "Boat" is dipping cigarettes in angel dust and smoking it. I got in because of my weed dependency and because I caught dirty urine from cocaine while I was on pretrial supervision before I went to jail.

I remember my probation officer had put a drug patch on me and I bagged up some drugs. Even with gloves on, my urine came back dirty. My P.O. snuck to my house one night, barged in, and started looking around, patting me down and asking, "What's going on?"

"Nothing, what do you mean?" I replied.

"Your urine came back dirty!" he said. Now, the first thing I thought about was I got a weed dirty from being around people while they smoked weed. Then he said, "You tested dirty for cocaine!"

"What?" I replied.

"You heard me, you tested positive for cocaine."

Man I almost threw up. I just knew he was going to violate me. I had to think fast. I said, "I'm sorry. I put some cocaine in a cigarette because I was depressed after my grandfather's death."

"Okay, I'm gonna give you a break this time because this is your first slip up, but you're gonna have to go to group." Because of that, I was automatically accepted into the drug program when I went to jail and didn't have to go for an interview.

Like I said previously, it was tough being in Allenwood FPC because it was full of non-violent criminals from all walks of life: stock brokers, embezzlers, drug dealers, and tax evaders. There was definitely a mixed bag in our group, so you had to watch what you said in groups and to others in your class. I almost got kicked out of the program for saying something a person in my class thought was racist and he brought it to the attention of the group in the drug program one day.

We went around the room like we did each day, saying our name and drug of choice when this Russian guy from NYC, who used to be a stockbroker, said, "TheArthur's a racist."

And I went, "What the fuck are you talking about?" I was thinking this muthafucka was trying to get me put out the program. I was going to beat his ass if I got put out.

The counselor looked over at me and said, "Quiet down and let him talk!"

Then the Russian guy says, "I was trying to talk to TheArthur in food service and sat down next to him and he told me to go sit with my peoples. I think it is racist to tell me to go be with the other Russian people." Just then, all the black people begin to laugh hysterically while he sat there with this dumbfounded look on his face and said, "What's so funny?"

One of the black inmates said, "He didn't mean go be with your peoples as in your race. 'Peoples' is slang for the people you normally hang with, your friends."

The Russian guy said, "Ohhhhhh!" and apologized. Funny thing: after that, he and I became real cool.

As I got closer to the door, I started to think about what I was going to do for money when I got home. I definitively was not going back to the streets and hustle. I had a chance to start anew after returning, but I was returning home as a black convicted felon with no job skills or college degree, a lot of strikes against me. I had hoped Black's record label would blow up and I could work there. I even came across a great contact in the music industry while I was in jail and ironically it was the Russian guy from NYC.

Black was sending me pictures and bios of the new artists on the label, and one day when I was looking at them in my cube, the Russian guy walked by and asked me what I was doing. I told him my friend had a hip hop record label back home that I was going to be a part of after I left.

He went, "Oh, yeah? Well, my brother's best friend is Tommy Motola and I can introduce you when we get out."

"Yeah, right." I replied sarcastically.

"No for real, no bullshit!"

I said, "WORD?!" I knew people in jail make up a lot of shit and make idle promises. While I was skeptical of his gesture, I was enthused about the prospect.

As the end to my bid got closer, I still continued to keep my routine: the drug program, working in the day, hitting the weights at night, and refereeing the A league games. One thing I was not lacking for in jail was a crisp haircut. First, my man from Philly who worked in the barbershop was cutting my hair for free because I photocopied his appeal that would have cost him a lot if he'd photocopied it himself. As the clerk in food services, I had unlimited access to the jail's copy machines. The people who worked in the barbershop were not supposed to charge you because it was their assigned job in jail, but if you didn't pay them with some cans of mackerels or tunas, either you would be waiting all day or you would get a fucked up cut. Anyway, my little hook-up ended when my man from Philly got a job in Unicor. I had to start paying this kid from Detroit, giving him two cans of mackerels and a bag of rice for a cut.

Three months before my release I had to tell my case manager my release destination so the halfway house could reserve a bed for me. I decided to go back to Buffalo, because I had to be there for Philip and Kenny and felt like I had so much unfinished business there. Plus, there was the possible music connection. After I put in my paperwork for Buffalo, I just waited for my release date and the date my bed would be ready in the halfway house. I called Black to send me some going home clothes. Of course, he came through, as always. I had not talked to Tasha in over a year and wasn't quite sure how I felt about her, but I did want to see her daughter Jada, whom I missed a whole lot.

My release date was December 2nd, and I called Black to let him know when to pick me up. It was a three-hour ride home, and I was informed the Federal Board of Prisons would give me five hours to report to the halfway house as though I were catching the bus. Knowing I would have two hours to kill, naturally I began calling to see what female I could get with before I had to report to the halfway house, but nobody was messin' with me.

The day of my release I was up early in my V.I. (visit) prison uniform, just walking around saying peace to everyone and giving away my bowls and do-rags and everything else I had collected while I was there. The Russian dude from NYC had left a day before me, but true to his word, he came by my cube to say goodbye and gave me three numbers to contact him when I was ready to pursue the music label. I was glad to go, but I had met some real good dudes in jail and had some good times in spite of it all. I would miss them, and I knew that I would probably never see any of them again.

I heard the magic words over the loudspeaker around noon: "Inmate Duncan, Inmate Duncan…report to R&D!" It was the call I had been waiting for for over two and a half years. I was going home at last. The C.O. in R & D gave me the money I still had on my books and the box with the clothes Black had sent. I walked out the same door I'd used to walk in. When I got outside, I saw Juney and Lee. Juney gave me a new leather jacket to throw on before I got in the truck and headed home. I didn't even look back. I was out!

I felt like Lot's wife from the Bible: if I looked back, something bad would happen to me. Doing time in a prison camp was a form of psychological torture. You had to stay somewhere you didn't want to be even though there were no gates or anything to stop you from leaving. So in essence, you had to mentally wrap the fence around your brain and fight the urge to leave to avoid the consequences. There were no markings on the campus where you were considered out of bounds, you just knew. Although surviving prison is not an accomplishment worth bragging about, I still felt good that I'd done my time with integrity. I didn't lie or pretend to be someone I wasn't just to fit in with the crowd. I chose whom I interacted with carefully. I'd done my time and left quietly. As I exited, I wished they would forget me like I was never there.

I wanted to put this all behind me, but getting out of jail as a convicted felon would add so many barriers, so much uncertainty. In jail, once I adjusted to my surroundings, it was easy to follow my daily routine. Now I had to go out and face the real world.

As I stared out the window with little to say during the three-hour drive back to Buffalo, I wondered what the future would hold for me. How was I going to support myself? Would I be able to get a job? Where was I going to live? Would I wind up back in jail? To say I was worried would be an understatement. I drifted off to sleep in my thoughts, and when I woke up, we were getting off the I-90 to the 33 expressway heading downtown. I was back in Buffalo.

Juney was driving and said, "Tone, you got about an hour before you have to be at the halfway house. Where you going?"

"Take me to see my grandma, fam."

Chapter 10

Halfway Home

I left Allenwood in December of 2002 and had to do six months in the halfway house. The halfway house I was assigned to was right in the hood and you could hear gunshots at night. It was a big brick three-story building on a residential street that sat way back from the street curb. In front of the halfway house was a house for the administrators and counselors. The halfway house had federal and state inmates; there was even a small partitioned area with four rooms for the eight women.

The state residents were wild; they could literally piss on the floor and not get violated. They used to smoke weed and drink and still be good. Plus, they did not have to pay to be there. On the other hand, if the federal prison residents got into trouble for anything, we would be sent back. We also had 60 days to find a job or be sent back. Then, once we found a job, we had to give the halfway house 15 to 20% of our pay for room and board. The halfway house resident supervisors gave us random piss tests, breathalyzer tests, and we had to attend our scheduled group drug counseling sessions at a counseling center.

To go out and look for a job, I had to fill out a slip stating where I was going to fill out an application. I also had a counselor I had to submit everything to for approval. She would give me about an hour per place to go and fill out an application. I also had to call when I got to my destination and get an employee to sign my paper stating "I was from a halfway house and had filled out an application". Yeah, like they were gonna really hire you after that! Then I had to call when I was leaving the place.

I tried to get a job in the mall at Kaufman's and got a preview of what the rest of my life may be like. During my job search, I had only filled out applications and hadn't been given an actual interview. Until now.

At Kaufman's, I went to their HR department to fill out an application. An old white lady came from around her desk and asked if she could help me.

"Yes, I just filled out an application for employment and I want to turn it in."

"Oh, well, I do the hiring and if you have time, I can interview you right now," she said with authority.

"Ok, that's fine," I responded. She instructed me to come around the counter and follow her to her desk and told me to have a seat. She sat at her desk and began looking at my application. I followed her eyes down the application waiting for her to get to the "have you ever been convicted of a crime?" question. I had checked yes and wrote down my conviction charge, which was "Conspiracy and Intent to obtain and distribute a controlled substance."

She turned to me and asked, "What crime were you convicted of?"

"I was convicted of trying to obtain a controlled substance."

"What kind of substance?" she inquired.

"Well… cocaine, ma'am."

"You mean crack, don't you?"

"Yes, ma'am, but I never got caught with any; that's why it says conspiracy."

"But you were trying to buy some to sell to your people, weren't you?"

"No, ma'am--I mean, yes, ma'am, I guess."

"Well, what do you mean, you guess? Either you were a drug dealer or not."

"That's okay, ma'am. Forget it." I got up and walked away feeling less than human. I knew my application would find its way to the garbage as soon as I walked off. And then it dawned on me that I would probably go through this for the rest of my life every time I tried to get a job as a felon. I started to understand why so many people go back to jail after they get out. I started to think that eventually I would too.

I continued to fill out applications all over the city for about a month with no luck and was about to start trying fast food spots. My time was running short to find a job or be sent back to jail when I caught a break.

This guy Black knew was a manager at a wheelchair van company that needed drivers. At the time my license was suspended for a ticket I didn't pay before I left, so all I had to do was pay the fine, pass a piss test, and get my commercial license, which I would receive class training to pass. When I went to pay the ticket, I went to the DMV instead of traffic court and ran into Tasha's mom, who worked there. She came from behind the counter and gave me a big hug. We were always cool and I talked to her occasionally when I was in jail. Then, out of the corner of my eye, I saw that Tasha worked there too.

When I left for jail she was working in a beauty salon, so I didn't expect to see her here. She was looking fine as a muthafucka too, as usual. I did not know whether it was love or lust, but I thought to myself, *Damn, I gotta hit that again!* Her jeans looked like they were painted on. I had heard through the grapevine she was dating some dude and he was not doing right by her, so I knew I had a chance. She seemed surprised but happy to see me. We talked briefly and then she told her mother that she was going on her lunch break. We walked out into the hall and I could not contain myself; I just had to grab that ass. Her reaction from me touching her let me know that she was missing me and still had feelings for me. We starting kissing and she took me into this empty room and locked the door. I threw her on the desk and started to take her pants off when someone tapped me on the shoulder from behind and said, "Yo, you holding up the line." His impatience brought me back from my daydream, as I was standing in front of Tasha's counter in a daze. After I regained my composure, I asked her about Jada and she gave me her number and said I could see Jada. She had brought Jada to see me a few times while I was in jail. Even after we had broken up while I was in jail, I would still call Jada over Tasha's mother's house to speak to her.

After I got the job driving the wheelchair van, this ex-baller had to use public transportation and get on the bus and train every morning and evening to get back and forth to work. Talk about coming back down to earth, but I wasn't tripping though. I was just glad to be free and back home again. Because I was driving, my counselor in the halfway house required me to have a cell phone so she could contact me at all times, which was cool. I just had to turn it in when I came in after work.

At my job, I drove all around the Buffalo area picking up senior citizens and mentally disabled people in wheelchairs and taking them to and from day programs, doctor appointments, hospitals, and nursing homes. The old people were something else; some were nice, some mean, and they'd curse you out if they were waiting a long time for a pick up. Sometimes you would hear the wrath from their family as well. The mentally disabled people would bug out on your van, some would even have seizures. I remember one client took off his wheelchair belt, got up, and got buck naked. I called the incident in to my dispatcher, but by the time I got him to his destination, he had put all his clothes back on like nothing happened and then had the nerve to ask me to sign his paper indicating that he was good on the van; he was funny as hell. After a while, I upgraded my commercial license to a bus license where I had a bus aide and was driving busloads of patients. Depending on my run, I would switch back and forth from a van to a bus.

I kind of liked the job too. There wasn't a boss looking over my shoulder, I could stop and handle business between calls before picking up clients, and I enjoyed working with the public. I could take a two-hour lunch if I wanted, go get a haircut, or go see a female. Funny thing: up until then, all the jobs I had were part-time, so I didn't know that after 40 hours I would get time and a half. After that discovery, I tried to work my ass off, but my counselor in the halfway house would only let me work five hours of overtime. Since I was living in the halfway house and not paying any bills, I started to stack my little money.

The halfway house was not as bad as I thought it would be. The food was good; it was like home cooking sometimes, especially after eating prison food for over two years. There were some good dudes in there too, as well as some damn fools. Some state residents would catch dirty urine, jump out the windows, and not come back. The phone situation left something to be desired; there were only three pay phones in the whole spot that had about 40 to 50 people sharing them. When you came in from work, you had to make sure you had quarters for the phone to make calls.

One time I had to press a dude to get off the phone and I was not even on that type of shit, but he was abusing the phone for hours. We had a little game room in the basement with a pool table and a bullshit ass universal weight set, but it was better than nothing. We also had a little TV room in the basement.

There were a few okay looking females who came through the halfway house while I was there. Shit, I can't lie; I've messed with worse and had been locked up for over two and half years.

This one shorty was feeling me and was pretty cute too. I couldn't blame her though; I was on swoll, all brolic and shit from lifting weights in jail. In jail, the C.O.s used to call me the "weightlifting ref" because I was busting out the referee's jersey. My man Drew started to call me "Tony Guns" because every time he came in the weight room he said I was doing arms. Well, anyway, shorty and I started kicking it in the TV room at night and she told me she dreamed about us having sex. I wanted to hit it, but there were cameras all over the place. So I chilled until one day this kid from Rochester said that shorty and another chick had a plan to sneak us in their rooms. Needless to say, I was with it.

On the night shift there was only one resident supervisor on duty, and her office was near where the ladies slept. The other chick took the supervisor into the kitchen to distract her while me and the other dude snuck in the girl's section.

I went in shorty's room and she playfully said, "Oh, what you doing in here?"

I said, "Ma, you already know!" I got up on the bed and started taking her clothes off when the other chick came banging on the door.

She yelled, "Yo, the resident supervisor just busted us in the other room!"

Now how in the hell am I gonna get out of this girl's room? *Damn! I'm about to go back to jail for a piece of ass I didn't even get to hit. I might as well hit it if I'm gonna get caught anyway,* I thought to myself. So, I tried to take shorty back to the bed, but then the other chick came back hammering on the door again saying, "Leave now! Leave now! The supervisor just went to the basement." I jetted out of the room to the girl's hallway, out that door, and then up the stairs to my room. I couldn't sleep for shit that night. I knew I didn't get caught, but I didn't know if the dude would tell or if they would review the video and see me running from that direction around the time the dude got busted.

I got up the next morning and went to work. I saw the same resident supervisor before I left. She handed me my cell phone without a word. Later on that day when I got back to the halfway house, the other kid was on shit. He thought he was going to be violated, so he got some weed and was in his room smoking with a bottle of Hennessy. I asked him if he heard anything and if the supervisor had told on him. He was sure she did, but she didn't and he wound up getting violated for dirty urine. After that, I told shorty I would catch up with her in the streets and stayed on my best behavior so I could do the rest of my halfway house time on home confinement.

When you first get to the halfway house, the counselors let you go home on weekends. Then after a while you can go to home confinement and only leave home for work, church, or approved outings. You had to have your own phone line put in for the halfway house supervisors and counselors to call and if you missed a call, you were in trouble. You also had to call them when you left home and then again when you reached your destination. Then you called when you departed and arrived back home. The resident supervisors would call you around midnight and that was normally the last call until the morning.

My brother Ronny had been in the halfway house for over a year after finishing boot camp and had been assigned home for a long time, so he knew the routine. He told me the resident supervisors who were most likely to call back after your good night call. I managed to stay out of trouble, so they let me do the rest of my time at home at my grandmother's house.

One night when the resident supervisor who didn't call back was on duty and gave us our good night calls, we decided to go around the corner to the local bar. It was summertime and we stayed out to about five in the morning and had a ball. When I got in, I grabbed the phone and put it next to my bed so I would hear the phone ring for the 8am switch shift wake-up call.

I fell asleep in my clothes and was awakened by my grandmother yelling down in the basement for me to come upstairs and get the other phone. When I got to the phone, it was my brother saying the halfway house resident supervisor was looking for me and had called him inquiring about me. I said, "What? I been here and they didn't call." He said they told him they called me three times and I didn't answer. Then it dawned on me. "Shit! Maybe the phone was unplugged." I ran back down to the basement and picked up the phone and heard a dial tone. Then I looked on the side of the phone to my dismay: I had turned the ringer off by mistake. All I could say was "FUCK!" I immediately called the halfway house staff to explain, but they weren't trying to hear any excuses. The resident supervisor told me to pack my stuff and come back to the halfway house and that I would have to face the decision of the BOP (Board of Prisons) director.

Needless to say, I was sick. I went back to the halfway house and luckily was not drinking the night before because I was given a breathalyzer test and put in a room all to myself. My timing for a fuck-up was ill-conceived. It was one week before Easter and I had planned on going to church and Tasha was supposed to bring Jada by after church where I could see her in her Easter dress. I had seen her a few times at Tasha's mother's house between work calls and lunch after I ran into Tasha at the DMV. When I first saw her after coming home, she ran down the stairs and jumped into my arms. I loved this little girl like she was my own and this love for her would change my life in the near future.

On the Saturday before Easter I had to call and explain to Jada that I couldn't see her but would stop by and see her over her nana's house the following week. The halfway house counselor wouldn't let me leave on the weekends, but she allowed me to go to work because they needed their money.

That week I had to meet with the halfway house director to tell her what happened. The following week I got the word from the BOP that my punishment was to spend the rest of my time in the halfway house, which was only about another month. My cousin Val had just arrived at the halfway house a couple weeks earlier because she was waiting for living quarters. I finished out the rest of my time there and hit the bricks. Goodbye and good fuckin' riddance!

Chapter 11

Choosing a New Path

A couple of days before I got out the halfway house I ran into one of Cindy's friends. I had poured a cold Heineken on her at a club once for talking shit to me back in the day, but we were cool now. Plus, she had started messing with one of my homies before I left. I was at work driving the wheelchair van and she asked me when I was getting out of the halfway house, and I told her Friday. Then she said, "Me and Cindy gonna come down the way and see you."

"Cool, I'll be at the bar," I told her. I didn't believe my ex would be coming to see me. As a matter of fact, I really didn't care. She wasn't trying to see me when I was locked up and now that I was home it would be some bullshit for her to try to see me. But of course Cindy showed up.

When they arrived I had mixed feelings and really didn't know how to act or what to say. I was standing outside talking to Juney when they pulled up. The friend blew the horn and yelled out the window, "What up, Tone?" I was surprised to see them.

I walked over, leaned against the car, and dipped my head in the window. I told Cindy's friend how nice her hair looked, knowing Cindy was her hairdresser. Cindy was looking good too. I hadn't seen her in almost three years, but I couldn't bring myself to compliment her. I had a lot of built up animosity towards her. If I said anything to her, I was sure an argument would ensue, and I didn't want to kill the atmosphere. I knew I had to deal with her sometime later to see her son, Kenny. Nevertheless, I was able to make small talk asking her how she was doing until her friend saw Black and Juney smoking some weed and she got out the car, leaving me alone with Cindy.

After her friend left, I honestly did not know what to say. I had so many questions in my head to ask her, but I didn't know how to ask without getting into an argument with her. Where's Kenny? Why didn't you let him come see me in jail? Why didn't you ever visit, write or answer any of my letters? Why did you come down here to see me after dissin' me in jail? Where ya man at?

Then Juney yelled, "Tone, you got a light?"

"Yea, hold on," I replied. I told Cindy that I would be right back and as I walked over to Juney, I tried to get my thoughts together.

I pulled out my lighter and lit my little Black & Mild cigar and passed the lighter to Juney.

Black said, "Yo, fam, what's up with you and Cindy? She see you come home shining and all brolic and shit. She must want you to hit it again."

I said, "Yeah, whatever. She got a man."

He continued with his inquiry. "She got a man? Yo, what the fuck that mean? Fuck that nigga. She came down here to see you."

I thought to myself, *Even if that's what she wanted, I couldn't take the chance that it wasn't and give her the satisfaction of turning me down or teasing me; she had done it before.* Well anyway, I never got the chance to see because the next thing I knew she yelled out to her friend that she would be back and drove off. I guess she was mad because I wasn't sweating her or paying her enough attention, but what did she expect?

I was hoping my first night out of the halfway house would get better, but there wasn't really anything happening at the bar. We decided to go out, but Black had to handle some business first. Me, Juney, and AO got dressed up and went to this bar uptown to kill some time.

When we got there we saw three honeys sitting at the bar alone. One of them I knew because I used to mess with her sister and she used to mess with AO. I found out that Juney used to mess with the other one, so that left one for me. They both went over to them and left me on the spot. My game was a little rusty, so I went over to Juney asking who he was talking to to spark an introduction. Juney introduced me and she in turn introduced me to the one I was trying to get at.

She and I talked for a while and went over to the jukebox to play some songs. Out of the blue she reached over and started feeling my chest. No bullshit this time! I smiled and thought to myself, "yeah, she feeling me."

Then Black called saying he was ready and to come pick him up to go to the club. I exchanged digits with shorty and she asked for a hug before I left. She hugged me and kind of squeezed on my arms and back. *Yeah, I can get use to this muscle shit,* I thought. After we left, I figured we'd probably never hook up after she found out I used to date her friend's sister, but that wasn't it. I talked to her and saw her a few times afterward and I knew she was feeling me but was hesitant. Ultimately, I think she didn't want to fuck with a dude fresh out of jail with a felony. She probably thought I would wind up back in jail. Little did she know.

A couple of days later I was at the park shooting around with the youngins when Lee drove by and said he was about to go around the corner to Black's mom's house. I walked around there about a half an hour later and saw Black's baby mama, a couple other people, and Black's mom, Ms. G, talking to this old head who was down with the record label in the backyard. I thought that was strange but didn't ask and figured Black would tell me what was going on. I small talked with Black's baby mama and then told her, "Let me go see what dude is doing." It was funny he hadn't come out yet.

She turned to Black's brother and said, "He doesn't know, huh? Well I guess I'll tell him." She turned to me and said, "Black in jail." The way she said it made me know this time it was very serious. He'd been in jail before and had done about two or three small one- and two-year bids before.

I found out that Black had gotten arrested in a hotel room allegedly trying to buy some drugs from an undercover cop with a whole lot of money. Black was facing life without parole, so he wound up coping out to 25 years. The hood was sick. The record label folded and so did a lot of dreams.

I still had my other dreams though, and I didn't know if they would ever be realized, but I was going to damn sure try! I heard someone say that in life one should always go with his A game. I had tried hooping, my B game, and I tried rapping, my C game. Even hustling, I'd lived that lifestyle for a while and didn't make any real money. I was a preacher's kid and my heart was never into that nefarious lifestyle and I knew I was dead wrong for doing it. Nevertheless, in spite of it all, I still had my A game. I was always smart as hell and my teachers even tried to have me skipped up a grade in grammar school on a few occasions. I kept a 98% average throughout grammar school and never studied. I decided I would go back to school, but with my felony conviction I didn't know what I could become, but the important thing was that I eventually took the first step.

After all that I was back to square one with my life, working every day driving the van/bus, saving for a car, and trying to figure out my next move. I had started to mess around with a few females, but nobody special. I was trying to make up for lost time with my family and kids. Philip was always over on my street because he was real close to my family and he partially grew up on my street. Tasha even let Jada come and spend some time with me. I was having trouble seeing Kenny because of his mother; all I got from her was venom. I finally just took it upon myself to have Juney drive by the beauty salon where Cindy worked to see if Kenny was around. I had heard he came there after school. I finally got a chance to see him after more than three years and initially he didn't recognize me. Of course, his mother didn't let him come see me in jail and he probably didn't get any of the pictures I had sent to him either. Plus, I had gained about 40 pounds. But it didn't matter; I was just glad to see him. He was 10 years old and had gotten big.

After a while, I began to talk more and more on the phone to my ex. Tasha was telling me about all the money she was making from this beauty salon working on commission. She said she was tired of making other people all that money and wished she could open her own salon. I saw a business opportunity and started to do the math and seriously began to consider going into the beauty salon business with her. To me, it was a no-lose situation with a small investment. I could continue working my job and let her run the shop and rent out the extra booths. Plus, it would give me an opportunity to get what I really wanted: her! I started to realize that I still loved her and wanted to do right by her. Honestly, I didn't know her motives, but I knew my intentions and I just hoped this thing wouldn't turn out ugly. I decided to take a chance.

I told her I would be willing to invest my savings in opening up a beauty salon and that she should start looking for a place. About a week later she found this storefront and called me to come see it. I was able to hold off from buying a car because my boss at the wheelchair van company started to let me take my work van home at night. I took my savings, rented the spot and bought chairs, work stations, and everything the place needed to become a beauty salon. Toward the end of completion I began to run out of money, so we went half on the rest of the stuff. A week before the grand opening, the spot where she worked got wind to her salon opening and fired her so we had to open up a little early.

Things were going well in more ways than one. Tasha and I eventually got back together and decided we were going to build a future together. With that, I knew marriage would have to come down the line because she kept stressing we had already done the boyfriend/girlfriend thing and she wanted progression in her life. I had basically moved in with her and Jada in her apartment just outside the city. I felt like my life was beginning to fall in place, but I also knew I still had my future to pursue and it had to be through education. I enrolled back at Erie Community College that fall. I didn't know where this was going to take me or what field of study I should pursue, but I just knew this was the right and first step for my future prosperity. I enrolled as a full-time student. Now my plate was really full. I was working 50 to 60 hours six days a week, had a business to tend, and was still mending relationships with family along with this new relationship with my ex.

At first, a lot of things in school were foreign to me. I didn't know how to use Microsoft Word to create documents. Shit, I didn't know how to type either. I also didn't know how to use the email address the school gave me, but I caught on quickly. Learning wasn't a problem for me. My first semester was going pretty well and I got my first grade on a paper I wrote in English: a B+. I was very excited. I decided to major in general studies because I didn't know what I was going to do. I just took classes that fitted into my schedule and the credits earned would go toward graduation. I wound up taking a US History class and a sociology class with the same professor that semester. His name was Dr. Shatner and he was one of the most distinguished professors at ECC. He was also head of the school's sociology department. He was a very smart little white man with graying hair and you could tell he truly cared about the students and his profession. I was in class with him four days a week and we began to build a good rapport.

One day after class he asked me what type of career I wanted to pursue. I told him that I didn't know but I always wanted to become an attorney. I had taken a business law class in high school and wanted to become a corporate attorney ever since. When I enrolled in CSULA, I was majoring in business management until I dropped out. After that, I kind of lost the dream and got sidetracked for many years thereafter. He asked, "Then why don't you? What's stopping you?" I felt comfortable enough to tell him I had a felony conviction and didn't know if I could still become a lawyer. He said, "I don't know either, but I'll check into it for you."

About a week later he asked me to stay after class to discuss what I had asked him. He told me that in New York I could still become a lawyer with a felony but it would be hard. He said that I could go through the process of obtaining my bachelor's degree, getting into law school, and graduating with a Juris Doctorate degree, then take and pass the New York State Bar, but then I would have to go in front of the Character and Fitness Committee. This committee, made up of local judges and attorneys, would decide whether I was morally fit to practice law in the state of New York. Thus, I could do all the before mentioned and they could tell me no. He added that they would thoroughly investigate my past. And then he asked, "Is that something you are willing to try and undergo? If so, I will help you all I can."

Once he told me there was no bar on my dream and that it would just be hard. I was more than willing to try. What isn't hard for a black man in today's society? What isn't hard that's not worth having? He really didn't tell me anything new; I already knew it would be hard. But I didn't have anything to lose; I was ready to go for it! Confidently, I told him, "Yes, I can do it!" We discussed my seven-year time frame and commitment and the grades I had to earn in order to be accepted into law school.

At first, things were going pretty well at the shop. We had about five or six booths and I believe we had four rented out. I was working and going to school and for the most part things were good except for being cramped in the little two-bedroom apartment. I was ready to progress in our relationship and knew Tasha was too. The next step was marriage. It never dawned on me about the commitment I was about to make, and I honestly never really thought it through. I just knew I wanted to be with her and no one else. I bought her a ring and then showed it to her brothers to get their approval. I planned to show her father the ring and ask for his daughter's hand, but I never got around to it.

I knew how Tasha was a romantic and how special she envisioned her proposal day. I had to plan when I was going to do it. She has a very big, close-knit family and they were always having get-togethers. On this occasion, one of her great aunt's birthdays was coming up and the whole family would be there, including Tasha's mother, sister, great aunts and uncles, grandmother, and cousins. I envisioned a perfect proposal would happen right in front of this big family.

The evening of the party I didn't feel well and stayed home from work that day, but I still went to the party and knew Tasha wondered why. I had only been around her family once or twice before, so I really didn't know anyone. I socialized a little but I was more focused on when and how I should propose, but her grandmother helped me with that. I told her I needed to talk to her, so we went into the bathroom. Family members who saw us go in there wound up telling Tasha because they thought I might have been getting cursed out or something. Tasha's grandmother didn't bite her tongue for any one. She was a loving, giving, and sweet lady, but she would cuss you out in a minute and go to church and pray for you. Well, anyway, I told her I wanted to propose to her granddaughter and she said she approved. Then, I showed her the ring and she was surprised because she didn't know I meant that night. She got very excited and said, "Don't worry about it, baby. I will let you have the floor to handle your business."

We left out of the bathroom and when we emerged, I saw some wondering eyes like, "what the hell were they in the bathroom talking about?" The family was singing happy birthday to one of the great aunts and then when they were done, Tasha's grandmother took the floor and yelled out, "I got an announcement to make!" Everybody got quiet and gave her their undivided attention and then she said, "Come on, boy!"

Just like in a movie, I walked over to Tasha in front of her whole family, probably about 30 people. I got on my knees and said, "I love you with all my heart and I want to be with you and only you. Will you marry me?"

She cried and said "yes!" and I put the ring on her finger.

Now, given the fact that Buffalo is a small city and I was pretty popular with the women from my old street running days, the news of our engagement spread fast. I got a lot of mixed reactions: some approved and were happy for me, some couldn't believe I was marrying her after she didn't do my whole bid with me. Some couldn't believe I was marrying her and not Cindy, and others just probably bit their tongue. One of my lady friends who had moved out of town cursed me out on the phone and another acted like she wanted to fight me at a club; but none of them stepped up when I got home. I didn't tell Cindy because it really wasn't any of her business or concern. Things were mad rocky between she and I anyway, and this would just be another reason for her to deny me from seeing Kenny. I figured she would eventually hear about it and call me, but she never called or said anything, so I didn't either. I let her find out the same way I first found out she was dating someone after we had broken up: through the grapevine. Plus, I didn't need any other issues, especially since I was about to have my share at home.

Eventually, Tasha and I started to have issues at the shop when the weather broke into winter. The storefront we rented had been divided by the landlord into two rental spots and there weren't enough heating vents to keep the shop warm. We had to turn the heat up really high to heat up our individual spot. Needless to say, we were also burning a lot of electricity. The bills were high and the girls who were renting the booths began to leave. But what can you do? They were independent contractors, here one day and gone the other. Pretty soon, Tasha was in there all by herself and I wasn't making any money from the shop. As a matter of fact, I started to pay out-of-pocket to keep the shop afloat. Tasha and I would split the bills, but she made more money than I did, so after the bills were paid, I was broke while she was off to the mall. This problem would eventually come close to splitting us up. The money issues began to turn into other issues at home and we even got to the point where we talked about ending the engagement and going our separate ways.

After cooler heads prevailed, we decided to get some marriage counseling from the pastor of our church. We met with the pastor and talked about our issues and concerns. Most of it was me, because I was at a breaking point. I was used to having money, taking care of my girl, buying myself nice things, and paying the bills from my days of hustling. Now I was working my butt off every day and living check to check and paying the bills at this salon that didn't benefit me. I was ready to close the shop or do something else.

The pastor listened and said, "Well, the first thing I don't agree with is ya'll living arrangement." And I think a light went on in both of our heads. We needed to make this right and get the devil out our household, so we decided to get married secretly the next week in the pastor's office. We were still planning to have the big wedding with all the trimmings, but we weren't going to make it if we kept on our present course.

The following week we got married and all the petty problems we had earlier seemed to start going out the window. Now we were one, not "your money" or "my money" but "ours"...even though it still took me a long time to adjust to being the broker half and having to ask my wife for money from time to time. I also had to learn how to express my love with emotions and actions as opposed to through monetary gifts. Believe me, it was a big adjustment.

We were married for about two months when we had to make a decision. We found a house, but we could not afford the postdated big wedding we had anticipated and still buy, fix up, and furnish it. Naturally, we decided to buy the house, and with that, we had to announce to everyone we were already married and there would be no ceremony.

We bought a three-bedroom house in the neighborhood around the corner from Tasha's grandmother. Tasha grew up in this part of town, which was opposite of where I had lived, so I had to adjust. We had the second floor attic turned into our master bedroom and now we had four bedrooms. We made sure we bought a big enough house for my son to come live with us and room for an expanding family. So the four of us moved in together, Me, Tasha, Philip and Jada.

Chapter 12

Life and Death

Around this time my grandmother's health began to deteriorate. She was having complications from her diabetes and some other ailments and was in and out of the hospital and wound up there on Thanksgiving, so we all congregated there. Philip wasn't looking too good either and had been drinking and urinating continuously for the past two days. His face seemed to get sunken in and he was extremely weak and throwing up. Finally, I took him to the ER and figured he had food poisoning or another minor ailment. Boy, was I wrong! We found out that he was a Type 1 diabetic and would have to take insulin and monitor his sugar levels for the rest of his life. This was a shock to the whole family, especially him.

I came home to get his clothes because he was going to have to stay in the hospital for a couple of days. I went in his room and saw all the juice bottles he had in his trashcan trying to quench his thirst not knowing he had diabetes. I sat on his bed and began to cry. I started to pray and asked God, "Why? Why?" I swore I would have taken this burden from him if I could, but I couldn't. I knew this would be very hard for Philip. He hated needles with a passion and getting him to stick himself and give himself shots four to five times a day would be a job in itself. We had to see nutritionists and counselors and several different doctors. We were given all these machines to test if his sugar levels were too high or too low, and prescriptions had to be called in several times a month. It was a lot. Philip wondered if he could play sports and what his physical limitations were. We were told if he maintained good sugar levels, he could lead a full active life. I even started to look up famous people with diabetes and found some in professional sports and other famous stars, but this would be a big adjustment for the family…and the family was growing.

The following year Tasha got pregnant with my second son. Although we had other kids, this one was special because we planned to have him and he was made by two people in love and married. Plus, this was my first start-to-finish-pregnancy. At the time I didn't care whether it was a boy or girl, I just wanted the baby to be healthy and was ready to be a father again, and this time a full-time dad from the start. Tasha was catching hell with the pregnancy; she was steadily throwing up everywhere we went including the mall and dining out. I felt bad for her and waited impatiently for the baby to be born, but tragically, I almost didn't make it to see the birth.

Val had decided to throw a birthday party at a bar on the other side of town. It was the side of town where I had moved to and everybody called it uptown. We called where we grew up downtown or down the way because we were so close to city hall and the courts, the sports arenas, hotels, and the commercial area. Traditionally, uptown and downtown didn't get along. It was nothing specific, just a couple of individual beefs where dudes were representing their hood and thought they were better or getting more money or had more women, like a competition. Since those were not real beefs, so I thought, I didn't see anything wrong with having the party there. I lived a few blocks away and never had any issues with anyone from uptown.

Of course, my family and a lot of people from downtown came to celebrate with my cousin. Val had gotten pretty popular through owning the clothing store. She had completed her bid like a trooper and didn't snitch and everybody respected that. I decided to go, and, of course, left the pregnant misses at home. The party went off without any issues and it was almost closing time when I made a plate to go but was stopped in my tracks by my brother Ronny. Everything went downhill from there.

As I was walking out the door, I saw Ronny talking to some chick and then some dude decided to chime in. My brother was trying to get her number and this dude was way out of pocket making little comments like she was his girl. Of course, Ronny's attention turned to this dude, wondering why he was all in this business. Now, Ronny is about 6'4" and weighs about 260 and was a little drunk and this dude didn't want it. But he was drunk too and was talking shit because this was his little hangout bar in his hood. I tried to squash the beef but some other dude he knew from his hood started to talk shit to my brother too. The next thing you knew we were all outside.

Dudes from that hood started to gather as my peoples from down the way started to come outside the bar to see what was up. Tasha's sister's boyfriend was from this hood and knew all those cats and tried to calm his peoples while I tried to calm mine. We had managed to get things under control, but the guy from uptown just kept talking shit.

Finally, Ronny reached across me and punched the dude in the face. I was standing between my brother and this dude holding my plate of food as my brother reached across me and made me drop my plate. When it hit the ground, I jumped to the left to avoid getting food splattered all over me. Shortly afterward, I heard gunshots.

I couldn't even tell you where the shots were coming from, and I wasn't trying to find out either. I ran and dipped behind a parked car until the shooting stopped and then immediately went to see if everyone was okay, but they weren't.

I saw Ronny running down the street holding his arm and it looked like he may have gotten shot. I yelled his name, but he didn't hear me. He was running with his man and then got into a car and sped off. I headed to my car to follow him but was greeted by a horrific scene as I ran back past the bar to get to my car.

As I looked around it was like a movie scene: things were going in slow motion to me and I saw people screaming and heard sirens growing closer and closer. I saw a crowd of people hovering over someone. I was a little drunk too and it started to dawn on me that somebody else may have gotten shot.

I remembered my lil' man Leon from down the way was right behind my brother ready to throw down for the hood when the fight started. I refused to believe he had gotten shot, but as I walked closer to the crowd I started to hear screams and see familiar faces. I got over to the crowd and saw him holding his chest around the same time as the paramedics arrived. They pulled up, pushed everyone out the way, and put him in the ambulance. I was numb; I could not believe what had just happened. Then it dawned on me how blessed I was. My brother and Leon were on my right when the shooting started and both of them got shot, so if I had jumped to the right, I would have gotten shot too.

My mind was racing. I heard someone scream that one of my cousins had also gotten shot coming out the bar. He had made it to his car before collapsing, so no one knew. The other paramedics on the scene got him out his car and laid him on the ground. I tried to get close, but the policemen were pushing people back and not allowing anyone near him. Then the paramedics lifted him up and put him in the ambulance. I jumped in my car and drove to the hospital to see what was going on. When I got there, the hospital securities wouldn't let anyone near the vicinity of the ER, which was their policy when there is a shooting victim. However, because of my job of delivering people to that hospital, I knew another way to get in the ER, so I parked and went in.

When I got to the waiting area for surgery in the ER, I saw all five of Leon's brothers and his mom sitting there. This was surreal. I asked how was he and one of his brothers said he was still in surgery and they didn't know anything yet. Since I heard my brother and cousin were at the same hospital, I left to check on them. I found my brother lying in a room with his arm all bandaged and bloody. He had gotten shot in his forearm, but he was ok. He told me our cousin had gotten shot in the shoulder and that he had seen him when they brought him in. He'd talked to him for a few seconds and he should be okay. I headed back to check on Leon.

About 30 minutes later, the doctor came out and said, "I'm sorry, he didn't make it." The room erupted. I had to stop one of the brothers from hurting the doctor. They started breaking and throwing stuff, and I just walked off. I just couldn't believe it. Out of the six brothers, he was the one I was closest to. He was a real good dude, a good friend and funny as hell. He was the first one from the hood with the crazy big downtown medallion. I used to call him "LEROY!" from the movie *The Last Dragon*. The crew watched all six of the brothers grow up and we used to chase their little asses off the block when we were out there hustling.

I felt even worse because this was my cousin's party and my brother's fight. I started throwing up! Damn! My little homey was gone and for a long time it was hard to face his mom and brothers.

Black called me the next day from jail and I told him what happened. I remember when the shoe had been on the other foot and I was calling him from jail inquiring about Petey after he was killed. Damn! Life can be a bitch.

A few months later, Tasha and I were ready for our child to be born. We found out we were having a boy. Tasha carried him past his due date, so the doctor had to induce her labor after a week.

I sat and studied in Tasha's hospital room while we waited for her to dilate. After about five or six hours, it was time. I looked forward to meeting my second son. I had heard all the horror stories about men fainting, and to tell you the truth, it wasn't that bad at all. I think the worst part for me was cutting the umbilical cord that was attached to him. After that, I was good and proud to be a new dad. I thought hard about whether to name my son the third after my dad and me, but I didn't. I wanted to name him in honor of my grandfather. I named him Elijah after one of the prophets in the Bible and gave him my grandfather's name as his middle name, James.

I wasn't scared of babies, but I needed a lot of brushing up on how to feed and hold them. I quickly got the hang of it. Since I was a natural light sleeper, I would be on baby duty every night.

In the beginning, I used to wake Tasha up to take turns, then I said, "What the hell" and started to treat it like my alone time with my baby boy. I was still working about 50 to 60 hours a week and had to get up at 6am, so there were times where I was exhausted and running late for my first pickup with the wheelchair van or bus. Then I would be sleepy when I had to go to class that night, but that was my life and I had to do what I had to do for our future.

Even with working six days a week and having a family, I did well. I finished the year-up with a 3.6 GPA and on the Dean's List each semester, and that was with some points being taken away for repeating two classes from when I attended this same community college over 10 years earlier and had received two Fs because I'd stopped going and didn't withdraw. I applied to SUNY-Buffalo (UB) and because of my felony, my application had to go in front of a review board. Dr. Shatner from ECC was an alumnus, so he wrote me a letter of recommendation and even called UB on my behalf.

I also got a letter of recommendation from a friend of mine named Chris who used to hang with the crew back in the day when we were smoking weed, drinking, and partying. I came to find out that even though he was hanging around with us, he was taking care of his business in school and had acquired a master's degree while I was wasting my life running the streets. I admired him for that; he had his priorities in order. Chris was a counselor and assistant professor at ECC and I even managed to take his class. I made sure I did all the assignments, homework, and regularly attended class because I didn't want to take advantage of our friendship. I think I gained his admiration and proved how serious I was about school and changing my life. After a lot of persistence, I was accepted into UB with the stipulation that I could not live on campus.

As my life at home was progressing, my grandmother's health was worsening. She started to have complications from her diabetes and eventually the doctor had to cut off her leg. Soon after, they had to cut off the other one. I was in disbelief until I saw her and by that time she wasn't really responsive because of the stroke she'd suffered earlier. My aunt was a nurse and was taking care of my grandmother at her house.

I'd tried to bring my son Elijah around so she could see him. Every now and then if she heard him cry in the other room, she'd yell out, "What y'all doing to that baby?" I can't lie, I had a false sense of hope that my grandmother would recover because of my job. I transported senior citizens all the time who had had their legs amputated or had strokes but had recovered and were now talking stuff to me in the van and going to day programs, so I thought my grandmother would get better in time. But that time never came.

I remember when she had to be admitted to the hospital for some complications and I had a drop-off at that hospital, so I decided to go and check on her while I was there. As I walked down the hall, I heard someone yelling in pain and it was a voice I had heard all my life but never under this type of duress.

I ran down the hall and into my grandmother's room to see her squirming in pain and the nurse said she was trying to turn her over. I yelled out to my grandmother, "Grandma! Grandma! It's okay." To my surprise, she knew it was me and said, "Tony, Tony, help me!" I started to cry as I held my grandmother until she calmed down. Then I called my aunt, who was already on her way back and had only left her briefly to go home and change clothes. That's when it first dawned on me that my grandmother wasn't going to recover. She was discharged from the hospital a few days later back to my aunt's house and about a month later I got a call in the middle of the night. My mother, who was back visiting from LA, called me on the phone. "Tony, your grandmother just passed away."

The funeral was at my grandmother's family church and at the same church as my grandfather's funeral. It seemed like yesterday when we all had congregated for my grandfather's funeral and my uncle had escorted my grandmother up to the front to see my grandfather in his casket when she turned to me and said, "He gone Tony. He left us."

When my grandfather died, I wasn't doing shit with my life. I was half-ass hustling, not going to church, out on bail and pre-trial supervision, and about to go to jail. When the call came to say a few words at his funeral, I was not worthy. When my grandfather died I was a disgrace and disappointment to him, but when my grandmother died, although I wasn't where I should have been in life, I was on the right track. I would not let my grandmother be buried without expressing my love and gratitude for my grandparents. I felt empty without them. I got myself together, stopped crying, and sat at the edge of my seat waiting to say my last respects to my grandmother.

When the call came, I sprang to my feet first and told everyone how we all loved my grandparents and how they loved us so much and would do anything they could within their power for us. I talked about how my grandparents had raised me and were so loving and kind. Then I spoke on how my grandmother always saw the good in everyone no matter what. I shared that my grandmother had spoiled me so much she was even willing to buy me McDonald's on Thanksgiving after she had cooked a full course meal. Finally, I said we all knew my grandfather wasn't gonna let his honey bunch stay down here on earth too much longer without him and now they could be together for eternity.

After I sat down, my cousin Matt got up and sang a song my grandmother used to love. He got so choked up that he couldn't finish.

Chapter 13

An Unfair Playing Field

Going into my last semester at UB I had a 3.5 GPA. I began to look into the process of applying to law school. I was scheduled to have enough credits at the end of the fall semester to graduate, but I still planned to walk the stage at the end of the spring semester in 2008. I also had started looking into LSAT prep classes. The LSAT was the law school admissions test you had to take to get into law school, and your score and undergrad GPA determined what schools would accept you and whether they would award you any scholarship money. Graduate school was strictly out of pocket; no government grants were available, just loans. Finally, I decided to call Chris, my friend that worked at ECC to get some advice. I told Chris that I wanted to be a lawyer and he told me that his cousin Jay had moved out of town and became a lawyer and that he would call him for me. As I continued on this journey, I started to realize that God was putting things in a particular order, directing my path and was just waiting for me to take the next step.

Jay was from Buffalo and I knew him from casually seeing him in the streets. We'd see each other, say "what's up", ask how it was going, and keep it moving. One night on my way home, my cell phone rang and it was Chris. "Tone, I got someone with me you need to talk to."

He passed Jay the phone, who greeted me with a "What up, fam?" He seemed very excited and proud that I was trying to go to law school and become an attorney like him. He sounded like the same ol' Jay too, cool as a fan. He hadn't changed since he'd become an attorney. We talked for a second about some old times and people, then he started telling me about what it takes to become a lawyer. Jay was impressed with my grades and asked me why I hadn't contacted him sooner. I told him I wanted to wait toward the end of undergrad to show him my grades as an indication of how serious I was about becoming a lawyer. I also wanted to contrast 'what I was going to do' with 'what I had done.' He respected that!

He asked about my felony and I told him I had done my due diligence and discovered there wasn't a barrier to me becoming licensed in New York. I told him I had just recently signed up for a LSAT prep course. Honestly, I thought he was just going to give me some pointers and send me on my way, but to my surprise, he got on board and rode with me from that day on. We started to talk three to four times a week about my progress and about his daily experiences as an attorney. We were both married with children, so that was another topic we shared and talked in depth about. He always used to say he needed some company and I didn't truly understand what he meant until later.

Prepping for the LSAT was an added burden. I was already working a lot of overtime and going to school full-time with a wife and three kids. Now in addition to that, I was taking the LSAT prep course two nights a week. I even had to pay about $700 for the course after I got some fee waivers. The worse part of the LSAT was the reality that it had nothing to do with the application of law; it was about logic and reading comprehension. By taking the LSAT prep classes, it gave me an opportunity to become familiar with test questions, strategies, and methods of compiling logical solutions under given timed constraints. I went to the various classes and studied as much as I could, given my other responsibilities. But I wasn't able to make the weekend practice tests, and I think that eventually hurt my test scores.

I sat for the LSAT and at the test site I was saddened by the lack of minorities there. I started to realize that I was embarking on whole new territory. I thought about what Jay had told me about "needing company." I also began to realize that all the people here were my competitors for spots in law school and the demographics did not favor me at all. The test was hard as hell, but I got through it and made a point of not leaving any answers blank. I did a lot of guessing, especially on the logical games.

The logical games had questions like: *There were 6 runners in a marathon: Adam, Bill, Charles, David, Eric, and Fred and they all finished the race one after the other. Here are the conditions in which they finished the race:*

-*Adam finishes after Eric but before Fred.*
-*Bill finishes before David.*
-*Charles finishes after Eric.*
-*David finishes after Fred but at some time before Charles*

Then the multiple choice question would ask: *Out of these four answers, which one contains a possible order in which the runners finished?*

Man! I read that shit and thought, *What the fuck?* But I had to get through this LSAT prerequisite to get into law school.

After I took my LSAT, I started to work on my law school application, specifically my personal statement. As I worked on it, I thought about who I could ask to write me a letter of recommendation. I had built up a pretty good rapport with a few professors at ECC and UB--so I thought. I reached out to Professor Shatner at ECC and he was delighted to write me a letter of recommendation. Next, I asked another professor at ECC, a lawyer whom I had taken a paralegal class under. He said he would write me a letter of recommendation, but he never did.

At the time, I was taking a Sociology of Law class at UB, which was kind of difficult but I did well and got an A-. The professor was a lawyer and I thought I had established a good relationship with her. I asked her to write me a letter of recommendation for law school and she said yes, but when I reached out to her again and again, she didn't respond. I was beginning to worry a little. It seemed like too many people were giving me lip service.

Luckily, I had a few other options. I was trying to get, at minimum, one letter from a professor who was an attorney. I had a business law class with an attorney professor and I asked him to write me a letter of recommendation and I honestly didn't know if he would do it. Since I was desperate, I decided to forsake the normal rule of common sense of if you don't know intuitively if someone will write you a positive letter of recommendation, don't ask. I had gotten a B in his class and to my surprise, he said yes. I sent him the forms to send with my letter and he actually did it. Finally, I asked one of my professors who was getting her JD/MBA and about to graduate from law school. She taught a class I took about law as related to films, which I enjoyed tremendously. She had moved back to Virginia after graduation but still wrote me a letter of recommendation. Naturally, Jay wrote me a letter too, but he could only vouch for me on a personal level.

Now I had to concentrate and finalize my personal statement. I didn't know how to approach it, nor did I know how I was going to go about trying to convince admission committees that an ex-felon was worthy of being accepted into their law schools over some clean cut, never-been-in-trouble applicant. In law schools, where image and rankings are everything, I knew a school definitely could not brag about me or make me their poster child for recruitment. I don't think the various alumni and donors would take too kindly to an admission committee letting in a black ex-felon.

I thought about it and with some advice, I decided to hang my hat on the changing of my life in my personal statement. I decided to be upfront with my felony conviction for shock value and would write about how I changed my life. I would include my getting married with a family, buying a home, working continuously for five years while going to school full-time and still graduating with a 3.4 GPA, and not having even a traffic ticket since my release.

I opened my statement with four words: I am a felon. Then, I talked about my new life contrasted with wasting my life, paying my debt to society, and how I wanted to make amends and give back to my community. After I wrote my final draft and got some feedback from Jay and my dad, I sent in my application and waited for my LSAT results. I received a waiver to apply to law schools for free because of my income, or lack thereof, and I immediately applied to about 15 law schools. I didn't want to leave my family, so I had my heart set on SUNY-Buffalo Law School. But I got some bad news and did not know if law school was still a reality.

UB was the one and only law school in my area. It was a second tier law school ranked in the top 100 and gave you a lot of bang for your buck; you couldn't beat it. It was a state school and only cost around $20,000 per year for in-state tuition, which was unheard of.

Schools that were ranked similarly cost $40,000 to $50,000 per year to attend, plus room and board. Naturally, if I got into UB I would stay at home and avoid all those unnecessary costs, made worse by interest rate loans. When I got my LSAT score, I started thinking I would have to go to a lower ranked school.

I got the email one evening and when I saw the 145 score, I was sick. For some reason, your LSAT score means more to the admissions committee than your GPA. I had a 3.4 GPA and needed a minimum score of 150 to 160 to secure a good chance of getting into UB's law school. I wound up taking the LSAT again, and the second time I second-guessed myself and got an even lower score. I decided not to take it again and just hoped I would get in with the score I had. My grades were strong, even though I was working full-time and had a family. I was hoping that some admission committee somewhere would take that under consideration. I knew my felony would be a negative too, so I wasn't feeling too good about being accepted. I began to wait patiently. But my scores wouldn't mean anything if I did not come clean from some situations I would soon face while I waited to get into law school.

In the first situation, I was just driving one night in my old neighborhood headed to my aunt's house when I saw this guy I was in the halfway house with. I didn't know him before the halfway house, but he was real cool and we had some mutual friends. He did a 10-year stretch and was heavy into bodybuilding and built like a tank. We worked out a few times together on the bullshit universal weight set in the basement of the halfway house. When I saw him, I pulled up to him and said, "Yo, fam, what you doing hanging out in my ol' hood?" I should have known better.

He looked in the car and when he recognized me, he said "Oh, what's up, Tone? I was just about to leave. I need a ride."

"Cool, jump in. Where you headed?"

"Around the corner…make a right up here."

"Alright."

Then he said, "Turn right, here." Then when we got to the next block, he said, "Make another right." Now I'm thinking, *One more right and we'll be back where we started from.* Then it dawned on me: this dude must be getting high! Sure enough, he told me to turn right again back onto the street where I originally picked him up. I pulled over. "Yo, where the fuck you going? This is the street I picked you up from."

He turned to me and said, "Tone, I'm fucked up man; I need a blast. Let me hold twenty dollars."

"What?" I replied. "Yo, you must be outta yo motha fuckin' mind. You getting high and you asking me for some money? Man, I got kids to feed!"

"Tone, I'm serious, I gotta get high and I know you got some fuckin' money!" As he turned towards me, I saw the deranged look in his eyes and knew he wasn't going to take no for an answer. I knew that look too well. It reminded me of the look my brother's father used to have when he'd come back to the house demanding money from my mother.

"Man, go 'head. I ain't got nothing for you!" But he acted like he didn't hear me. He started to tense up and stared me down. I realized this confrontation was about to get physical. Thinking quickly, I thought I might be able to bluff my way out this. Angrily I said, "Oh yeah!" I start reaching under my seat like I was going for a gun and said, "I got something for you right here!"

He put his hands up and yelled out, "No! No! Don't shoot me!" He got out my car and ran. I sped off, heart beating a mile a minute. Damn, that was a close one.

The next situation started out innocently from a much needed vacation. My cousin Greg was throwing a party in Charlotte, NC during the CIAA (HBCU college basketball tournament) and asked me if I wanted to go. I told him my money was pretty tight and I couldn't just jump up and take off work. He said it was just for the weekend and that he had a hook-up for a buddy pass plane ticket and it would only cost me $50 round trip.

I told Tasha and made arrangements for somebody to take my Saturday shift at work. I was going to stay at my other cousin Joe's house in Charlotte while I was there, so I didn't need any money to stay in a hotel. Joe had this big house and lived by himself. He was always up for company and had been trying to get me to come down and visit for a long time. So I went home after work, packed, and got dressed up since we were leaving that night and going straight to the party from the airport. My brother Ronny was going too, and my cousin said he would pick both of us up.

I got my things together and waited, then I heard them blowing outside. I grabbed my bag and went and got in the car. My cousin Greg had his man drive to drop us off at the airport, so he could drive his car back home. I started to look forward to this trip. I hadn't been out of town without Tasha since Greg and I had gone to South Beach before I got married about five years ago. Not that I was trying to cheat; I just needed a little getaway and this was a cool man's trip. But my excitement was short-lived and quickly turned into total fright and anger.

As we got into the airport parking area and headed toward departure drop off, Greg turned to his man and went, "Oh, here, I forgot to put this up." I couldn't believe my eyes as he handed him a sandwich bag full of bagged up crack.

I said, "Yo, what the fuck is that?"

Nonchalantly Greg said, "Oh, just some eight balls. Don't worry, I got a stash spot."

"Stash spot? Fam, we are at the airport and if we get stretched they're going to bring the dogs out and everything!" All I could think about was going back to jail for this bullshit. I was still on supervised released and about to finish up my last year in two more months. This would end any dream I ever had about getting into law school. How was I going to explain this? In my personal statement I wrote about how I had changed my life and didn't hang around with these types of people, places, and situations anymore. The more I thought about it, the more I thought about jumping out in the middle of the airport traffic. But I saw the airport police sitting on the side of the road and I didn't want to draw any attention to us. Needless to say, I was sick! This was some bullshit and the funny part was that I was the only one who seemed to have a problem with it; they made me feel like I was the one tripping. Naw, I wasn't tripping, I was just thinking about my future! We parked at the curb and the skycap came over and I practically ran him over trying to distance myself from this potentially tragic situation.

To make matters worse, we got bumped off our flight and had to take different planes to Charlotte. Of course, my plane had some engine trouble on the tarp. I sat on the plane for about an hour, and then over the intercom the captain announced that the plane had to be repaired and asked everyone to disembark. I could not ignore these happenings. It wasn't meant for me to go to Charlotte. Instead of catching an alternate flight, I just went home. It was a signal letting me know my destiny wasn't about hanging out and out-of-town parties. I needed to stay focused and keep my eyes on the prize. Since this was a last-minute decision, I didn't think about the repercussions of going to Charlotte. I hadn't even requested a travel pass from my probation officer, which normally took a couple of days to obtain. Thinking clearly at last, I questioned whether the trip was ever worth it, knowing all I could've lost in the process. No sir!

Subsequently, I started to receive letters back from some of the law schools I had applied to. Out of the 12 to 15, I got accepted to about four, including Detroit Mercy and Dayton. After each acceptance letter, I contacted UB to show them I was a worthy candidate. I was continuously reminded by UB that applications for law school were still being reviewed. Curiously, I got a letter of denial from Thomas Cooley Law School, a bottom tier law school where students go when they can't get into any other law school and usually transfer after their first year. Thomas Cooley informed me that per the admissions committee and because of my felony, I could not even apply there anymore. To this day I still wish I would have saved that letter so I could sue their asses for discrimination.

A few weeks later I received a letter from the UB admissions office. It wasn't a package, just a letter. Normally acceptance letters come in packages and notice of denials come in letters. I wasn't feeling good as I opened it. I read it and it said I had been put on the waiting list. "Well, that's better than a denial," I told myself.

Chapter 14

The Waiting Game

While waiting to hear back from UB, I had a whole lot of other things going on in my life, good and bad. The good thing was I was about to finish my supervised release. Although I had been working continuously and full-time since my release with no police contact, had graduated from a community college, was married with a family, and was attending a four-year college, my sentencing judge still denied an early termination of my five-year supervised probation. The five years would be up and would conclude 10 years of my life dealing with the federal authorities. I was initially arrested in '98, put on pre-trial probation for two years before I went to jail for two-and-half, and served six months in the halfway house and five years of supervised released. Thank God that part of my life was finally over. I always said that I was going to smoke the biggest fattest blunt of marijuana after I got off probation, but things had changed and I was on a mission.

And the other good thing was my pending graduation from UB. It was a big deal to me and my family, but I didn't know how much of a big deal it really was. My mother still lived in LA and came to visit every summer anyway, so this summer she just came around my graduation date. I didn't know that my uncle would fly in from the West Coast. My cousin, who was a corporate exec, came in from Manhattan and Jay drove up from DC. Then to top it all off, my father flew in from LA. My father had never been here before, so I knew this was special. Since everyone was coming in, my wife and I decided to throw a party the day before my graduation. At the party I had the pleasure of sitting at the table with the three men in my life I respected the most: my dad, my uncle from the West Coast, and my cousin Matt.

The next day I walked the stage and was happy, but I was ready to go on to the next step. Before that, I had a matter to deal with regarding my two-year-old son.

About a month prior, my son Elijah had developed a lump on his thigh and it began to get bigger, forcing us to take him to the doctor. The doctor sent us to a specialist and the specialist referred us to a surgeon. We were told he had developed some form of cyst that was retaining fluid and they had to go into his leg and remove it. It was a one-day procedure and not major, but shit, I've never had any type of surgery and now my son was about to have an operation.

We scheduled the operation the day after my graduation because we didn't want to prolong it. We went to the hospital early the next morning. I put the gown on Elijah and then he played until they called his name. I took him in the room and was okay until they put the mask on his face and put him to sleep. I'm not gonna lie, that shook me up.

About two hours later, the nurse came out, said everything went fine, that Elijah was still asleep, and that either I or my wife could come wake him up and go with him upstairs to his room for observation. I decided to go.

Elijah woke up screaming and hollering and I looked at his leg and it looked like it was excruciating. The doctor had put a draining tube in his leg to collect the fluids that we were going to have to empty.

The hospital discharged him after a few hours and I could see that he was happy to go. Even more so, he wanted to walk. Even though he had just had surgery on his leg, my little man didn't want anybody to carry him. He walked out of that hospital on his own like a trooper.

As the summer progressed, I began to see how unrealistic it would be for me to leave my wife and kids to go to law school out of town. I still hoped and prayed that I got into UB Law School. I didn't accept any offers to attend law school out of town, not wanting to hold up a spot for another applicant. At the same time, I was aware that summer was winding down. Around this time there was a community legal forum at this big church where a lot of judges were going to make an appearance and speak to the public; so I went to see if maybe someone could assist me.

As this black judge named Judge Connor was leaving, I took the initiative and caught him, introduced myself and told him I was trying to get into UB Law School and was on the waitlist. Judge Connors instructed me to put on a suit and go up to the law school without making an appointment. He said to ask to speak to the Dean of Admissions when I arrived and tell them that you will wait as long as necessary. Then when I talked with the dean, ask him what could be done to get me in.

I took the judge's advice and went up there the next day, but it didn't help. A couple of weeks later, I got a rejection letter. I was sad, but not defeated. I figured I would just get my application in earlier next year and stay hopeful; I had at least made it on the waiting list.

I went back to work as a driver and started preparing my materials to re-apply for next year. The early application admissions date was approaching in September and it was already August. I realized there was a possibility I wasn't going to get into UB, so I dedicated my efforts on trying to get into a school close to home. I wound up applying to the two closest law schools to Buffalo: Syracuse, two hours away, and Cleveland Marshall (CMU), about three-hours away. CMU was the school where Jay had received his JD and wasn't much more expensive than UB after paying out-of-state tuition. And to top it off, the school had a minority diversity admissions program aimed at getting more minorities into law school. I applied through the program and got in. My intention was always to get into UB, it was just a matter of waiting patiently. If I didn't get in, I would have to leave my family and convince Tasha this course of action was best for the future of our family and that wasn't going to be easy. Plus, I had just started to reconnect with Kenny. His grandmother started to bring him by my house to see me unannounced to Cindy In the meantime, I was about to get the ultimate test of my character and how much I had changed from the street person I used to be.

I was at work one winter day when I got a call to pick up a lady who was going to the methadone clinic to get her daily meds. Since she could walk, she sat in the front seat with me.

When we got to the clinic, I pulled directly in front of a walkway leading to the entrance that had been cleared of snow. She said thanks, got out, and said she would be right out. I sat there waiting when I heard someone yell, "Move that fucking van!" As I looked up, I spotted this frail ass white guy walking across the street headed towards the clinic with his girlfriend. He said, "Hey, you, you fuckin' asshole, I said move your fuckin' van!"

I rolled down my window and said, "Who the fuck are you talking to?"

"You, you fucking asshole."

"Shut the fuck up, you fucking fiend!" I replied.

"Who the fuck you calling a fiend, you fucking nigger?" And then, right there, I lost it!

I jumped out of the van and ran over to his little frail ass. He was about 5'8" and looked as though he weighed about a buck oh-five and I'm 6' 3" around 250. I'm thinking to myself, *I'm about to kill this white boy.* The funny part was that he wasn't backing down either. We were face-to-face in the street and he was still talking shit. Maybe it was the drugs or because his girlfriend was there, but he was acting like he wanted it and I was about to give it to him. I could smell the foul odor on his breath while he was still talking shit with about three teeth in his mouth. All of a sudden, something clicked inside me and brought me back to my senses. I said something, but I know it was God. I thought about going back to jail and everything I was risking, including my job, law school, and my future. And for what reason, beating up a dope fiend? I began to back up and told him he was right and that I didn't want any trouble.

When he sensed I didn't want to fight, he began to talk even more shit and started to call me a punk and a bitch. Man! It took all my God-given strength not to beat the shit out of this dude, but I didn't and I got back in the van and closed the door. But he went to the front of the van and spit on the windshield. I hit the windshield wipers and the fluid sprayed him. That pissed him off even more. He went over to the passenger window I had left down. I saw him headed in that direction, so I hit the switch to try to roll up the window. It didn't go up fast enough and he spit into the window and it landed right on my coat. I was so disgusted and in utter disbelief that I just sat there as I watched him walk into the clinic, still calling me names.

I had never ever been so disrespected in my life. Not when I was hustling, not when I was fighting in the clubs, not in jail, not in the halfway house, and not even by the police. I felt more respected when I got jumped in the club!

My heart was racing and I had so much anger in me I thought I was about to explode. I found some napkins in the glove compartment and I wiped off my jacket and waited for my client to come outside. When she returned, she got in and I left like nothing happened.

The crazy part was he told his clinic counselor that I had assaulted him and they called my job trying to get my name to press charges. I could not believe it. The incident and efforts to file charges really shook me for a while. My job wasn't in jeopardy but if I got arrested, I would have to disclose the incident to the law school's admissions committee.

About a few weeks after this incident, I received a letter from UB. Yes, I said letter, so I knew before opening it that there wouldn't be an acceptance package. I opened the letter and saw to my disbelief that I had been put on the waitlist again. "Ain't this a bitch?" I said to myself. This also opened up a whole new can of worms because the program I was accepted into in Cleveland started in June and the waitlist process could drag out the entire summer. I had to make a choice. As May came around I started to stalk the mailman. It was agonizing going to the mailbox and wondering each day. Then, I almost got caught up in another bad situation.

Things not happening as I had hoped made me paranoid about going anywhere. Even though my situation was less than perfect, I still felt that sooner or later karma had to set in for my past wrongs. I had stopped going out and I only attended mature events with my wife for the most part, but my man Juney was turning the big 4-0 and was throwing a party down in my old hood at the old bar where I used to hang out. I decided to go and holla at my man and join the celebration. Tasha didn't want me to go, but I told her I wouldn't be long. Believe me, I was back home quicker than I expected.

I went into the bar and everyone was surprised to see me. I had separated myself from old people because I didn't have much in common with my old friends anymore. I didn't smoke weed anymore and I barely drank alcohol, maybe a beer or two.

I walked around the bar and said hi to everybody. The place was packed. Besides being Juney's birthday, it was also a holiday, so a lot of people had crowded up in this little bar. It reminded me of back when I was running the streets and we used to have the bar crowded every night.

I went up to the bar and got me a beer, but I felt out of place. This wasn't my spot any more or a place where I was comfortable. There were a lot of new young faces I didn't know or trust. I needed to go outside; it was too crowded and too hot in the bar and I felt like something could happen at the drop of a hat.

I went outside and stood on the side of the bar for a minute and talked to some people. My man had bought the Arab store across the street from the bar, which was still open, so I decided to go over and see how he was doing. I walked in the store and saw his girl behind the counter and asked where he was. She told me he was over across the street in the bar. I informed her the bar was packed and I hadn't run into him.

Shortly afterward, this kid came in telling me how I had inspired him to go back to school. As I was talking to him, my man's girl asked me if I could stay in the store until she went in the back for a minute. I said sure and continued my conversation. Soon a few customers started coming in and I told them to hold on a minute, the owner would be right out.

This guy came into the store followed by two girls. One girl says to the guy, "Why you just punch my cousin!"

He replied, "What? Who is your fucking cousin? I ain't punch nobody."

The other girl said, "Yes you did. I saw you." Then she punched the dude in the face. In short order, one of the girls' boyfriend came running into the store from the bar and they proceeded to jump this dude in the store. They tore up the place, knocking down racks of chips and everything. I could not believe what I was seeing, but I knew I didn't want any part of it. I sidestepped past the ruckus and made my way outside where I threw my beer in the field, got in my truck, and took my ass home.

As I was driving off, I could hear sirens. I couldn't believe what had just happened. I had gone across the street to avoid trouble and trouble had found me. That incident let me know I had to stay away from down there no matter the occasion.

I called Tasha and told her what happened and that I was on my way home. After that, I hung up and jumped on the expressway to the house. I reached for the knob to turn up my radio, but before I could, and as clear as day, I heard, "I told you not to go down there." It was so real I turned my head to see if someone was in my backseat. No one was there. I realized it was the Lord speaking to me. I learned obedience that night.

For the next week or so, I continued to stalk the mailman with no word from UB, and the date to start school in Cleveland was coming close. I had to make preparations to have a place to stay if I was going. CMU had set up some summer dorms for the program, but because of my felony, I was ineligible to stay there. I had to find a place on my own.

About a week before it was time to leave, I called UB and there was no decision on my application, so I had to pack up and make arrangements to head to Cleveland. The summer class I was taking was three days a week and I decided I would go and stay in a hotel the two nights between classes. That way I didn't have to sign a lease in case I still got into UB. This also allowed me to be home half the week with my family.

I would get up at about 5am on Monday morning and drive three hours to make my 9am class and leave going back home on Wednesday right after class. I know it sounds crazy, but I had to do what I had to do to achieve my dream. I attended class throughout June and July going back and forth each week. In the process I got yet another rejection letter in the mail from UB. That shit just wasn't right!

Chapter 15

Sacrificing For a Greater Good

As the end of the summer came, it was time for my first law school final exam. The name of the course was Legal Processing and the professor was notorious for giving hard quizzes and exams. After the last day of class, I had about a week to prepare for the final. Then on the day of the final, Tasha decided to come with me to Cleveland and go shopping while I was taking my exam.

About halfway there I started to hear a noise from the rear of my truck that started getting louder and louder. It sounded like the wheels were going to fall off. I stopped the truck about three or four times on the side of the road to check things out, but I didn't see anything. Because I had to pull over so many times on the way, I was in jeopardy of being late and missing my final exam.

When I got to the city limits, I called a kid I had met at CMU and asked if he knew a mechanic. He met me at the law school and said his mechanic friend was on the way. He stayed with my wife while I ran in to take my three-hour exam.

I couldn't concentrate thinking the problem with my truck might be major and how much it would cost to get fixed, but eventually I managed to get focused. After I finished the exam, Tasha was still with the car and told me my friend's mechanic couldn't fix it and that I needed to take it to a shop. By that time it was late, so we found a hotel and had to spend the night. The next morning I was able to find a mechanic at a gas station to fix the problem for about $300 and we headed home that afternoon.

A few weeks later I packed up my stuff and headed back to an apartment I'd found on the Westside of Cleveland. I hated to leave my family. Philip was 18 at the time and he had started to venture out in the streets, experimenting with alcohol and weed even though he was a diabetic; that worried me immensely. Jada was 12 and Elijah was three and I just couldn't stand being away from them, but I didn't have a choice.

It didn't seem like UB's law school was going to accept me. I truly believed that going to Cleveland would benefit my family in the long run. For too long I had not constructively taken advantage of my God-given ability, and now it was time for me to reach my full potential. I was focused and nothing could deter me.

My apartment in Cleveland had some issues, but it wasn't anything I couldn't deal with. There were times when I couldn't sleep because the old head next door was blasting his music. I remember one evening he must have played the song "The Ghetto" about 20 times in a row. I used to go over there and ask him to turn the music down and he'd be drinking and offer me a drink. The walls in the apartment building were paper thin. I couldn't study there, so the only time I was there was when it was time to eat and go to bed. I pretty much kept the same schedule that I did in the summer, except

I added a day and was attending full-time. I left to go back to Buffalo after my Thursday afternoon class and would be right back for class on Monday morning.

I was really lonely in Cleveland and underestimated the environmental difference and culture shock. I'm a very intelligent person and can hold my own with anyone in any type of conversation, but what do you do when everybody is talking about something you have no interest in or an opinion about? I was around all these new people and had almost nothing in common with them except for the fact we were in law school together. I was older than everybody and not from the area. I didn't want to hang out and get drunk and my background was different. I thought about what Jay said to me about wanting company, and now I know he meant that in more ways than one. Our transition from the streets to this professional law career set us apart and very few could relate and identify with what we went through to get here. I really felt out of place and didn't hit it off with anyone except for a couple of dudes from NYC and my man from Cleveland who had helped me when my truck had broken down. We had a lot in common; we were both older with families and had pasts we were trying to leave behind. I had to try to adjust to being away from my family, living in another city with no social outlet, going to law school, and the fact that there were few minorities at the school.

For most of my life, people said I had a mean looking demeanor, so I tried to make a conscience effort to smile more and to be more approachable. I tried engaging in conversations that I didn't even care about. Ultimately, I started to feel fake and just resorted to being me. Besides, I had no intentions of staying there and the only people I needed to establish a relationship with were the professors and I didn't do a good job of that my first semester.

As a matter of fact, I did such a bad job my first semester in law school it almost became my last. I would see everyone line up after class to ask the professor questions and believe you me, I had questions too but I didn't bother to stand in line afterwards to ask. I experienced many cultural differences in law school that I wasn't used to. One was that I felt like the students were sucking up to the professor by waiting to talk to him after class. Because of all I had been through and my age, I felt like I didn't have to stand in line to talk to nobody; professor or not. I thought I was smart enough to get through law school without doing that. Boy, was I wrong!

To top things off and make matters worse, students were hiding books that everyone needed. CMU was very competitive and I learned that the hard way. I found out that the TA (teacher's assistant) for my contracts class was holding tutoring sessions that only select students knew about. Now, I'm not going to say the tutoring session was just for the white students, but I was initially approached by a student from South America who looked white asking me if I would be in attendance for the TA session. Needless to say, when I went to the session, I was the only black person there out of approximately 30.

All the students had begun to clique up and like I said before, I really didn't have anything in common with them. The few I was cool with weren't in my classes. I carried on a conversation or two but that's about it. I found myself air hustling (secretly listening in) around conversations so I would know what was going on and wouldn't miss out on something. I had to air hustle to find out my torts professor was teaching the class from a first year bar prep book he had written. All I could think of at times was home and family, but I had to do well here so I could get the grades to hopefully transfer to UB. After my first semester grades, that possibility didn't seem realistic.

I finished my first semester and had a paper due and final exams. My legal writing paper was due a few weeks before finals, which gave me time to study. I studied hard! I studied so much sitting at a desk that my ankles began to swell up from fluid. After I finished my exams I was very excited. It was a feeling of relief and accomplishment. I packed my stuff at my apartment since I wouldn't be coming back until after the New Year and the following semester wouldn't start until February, which gave me a nice little break to spend with my family.

It was the holiday season and I was home for Christmas. I was relieved that my tenant who stayed over Tasha's beauty shop was finally moving out. Tasha and I had purchased a two-story building so she could move her salon to a better location and we could rent out the upstairs for added income. The tenant and I had mutually agreed to break his lease because he was getting on my nerves. If it wasn't one thing with him and his girl, it was another.

First, I told the tenant not to park in the driveway on Wednesday through Saturday when the shop was open because the driveway was designated only for pickup of customers and employees. Tasha had to call me in Cleveland and I had to call his country ass. Yeah, he was country as hell. I think he was from Alabama and that was one of the reasons I let him and his girl rent the apartment. I figured since he wasn't from around here he wouldn't know too many people, which would decrease the likelihood of him having a bunch of dudes hanging around the shop. Well, anyway, I told him he could use the washer and dryer in the basement but to remove all of his clothes when he was done. Naturally, this guy and his girl left drawers and panties in the dryer, and when Tasha's assistant goes to wash and dry towels for work, she's not trying to touch anybody's underwear.

I had to call to tell him not to use the driveway or washer and dryer, just to eliminate the problems. Then, Tasha started to smell strong weed odor coming through the upstairs vents. A lot of Tasha's customers are older church going folks, so this didn't sit well with them. Tasha told me the smell was so strong she was scared her customers could catch a contact. So I had to call him again. Mind you, it was bad enough I was away from my family and law school was hard enough, but I also had to deal with this clown. I told him not to smoke when the shop was open or put up some air fresheners and towels under the door or something. I swear I was just tired of this dude and wanted him to go. I thought I would deal with it when I got back home, but he beat me to the punch.

It was right before finals were about to start and I was already uptight and stressed out. The tenant called me on the phone and said someone hit his car last night while it was parked on the street. I said, "Okay, why are you calling me and not the police? What, you don't have insurance or something?"

"Yeah, I got insurance, but this happened because I had to park on the street. If I can't park in the driveway, I want to break the lease." Now by that time I was vexed; I was trying to keep my composure, but I couldn't.

I told him, "Yeah, you can break the fucking lease, but you ain't getting your security deposit back!"

"Fine," he said, "I'll be out by the first." That was cool with me because I would be back home for my semester holiday break and could make any needed repairs and show the apartment to a prospective new tenant.

It was around December 20th and Tasha told me her assistant expressed a willingness to rent the apartment over the shop and wanted to see it. I called my tenant three days in a row and left a message telling him I wanted to show the apartment, but he never returned my calls.

One day while I was at the shop visiting Tasha her assistant asked about the apartment again. I called the tenant again and he didn't answer or call me back. Since I had the key, I let myself in and I could not believe what I saw.

As I looked around the apartment, I saw hydroponic lamps and weed plants throughout. There was a mattress on the floor, a computer, and stacks of *High Times* magazines. This dude didn't even live up here, he was using my apartment to grow his weed. I almost passed out! All I could think about was going back to jail or being caught up in this scandal with headlines reading, "Ex-Con Law Student Uses Hair Salon as Weed House." It would be over for me! Tasha came upstairs, saw the weed, and freaked out. She started screaming and hollering, "This shit gots to go! I ain't going to jail for nobody!" Luckily, her brother was a cop, so she called him and he calmed her down.

Now I'm heated. I get back on the phone and call this dude again and it goes to his voicemail. I left the following message: "What the fuck are you doing growing weed in my apartment? You got five minutes to call me back and get this shit out!"

This time he called me back and said, "What are you doing in the apartment?"

"What? What the fuck you mean, what am I doing in the apartment?"

"That's my shit."

"I called you for three days and you didn't answer, so I let myself in to show the apartment. All I know is that you better come here right now and get this shit out."

He said, "But I'm at work."

"I don't give a fuck! You better come and get this shit! You got 15 minutes."

About 10 minutes later he came speeding down the street. I thought about just taking his shit and giving it to my peoples down the way, but that was the old me. Plus, I had to go back to Cleveland and didn't want any repercussions at the shop while I was gone.

It took him a few trips, but he finally got all that shit out. I called my man and had him fake like he was coming to the shop to see me and had him follow the tenant to see where he was taking all that shit just in case there was trouble down the line. Damn! There's always something going on!

As the new year came in, I began to check my law school account for my grades and my hopes of becoming an attorney became bleak. I got a C+ in Legal Writing, and that was my best grade. Besides that, I got a C, D+, D, and a D-. To stay in law school I had to maintain a 2.0 GPA and I was well below that. Besides that, transferring now seemed to be out of the question. I think the worse part for me was that I thought I'd studied well and had understood the material. I began to doubt myself and whether I was built to become an attorney. This was a turning point for me. If I didn't kick ass next semester, my aspiration of becoming a lawyer would be over and I would be put out of law school.

Chapter 16

Beyond My Imagination

I called Jay and told him about my predicament and he was surprised to hear I didn't do well on my exams. We would frequently talk on the phone about what I was studying in class and he felt like I had a good grasp of the material. He asked me if I knew about conclusory analysis and told me he'd had this issue when he first got into law school and that it affected his grades. He told me that in law school exams you have to show how you arrive at your conclusion in order to get points. I was never told this and when I got my exams back, I could see my shortcomings. I felt better now; I knew what I had to do. The next semester would be critical.

I met with my Contract Law professor and we went over my exam and he encouraged me. I asked him to challenge me in class for the upcoming semester, and boy did he ever. He started to call on me every class, which motivated me to be prepared, and he even asked me for feedback when someone else had already answered the question. Because of this interaction, I learned how to be prepared for all my classes and how to think outside the box. My professor taught me that law is not black and white, much of it is gray and most of the time it's not just one answer to a question or issue.

Additionally, I stopped going home every weekend, which allowed me more time for studying. Sometimes it wasn't a good idea to travel anyway; it was wintertime and Ohioans were in denial about their snowfall and used their snow plows sparingly. Sometimes in downtown Cleveland you had to walk through slush and inches of unplowed snow. I remember when it took me about five hours to drive home, which was normally a three-hour trip. It took me about two and a half hours to get out of Ohio because of unplowed highways.

I did okay the following semester. I got an A- in Property, a B+ in Legal Writing, a B in Contracts & Civil Procedural, and a C+ in Torts. I was good as far as any suspension for poor grades and even thought I might be able to convince UB to accept me as a transfer student. I knew it would be a long shot, but I had to try.

I had tried to secure a summer internship back home through Cleveland Marshall's career services, but their connections in Buffalo were limited. I was going to have to make something happen on my own. I ran into the lawyer who defended me on my federal criminal matter during one of the weekends I was home from law school and told him what I was doing. He congratulated me and told me to call him if I ever needed anything.

I decided to take him up on the offer. I sent him a cover letter, writing sample, and my resume in hopes of obtaining a summer internship. I talked to him before I left and he told me to call him when I got back to Buffalo. However, this opportunity never panned out. I didn't know what I was going to do as far as gaining some legal experience for the summer. Ultimately, bills still had to be paid, so I went back to work with the wheelchair van company. I had hurt my back taking people in wheelchairs up and down stairs before I left for law school, so now I was only picking up people who could walk. I had come to the conclusion that I was at a disadvantage because I went to school out of state and all the summer internships were filled during the school year and I wasn't going to be able to get any legal experience during the summer. But God had another idea. Little did I know I would get an invaluable legal internship that summer with a judge who would become a lifelong mentor.

Some may call it luck, but I was blessed that Tasha's mother and cousin grew up in the projects with a highly respected judge. My wife's cousin called the judge to try to get me an internship for the summer. I was told to come to the judge's chamber on a specific day and time. I assumed that there would be an interview for the position, so I prepared a cover letter and resume, suited up, and headed down to the court house on the scheduled day.

The courthouse brought back a lot of bad memories. The only time I had ever come to the city court building was when I had a case pending against me or to bail out one of my homies. I was really nervous, not to mention that this particular judge had a reputation in the city for being a bitch. In other words, she wasn't going for shit. My biggest fear was knowing I had to disclose my past in the interview. How was I going to tell a person who puts people in jail for a living that I was an ex-con and I should be her intern?

I arrived about five minutes early and rang the bell to her chambers. Her secretary inquired to who I was over the intercom. "TheArthur Duncan," I said nervously. "I have an appointment with Judge Johnson." She buzzed me in.

I walked to the secretary's office and had a seat. As I sat, a court officer came in and I got an uneasy feeling that he was watching me.

He stayed in the office the whole time I was waiting, and then finally the judge called her secretary and asked her to show me to her chambers.

I walked into Judge Johnson's chambers and saw dozens of awards and plaques on her wall. She also had pictures of herself posing with a lot of prominent individuals, which only served to make me even more nervous. I introduced myself and we engaged in small talk about her knowing my in-laws before she told me what I would be doing as her summer intern. *Summer intern?* I thought to myself. *She didn't even interview me and I got the position?*

When she told me where I would be seated during court proceedings it dawned on me that I had been given the internship, but I knew I still had to disclose my past to the judge. I said, "Wait one moment, judge, I need to tell you something. I have a felony conviction and served three years in jail."

She said, "Okay, thanks for the disclosure, but don't tell anyone else."

After that, we left her chambers and she introduced me to the court officer whom I thought was watching me. He shook my hand and said, "Welcome. I heard that we were getting a new male summer intern soon and I was wondering if you were him."

We proceeded into the courtroom and I sat up on the bench with the judge, the court clerk, and the court reporter. I could not believe it! I thought about all the times I was on the other side facing the bench, now I was sitting on the bench with an actual judge during court proceedings. Funny thing, I knew it would only be a matter of time before I saw someone I knew. Sure enough, I started to see some familiar faces. They would see me up there with the judge and would do a double take. A few guys gave me the head nod, like, "I see you doing ya thing." Others were just amazed and when I tried to acknowledge them, they'd turn their heads like they didn't see me.

Oh well!

On one occasion, I had to physically leave the bench. This crackhead I grew up with down the way kept trying to talk to me while she was standing in front of the judge. I gave her the "shut the fuck up" look, but she still kept whispering loudly, "Yo, I need yo number." I shook my head and looked the other way but she kept trying to get my attention. "Yo, Tee, I need your number!" The judge started to get angry and told her to pay attention before turning to me and saying, "Go in the back!"

I was learning a lot in city court and meeting a lot of local people in the legal profession. I found out how much of an honor and privilege it was to be this judge's intern. She was highly respected in the legal community. People even started to treat me extra nice and say stuff like, "tell the judge I said hi and that I helped you out."

As the summer was beginning to wind down, I was again in the non-envious position of waiting to hear from UB Law School for the fifth time (two years on the waitlist and two rejection letters). I told the judge I was trying to transfer to UB and she called the law school on my behalf and even helped me with my transfer letter. As the days passed, it got close to when I had to return to Cleveland for classes and I still hadn't heard from UB. Classes were starting in two weeks, so I had to start getting my stuff together. I had missed the deadline to give the apartment manager in Cleveland notice if I was moving out, so they automatically renewed my lease which was great considering my situation.

But yet again God had other plans and was continuing to intervene in my life. One week before I was about to go back to Cleveland I attended Jay's kids' birthday party. Jay would bring the family from Washington DC back to Buffalo every summer and give his kids a birthday party so they could see and celebrate with their relatives here.

The same judge, Judge Connors, whom I'd met at the community legal fair came to pick up his wife and kids from to the party. He knew Jay and had helped him on his journey to become an attorney. He asked me how law school was. I said, "It's okay, but it's hard being away from my wife and kids. I submitted my transfer application to UB and I still haven't heard from them and I go back to Cleveland next week."

"Oh, yeah?" he responded. "Let me make a few calls and I'll touch bases with you in a couple of days." I left the party encouraged, but time was of the essence. A few days later I got a call from UB and got in. I just had to make up the classes I had gotten Ds in at Cleveland, which didn't present a problem as long as I could stay home.

I hung up the phone with a sense of relief. All I could do was thank God! I knew it was nothing but Him that had brought me this far. He was moving mountains and opening doors in my life.

I bought a bottle of Moet and went to the beauty salon to tell Tasha the great news. I walked in the salon smiling. Tasha said, "Babe, what are you all happy about?"

"No reason, I just decided to buy this bottle of Moet."

"What? Did you get into UB?"

"Yep, I just got the phone call!"

She screamed for joy and the whole shop came to see what was going on. "Tone got into UB! Tone got into UB! My baby gets to stay home!" Everybody in the salon jumped for joy! They knew how hard it was on Tasha with me being gone. I called Jay, Judges Johnson and Connors, and my parents in LA. When I got home that evening, I told Philip, Jada, and Elijah that daddy was staying home and they were very happy. This was a good day in the Duncan household, to say the least. I had finally gotten into UB after two denial letters and a year away from my family. Only by the grace of God!

When classes started at UB, I didn't know what to expect. I wasn't looking forward to going through the not knowing anybody stage, but I was in for a pleasant surprise. I soon find out the students at UB, particularly the minorities, were my kind of people. I felt comfortable almost immediately at UB. Maybe it was just me letting my guard down. Or maybe it was just a New York thing because a majority of the minority students were from NYC, Rochester, and Syracuse, and a few were even from Buffalo. When I was in Cleveland, everybody was kind of standoff-ish and I felt like if I didn't say anything to them, they definitely wouldn't say anything to me. But my NY people were different; they were in your face like "What up Fam?" "What's good?" "My name is so and so…" And it didn't hurt the atmosphere that there were some fine female law students there. I wasn't trying to get at them, I just like to be around and socialize with confident, nice looking people.

My new classmates were so cool that I started to hang out with them outside of class. We'd go hit a bar on school bar night, go to an event, or just have a get-together at someone's house. I felt like I was getting some of the college undergrad social life I had missed out on by being a non-traditional student. And Tasha was cool with it, as long as I wasn't hanging out with my old friends in my old hood. She worried about me getting into trouble, but shit, I did too; I knew I had to keep my nose squeaky clean.

Tasha and I had a big decision to make. We talked about having another baby, but only if I got into UB law school. We decided we would have one more baby and were praying for a girl. After a few months, we found out that God had answered our prayers.

Back at school, I joined and was very active in the Black Law Students Association (BLSA). I went to every meeting and event. I even went to the northeast region annual convention in Connecticut at the Foxwoods Casino. The president of the BLSA rented a van and we drove up about eight deep. Others students came up to compete in the Thurgood Marshall Mock Trial and Fredrick Douglass Moot Court competitions. Besides that, we had fun. We gambled a little and went to seminars, meetings, and parties. Although I was married and older than everyone, I enjoyed hanging out with my new classmates and future colleagues.

I got all Bs my first semester at UB and knew I wasn't going to be an A student. I didn't have the time to study like the young unmarried students. I still had my grades from Cleveland on my record too, so I knew I had to make up for those subpar grades by adding to my social network. I was looking for something to set me apart, so when I heard the president of BLSA, who was only in her second year, say she wasn't going to run for president next year, I sensed an opportunity. I thought about it and talked to a few students to see if they would support me and they said they would. I knew it would be a lot of work and sacrifice, but like I said, I knew I wasn't an A student, so I had to have other things on my resume that stood out. There were a lot of great advantages that could be gained through that position. Plus, I knew it would look great on my record when I went in front of the Character and Fitness Committee. It would show my leadership ability and that people trusted me to lead them. It was a go! But I didn't know if I had competition for the post. I didn't really campaign hard until the election got close, remaining dubious whether classmates would vote for me.

About a month later, the law school had its annual Students of Color dinner where the minority students about to graduate were honored with awards as well as prominent minority alumni in or from Western NY. I wasn't aware that each president of a Student of Color Association, namely the BLSA, LALSA, and APALSA, gave an award to the most deserving active member of the year. I heard the president of the BLSA talking on the podium about a person who was very active in the association and had turned his life around. I thought to myself, *Damn, is somebody else here like me?* Then I heard my name. I had to man up because I almost cried, but I kept it together and went and got my award. I was shocked! After that I was pretty much a shoo-in for the position of president. The one student who thought about running told me he would just be my vice president. I ran unopposed and was told to turn my back for the hands up vote; I'm pretty sure it was unanimous. Once it was official, I called Jay and Judge Johnson and told them the good news. My presidency didn't start officially until the fall of the next year, but as soon as school was out, I started to use my presidency to my advantage in a big way!

Chapter 17

Breaking Through

My cousin in Manhattan gave me some sound advice and told me to practice on my elevator speech. You know when you get about 30 seconds to talk to and impress a powerful individual. Well, with my new appointment, I now had my elevator speech opener and was going to use it to the fullest. Funny thing though, I didn't practice it but I knew what I would say and I got the opportunity very quickly. One of my classmates from Brooklyn invited me to a local politician's house he had met in Albany during a networking event. I started not to go because I was tired, but I forced myself to go and boy, did it ever pay off!

As I pulled up and was about to get out, a black Tahoe with tints pulled up behind me and I instantaneously got a flash from the past and thought it was the police. I slowed to see who would get out before parking. I was pleasantly surprised to see it was the mayor of

Buffalo and that I had him all to myself with no one else around trying to get his attention. I was suited up, so I felt comfortable approaching him.

I walked over to him and extended my hand and introduced myself. "How are you, Mr. Mayor, my name is TheArthur Duncan, President of the Black Law Students Association at UB law school."

He said, "Oh?" and I could see he was impressed. He shook my hand. "So, TheArthur, what are you going to do after you graduate? Are you going to leave Buffalo?"

I said, "No sir, Mr. Mayor. I'm from Buffalo. I'm going to stay here and make a difference."

"Well, we're going have to talk then, TheArthur," he replied.

By then we had made it to the door of the party. I'd had my minute with the mayor and believed I'd made the best of it and made the first of my good impressions that night. I entered the event held at a prominent state legislature's house, and when I met her she seemed very nice. She shook my hand and said, "Hi, I'm Sharon Franklin-Jones." I had heard a lot of great things about this lady and it was an honor to meet her. I also met a local councilman named Mr. Miller who was real cool and down to earth. He asked me what I was doing during my summer break and I told him I was looking for some summer employment that would give me some practical legal experience. He gave me his card and told me to come by his office next week and he would try to help me. It turned out to be a great night. I exchanged information with Mrs. Franklin-Jones before I left and even the mayor came and said goodbye to me before he left and told me to make an appointment to see him.

The following Monday morning I suited up and went to see Councilman Miller from the party. He offered me a paid part-time internship. He told me to call the DA's office and to give them his name for a summer internship. I told him about another summer internship at the city's law department and he said I could do either.

I called the DA's office later that day and left a message on the voicemail. The person in charge of summer internships called me back later that day and set up an interview. I hung up and I had to pause for minute and think. I was about to interview for an internship with the DA's office. Unbelievable!

There was no way in hell I was going to work for the DA's office. I have seen too many friends, family, and myself on the other side and I just couldn't work for them. But of course I went to the interview; I felt privileged to walk in there and say I was there for an interview.

Once again I put on a suit and went downtown about a week later for my interview. After about 15 minutes, the person I was interviewing with came out introduced herself and apologized for the wait before escorting me to her office. I could tell she was a big wig by the way everyone addressed her. Finally, we got to her office. My assumption was correct. I noticed all of her accommodations on the wall, like Judge Johnson's chambers. I thought to myself, *If only she knew.*

During the interview we talked and laughed, and she told me she was good friends with Judge Johnson. She informed me that she had taken the same bar review I was a rep for and we discussed family and finally she offered me a position. I told her I had another opportunity at the City of Buffalo law department, that I appreciated the offer, and would let her know by the end of the week.

I had an interview with the law clerk at the law department the week before and was very interested in working there doing civil law. The next day I got an email from the law clerk at the law department telling me when the internship at the law department started, so I called the lady in the DA's office, thanked her, and respectfully declined her offer. Then I called Councilman Miller and told him what I had decided to do. As his intern, he officially assigned me to the law department for the summer.

Tasha was due at the end of June, but since the baby was a week late, the doctor chose to induce her labor. We went to the hospital one morning and she was given medication. We waited and waited, but she wasn't dilating. They gave her some medication to help with the process, but she still wasn't dilating very much, so the doctor consulted us about a possible C-section. Now, I know women have babies via C-section all the time, but there was no way I wanted them cutting my wife's stomach open if they didn't have too. I prayed she would start dilating at a faster rate. I think we had been there about 12 hours. The doctor and nurses were in and out checking on her. Finally, she dilated enough to have the baby. It was time and the baby wasn't coming out by herself, so Tasha had to bear down and push!

I held her hand and one leg while she pushed and pushed. After a while, I saw this little head with all this hair coming out. We had already named her Lea and she was simply gorgeous! Tasha was bleeding pretty heavily afterwards and was real cold. The nurses brought blankets to put on her, but she was still shivering. I was a little worried, but I didn't let Tasha know it. This was it for us, no more babies. I wasn't going to put her through this again.

Back at work, I took the internship very seriously. At times, the lawyers would go home for the day and I'd be left in the law library still working. I learned a lot that summer about practicing law in the real world. Law school was all about theory and old cases; these were real cases. The two attorneys I was assigned to took the time to help and explain things to me. I was glad I decided to work for the law department that summer.

I began to get ready for my third and last year of law school and the BLSA presidency. Before I could focus my attention there, I got a call from state legislator Franklin-Jones. She told me she had a temporary job available and felt that I would be perfect for the position and invited me to come to her office and talk. I got off the phone and could not believe how blessed I was. God was ordering my steps, one blessing after another. Things were so surreal that I felt like I was undeserving for all the bad things I had done in the past and that sooner or later my luck would run out and things would start to even out with bad things happening to me. But by God's grace it didn't.

I met with Mrs. Franklin-Jones and she told me she had an idea for an educational initiative that was premised on the fact that the high school graduation rate in Buffalo was around 35%. Her idea was to go into the elementary schools and mentor and provide resources for the students in the failing grammar schools. She was instrumental in passing legislation and acquiring funding for some state educational funding and wanted her constituents to be able to take advantage of it. I was excited; more so because she thought that highly of me to want me to be a part of her vision. I knew I had to disclose my felony with her. I wanted her to know who she was dealing with so there wouldn't be any shit later on.

When I told her, I didn't know how she would react, but she smiled and said, "That really confirms that you're the perfect person for this. You've been on the other side and are an inspiration that people can turn their lives around."

This new job started around the same time classes started. Now I had this new job and had to keep up my grades. I was also the president of BLSA and still had to be a father and husband at home. I scheduled all my classes in the afternoon and evening so I could work for the state assembly in the morning. My job at the state assembly mainly consisted of community relations, meetings, and contacting and interacting with local community organizational leaders and politicians. I managed my time pretty well and even took advantage of my connections through my new position.

As the president of BLSA, one of my duties was to promote interaction between the local community and the law students. My first idea was to bring the local lawmakers to the law school to give the students a chance to meet them. It would also provide the local lawmakers a chance to meet the next generations of lawyers coming out of the local law school. I invited my boss, a former state senator, a county legislator chairperson, and Councilman Miller. It was a great event. Even the event planner for the law school was excited and could not believe I'd gathered all of those politicians together.

Next, I enrolled in a trademark class for the upcoming semester and my man Jay was a trademark guru. He had worked for the U.S. Patent and Trademark Office as an examiner and then went on to the private sector and worked at two law firms and had recently gotten appointed to be one of the nine members of TPAC (Trademark Public Advisory Committee) by the Secretary of Commerce. I told my trademark professor about him and the two of them exchanged emails and set up a time for him to be a guest lecturer in my class. I also made it possible for him to speak to the BLSA afterward. By coincidence, he wasn't able to come to Buffalo until the end of the semester, which happened to coincide with my trial tech class trial, so he was able be there and watch his boy in action.

I'm not going to mince words, but my trial tech class was NO JOKE! Now I understand what is meant when they say when a lawyer is on trial, the case consumes him/her. I did trial tech work in my other classes as well as at work. I would pull over from driving to write stuff down I thought I might forget. I put added pressure on myself by taking Judge Johnson as my trial tech professor. She was on me from the start and pushed me to do well.

Normally in a trial tech class two classmates are paired up together and share the duties of the proceeding trial. For example, one person does the opening argument and the other does the closing argument and each would get a friend or relative to be a witness and do the direct examination on his witness and cross examination on the other party's witness. However, my class did not have enough students, so I had to do the whole case myself. I had to get two witnesses and prep them, do the motions, do opening, both directs, both crosses, and the summation. To top it all off, the judge made us memorize our case presentation. In other classes they were allowed to use paper or note cards for openings, examinations, and closings. I think I alluded to the extra work in class and the judge let me have it. She said, "You're not gonna have a partner in the real world and you have to follow the rules of the court and that's whatever the judge allows." I took her admonishment as a challenge and an opportunity to see if I was built for litigation.

My case was a civil matter where I was the defense attorney in an accident in which the plaintiff had left a bar drinking and was suing my client, who ran a light trying to get her sick child to the hospital and crashed into him. I wound up going up against two other 3Ls (3rd year law students), and one was already on the law school's trial team with a lot of experience. My family came to the law school and viewed the trial and even one of my local attorney friends came out in support. I got my cousin Val and my man Chris to be the witnesses and they both did great jobs.

The plaintiff attorneys put on their side of the case first and called their witnesses to testify. Afterwards, I got up and did my cross examinations and did a great job. You can tell when witnesses get argumentative and say something inadvisable and look over at their lawyers. I had both of their witnesses making admissions. I also prepped my witnesses very well and took the sting out of the plaintiff's cross by having them admit things on direct. When the panel of judges came back, they voted for comparative negligence. So basically both parties had faults and a separate trial would have to award damages. I was very excited about how I'd performed in the trial and somewhat relieved it was over.

As I walked out with my family, the professor who wrote the case and ran the trial team for the law school approached me and told me I'd done an excellent job. He asked me if I wanted to be on the trial team for the school. I was extremely honored, but I told him I doubted I had the time since the trial team practiced almost every night. I already had too much on my plate and didn't want to neglect any commitments. I told him I would think about it and let him know, but after talking it over with Tasha and a classmate on the trial team, I knew I didn't have the time. I emailed him and told him no thanks. Nevertheless, this was my confirmation that I indeed had the talent to litigate!

The next semester I organized a minority judicial panel that continues to this day. Because of my internship in Buffalo City Court and my friendship with a number of judges, I was able to get a federal magistrate, a NY Supreme Court Justice, an Erie County family court judge, and a Buffalo city court judge to come to UB for the seminar. This event was a big success, even though I still could not get any non-minority students to attend. I wondered what commitment could be so pressing as to keep them from the presence of these judges with all of their vast experience and knowledge. For some reason, non-minority students thought the BLSA events were just for the minority students. I personally invited them to attend, but they did not and would not. The only event I got the non-minority students to attend was our bar night. Now that I think about it, I coincidently chose to give a bar night at the place where they were going to hang out that night anyway.

While this was happening at school, my temporary job with the state legislator had ended and I was able to get a job as a clerk in a law office. I hoped that if I did well, I would be hired as an attorney after I graduated and passed the bar. I had started my last semester of law school and boy did I have senioritis. I had outlines for all my classes, so I only went to the classes where the professor took attendance, and even in those classes I would go to the restroom and wind up in the lobby talking for the rest of the class.

Toward the end of the semester we had the annual Students of Color Dinner in honor of the minority alumni and the graduating class. As the BLSA president, I had to make a speech about our student organization and what we accomplished during the year and give out the BLSA president award. I got up in front of distinguished alumni, judges, big firm partners, and law school administrators and talked about what BLSA had done this past year. It felt great because I brought Tasha with me and she got a chance to hear me speak in front of all these important people. She was very proud of her man.

Soon afterward, I got a call on my phone from a NY state parole officer. He said, "May I speak to TheArthur Duncan, please?"

"This is TheArthur Duncan, how can I help you?"

"This is NY State Executive Parole Officer Coleman and I have been assigned to your case regarding the certificate of relief from disabilities you applied for." This certificate was the closest thing one could get in New York State in getting all of your rights back, besides a pardon. Judge Johnson told me I would need one when I went in front of the Character and Fitness Committee. I had applied for it about a year and half ago and apparently NY State Parole Division was backed up and was just now reviewing my application. The application was about 10 pages and detailed my past. The application was so invasive that it even asked about previous girlfriends and people you'd previously lived with. Hesitantly, I wrote Cindy's name on the application but didn't put an address because I honestly didn't know where she lived at the time. I just hoped she wasn't contacted somehow. Only the Lord knew what she might say.

Coleman asked me what I was doing with my life and told me to call him after I'd finished with my finals so we could do my formal interview.

I called him right after I finished my finals and he didn't answer, so I left a message. A couple of days later I was sitting at home with my daughter Lea and the house phone rang.

"Hello?"

"TheArthur, this is the Executive Parole Officer Coleman. Can we complete your interview tonight?"

"Sure," I said.

"Then open your door, I'm right outside your house." I guess his M.O. was sneaking up on people. Regardless of all the positive things I told him I was doing, he still felt the need to show up unannounced trying to catch me slipping. But shoot, I didn't care, I was good. I opened the door holding Lea and invited him in. He came in and told me how nice my house was and went over my application. He kept smiling and talking to Lea, saying, "Your daddy is gonna be a lawyer." This was the validation I was looking for.

Chapter 18

One Down….Two to Go

I started to plan for graduation and, to my surprise, family members were flying in from all over to attend. My mom and dad were coming from LA, my uncle from the West Coast, my cousin from Manhattan, and, of course, Jay. It was just like when I got my undergrad degree. I was happy, but this posed a big problem: the law school was only giving out five tickets per student for the graduation, so I had to hustle up some tickets. I needed 14 in order for everyone to attend. Luckily, I was able to get enough tickets to everyone's satisfaction. The day before graduation, the law school had its award ceremony and I got an award for trial tech excellence.

On graduation day I was very happy, but by no means was I satisfied or ready to really celebrate yet. I had a few more hurdles to jump over before I could accomplish my goal, which included the bar and the Character and Fitness Committee, one more daunting than the other. I put my robe on backstage and marched out with my graduating class. There were thousands of people there: all the law school administrators, distinguished alumni, and politicians with their ceremonial robes. At the conclusion of the program, we were individually called on the stage to be hooded, signifying the obtainment of a doctorate, and to shake the dean's hand. I got close to the stage and as the person in front of me went, I began to finally smile. "TheArthur Duncan!" I walked up on the stage and raised my fist in triumph. I had accomplished somewhat of a miracle, being a black man from the inner city with a drug-related felony graduating from law school at age 42 with a wife and five kids. After the ceremony, I took a lot of pictures with my family and friends, including a very special one with my dad, Philip, Kenny, Elijah, and I.

To celebrate, we had a small cookout at my house the next day with family and friends. I enjoyed it but knew come Monday the fun would be over and my bar review would start first thing in the morning. This was a two-month process of straight bar review and study and everything else had to take a backseat.

The bar review sent me these six thick 400- to 500-page review books full of practice exams, statutes, and cases. The class cost me about $4,000, but I got a discount because I was a representative for my bar review and had signed up a few people. Still I ended up dropping about $1,500. The class was a four-hour video Monday through Friday and a six-hour session on Saturday and the bar review instructors encouraged us to take thorough notes. My typing skills were nonexistent, so I wrote my notes by hand. After falling behind in the lecture with my hand cramping from so much writing, I decided to watch the videos online alone so I could pause and go back if I needed to.

For the months of June and July I watched the four-hour videos, which took me about five hours to finish, and then studied for another five to six hours every day. Every now and then I glanced at Facebook or ESPN, but besides that, studying was all I knew.

The videos concluded about three weeks before the exam, giving me three weeks to digest all the info I was given and the 400 pages of notes I had taken. Over the next three weeks my plan was to condense my notes, take practice tests, and study my MNEMONICS, which are acronyms of law issues to help you remember their elements. The test was on the last Tuesday and Wednesday of July. I got a call from the bar review professor out of Long Island on the Sunday before the test. He told me not to worry and not to do any heavy lifting before the test. I appreciated his call and couldn't believe he personally called people.

Of course, the night before the bar I couldn't sleep. I stayed up praying and just thinking to myself. The exam started the next morning in the Buffalo Convention Center at 9am, but the NY State Bar Examiners recommended that all test takers arrive at least an hour in advance. I knew the line was going to be long at the convention center from seeing it personally last year, so I had Tasha drop me off at 7:30am.

When we got downtown, I could see the line had formed down the street and around the corner headed into the convention center in both directions. I told Tasha to just let me out and come back around 5pm. I waited in line for about 45 minutes before I got inside. Security was tight, and we were only allowed to bring a transparent small Ziploc bag with a small snack, personal ID, writing utensils, and laptop if you were typing the answers to the essay questions. I finally checked in and went upstairs. There were a few thousand people inside. I found my designated seat, got set up, and went to the restroom. On my way back, I saw some of my classmates from UB, so we chatted for a while until the PA announced for everyone to take their seats.

I sat down and at the stroke of nine the PA announcer said, "You may begin." I put in my earplugs and opened the test booklet. The first part of the morning session consisted of 50 NY multiple choice questions and the second part consisted of three essays, and we were given a combined three hours and 15 minutes to complete both. One hour was allocated for the 50 multiple choice questions and 45 minutes per essay question. This is where everything went wrong.

There were two types of multiple choice questions I had studied for: the NY multiple choices and the MBE multi-state questions, which were written using different concepts. The NY questions had a right answer out of the four choices while the MBE questions technically had two right answers but one answer was better than the other. The MBE questions were deemed more difficult. We were given about a minute and 10 seconds for each NY multiple choice question as opposed to about one minute and 45 seconds for the more difficult MBE questions.

In the middle of answering the NY multiple choices I realized I had created a problem for myself. I had done mostly MBE questions for practice tests while studying for the bar and had gotten into a time rhythm for MBE multiple choice questions, which proved to be too time consuming. I'd concentrated on answering the NY multiple choice questions in the time allotted for the MBE questions. By using the improperly allotted time to answer the NY questions, I had used too much time and had to rush through the remaining questions. Because of this mishap, I had gone into the time allocated for the subsequent essay questions, causing me to rush even more.

The time issue began to have a snowball effect, and my poor typing skills made things worse. I was making a lot of typing errors, trying to make corrections, and I eventually had to do a retype. I was continuously looking at the time I had left and started to panic. I glanced over to my left and right and saw other people were just typing away. I could see paragraph upon paragraph with typed answers to questions while I was struggling to type sentences. I couldn't type it out fast enough to make up for lost time. My panic mode continued from bad to worse.

I thought about getting up and quitting and just taking the exam again in six months, but I had come too far. I pulled myself together and finally finished my first essay. I looked at my watch and saw that I had less than an hour to do two essays, which wasn't that bad, but I couldn't concentrate. My mind was racing! I kept reading the second essay question over again then started to write, but it seemed like I was missing something. I read the question again and saw I was misunderstanding what the question was asking. I ended up erasing all of what I had written and started again. Sadly, by the time I finished the second essay, I had only about 10 minutes left in the morning session. I read the third question quickly and just started outlining and writing what I could before the PA announced for us to stop writing. All the while the test proctors were around eyeballing everybody and making sure we stopped writing.

After the tests were collected, they dismissed us for lunch. I ran into one of my classmates and we decide to have lunch together. Boy, was that a mistake. He started talking about the test and some issues I didn't remember seeing. While attending law school, I never talked about a test afterward but I let him talk since I had rushed through the last two essays and wanted to know if I had missed anything. Regrettably, it sounded like I did. But I knew I still had the afternoon session and tomorrow to kick ass, so I was somewhat optimistic.

We headed back after lunch and I went and sat at my seat until the test began. I was determined to manage my time better. The afternoon session consisted of two essay questions and a MPT, which was similar to writing an office memorandum of law. We were given three hours to complete the afternoon parts: 45 minutes per essay question and an hour and a half for the MPT. I finished my first essay in about 45 minutes and my second around 50 minutes, so I had an hour and 25 minutes to do the MPT. I took my time and was ready to complete the task. The problem for me was I didn't do any practice MPTs because I thought since I worked in a law office and wrote memorandums of law all the time I wouldn't have any trouble.

The MPT included a library of info and it was the reader's job to discern what was relevant and write the best memo in the allotted time. It took about 45 minutes to thoroughly review all the facts, cases, and statutes, which allowed only about 45 minutes to write the memo. Initially, I wrote a couple of paragraphs in my memorandum of law that I supported with facts from the material, but after that I didn't know what to write. I started to look at my watch again and started to worry about the time. To save face, and hopefully get some points, I started to write down anything I thought was relevant. Then the PA announcer ordered us to stop writing I got up and left after the proctors collected my test, not feeling good at all about the exam and knowing that tomorrow would come too soon.

The second day was all multiple choice, and the bar officials only allowed you to bring a number two pencil and your lunch. The two sessions were three hours each, which included 100 MBE multiple choice questions in the morning and another 100 in the afternoon. I had a pretty good pace going when about an hour and a half into the morning session the woman next to me raised her hand and told the proctor she was finished. About 10 minutes later the guy on the other side of me raised his hand to say he had finished. It made me feel like I had missed out on something. I started to doubt myself and thought about yesterday and really lost my concentration for a while. Then I caught myself and labored on. I finished the morning session and took all my time.

I went to lunch alone on the second day and came back ready to get the test over with. The two people I sat between during the morning session did the exact same thing for the afternoon session. I swear I wanted to just smack the shit out of them! I turned in my Scantron and test when the time was over, then walked out knowing that the waiting game had begun.

I went back to work the first week of August knowing that the bar results normally didn't come out until November. Basically I had three months to wait. I swear I must have gone over that test in my mind about 2,000 times, convincing myself I'd passed then later coming to the conclusion that I'd failed. My application for admission to the NY State Bar was due by the end of September. The bar application was very thorough, about 10 pages long, and included criminal background questions. Since I knew those types of questions were on the application, I was ready with all my dispositions from my arrests. Questions on the application asked about arrests, for what reason, the disposition, and an explanation. I disclosed everything, because I knew how important honesty was at this phase of the game. The NY State Bar needed to be able to trust my word to let me practice law. I countered my negative arrest record with a letter from my pastor and the state legislator I worked for. I also got character reference affidavits from Judge Connors and my man Jay. I got legal employment affidavits from my current employer and Judge Johnson. I also included my NY State Certificate of Relief from Disabilities, so I felt like I had a strong argument regarding my rehabilitation when I went in front of the Character and Fitness Committee after I had passed the bar.

By the time October came around I was on pins and needles. Everybody made it worse by asking me every day if I'd passed the bar. As October concluded, I knew the results would be coming soon. The notification comes via email, and I monitored my phone each night. Then one night, the results came.

I had fallen asleep in my family room when I heard my phone going off. It was a text from one of the attorneys at my job that read, "Check your email, the bar results are out." I went to my email and saw I had gotten an email from the NY Bar Examiner's Office. I could feel my heart beating like it was gonna jump out my chest. My eyes were still a little blurry from waking up, and as I opened the email I tried to focus on the small print. "The NY State Board of Examiners would like to notify you that you did NOT pass the exam taken in July." I was sick, numb, and dead to the world. What was I gonna do now? I couldn't take the exam again for another six months. Would my boss hold a position for me during a retake and allow me to go out on leave to study? What would my family and friends say? For now, all I knew was that I had to go upstairs and tell Tasha.

I went upstairs and tapped her. She woke up and said, "What's wrong?"

"I didn't pass, babe," I said.

"Didn't pass what," she said, as though she knew I couldn't be talking about the bar.

"The bar. I didn't pass the bar." She sat up in the bed and began to cry and I just sat there in silence. Then she asked me how far I'd been from passing. I said I didn't know and looked at the email again, but this time I scrolled down to my score and a breakdown of each part. After reviewing the results, I had to add another emotion to what I was feeling: MAD! I had failed by three points! I needed a 665 and I'd gotten a 662. I was so pissed! All I could think about was my disorganization and lack of time management skills on the first day of testing, which forced me to rush through later parts of the exam. I saw I had missed all those points on the third essay that morning when I had to rush through and outline and the office memo I had neglected to prepare for. I had come too far not to triumph, but failing this test put my family's life on hold for another six months!

When I logged in on Facebook, I could see that almost all of my classmates had passed and were celebrating. I felt sick but I had nothing to be ashamed of. I went to work the next day and told everyone the bad news. My boss said he would support me through my retaking the bar, so I felt a little relieved. God had brought me too far to leave me, and that's when I knew it wasn't time yet. I knew the Lord was dealing with me and ordering my steps, so I just had to continue to be faithful and obedient to Him. I felt like God was testing me to see if I would still seek Him when times got a little tough and things didn't go my way. With that resolve, I began praising Him even more.

Chapter 19

God First!

Just to backtrack a little, I had joined my wife's family church after we'd gotten married and I was starting to get a little more involved in church. I had even been appointed a trustee until I had to leave to go to law school in Cleveland. I was pretty much content at my wife's church; all her family attended there and the atmosphere kind of reminded me of my grandfather's church back in the day. It was a Baptist church with pretty much the same type of program. My wife had basically been going there all her life, but her friend invited her to this new church with a new young pastor. I was going back and forth from Buffalo to Cleveland around the time and using the weekends to study, so I wasn't attending church on the regular. When my wife told me she had started to visit this new church that had a young pastor on fire for the Lord, I had to hear him.

I got the chance to attend the church a few times while I was still attending law school in Cleveland. The church was in my old neighborhood down the way and I was trying to get away from my old hood. But the Lord had other ideas.

Tasha and Jada had joined this new church by the time spring semester ended in Cleveland and I came back to Buffalo for the summer. Tasha attended on Sundays with enthusiasm and even went to Bible study on Wednesdays. She began telling me about all the things she was learning in the new church. She was even re-reading the scripture when she got home. I began to get a little jealous of her. I wanted that zest for the Lord, so I couldn't wait to give this new church a chance. I had attended this new church a few times previously, but I had other things on my mind, like not flunking out of law school and money issues with my student loans. Even more than that, I didn't want to be in my old hood. Despite the possible upside of attending, I didn't want to give this church a chance even though I could see the pastor was on fire for the Lord. Also, I didn't want to blindly follow my wife to a new church. I had joined her family's church before on general purposes but this time I wanted to see how the services were conducted each week, meet the people in the congregation, and, most importantly, wait on God.

Attending the church week after week, I was seeing and having the same positive feelings as my wife had expressed. By growing up in the church, I thought I knew the Bible pretty well and with my time in jail I studied a lot of scriptures, but now I was getting clarity. I was being fed! The pastor's sermons were so clear and he brought forth understanding. He preached on subjects I had heard a hundred times, but when he preached on them he made me think and look at biblical and day-to-day moral issues from another perspective. He brought out points no other preacher did and backed them all with scriptures. I was convinced and felt like I'd waited too long to join. When I finally did, I felt like the Devil had taken a backseat in my life, no longer holding me back.

Coincidently, my oldest son Philip was at church the Sunday I joined with one of his friends. He had moved out a couple months prior. After I went up to join, they got up and joined too. All I could do was cry. My son was 21 at the time and had started to get in a little trouble. I met him about halfway to the altar when I saw him coming up and embraced him in the middle of the church. I just cried and told him how much I loved him. A couple of weeks later, Philip got baptized. I prayed that this would be the beginning of him turning his life around.

I was learning so much from this pastor on so many levels. Besides the word, he led by example. He was caring, genuine, and humble. He was so humble that he allowed another pastor to come to the church and pray for him, which I had never seen before. A lot of ministers may think they might lose members to another pastor by being so humble in front of his congregation, but my pastor didn't buy into any inferiority complex. He wanted any and all blessings and prayers he could get and he'd tell you too. From his example, I also learned that it's okay for a man to show out, dance, clap, and holler for the Lord. A real man is not embarrassed by his love for Christ and will get up and confess it and doesn't care who is looking or what anyone thinks. For the first time in my life, I was shouting in church, crying, waving my arms, dancing, and being spiritually filled. I thanked God for my new church home!

As time went by, I started to meet more people in the church, talking and socializing with some. I joined the men's ministry, which met at the church every second Thursday of the month. My wife and I started out sitting in the back each Sunday and worked our way up to a pew about three rows from the front and sat there every week after I transferred to UB's law school. I was juggling a lot at the time with law school, so I still had to miss church sometimes to study. I would have brief conversations with the pastor when I missed church, informing him of my school schedule just to let him know I wasn't missing church purposefully.

One day at service the pastor let a few members express to the church what they were thankful for. Of course Tasha blew up my spot. The pastor passed her the microphone and she walked up in front of the congregation with tears in her eyes. I honestly didn't know what she was gonna say because we had a lot to be thankful for. We owned our home and beauty salon, we had beautiful kids, we had our health, and we had many other blessings. But she got up there and talked about me being in jail, coming home and working, going back to school, and now about to graduate from law school next year. Her testimony brought tears to my eyes.

Around this time, Tasha had given birth to Lea and we thought about who we should name as the godparents. We took godparenting seriously and wouldn't just pick anyone since the godparents are supposed to take care of the child if anything happens to the parents and the immediate family. We picked my cousin Val and my wife's best friend and her husband to be Elijah's godparents. This was a no-brainer though. My wife and I talked it over and decided to ask her cousin and her husband to be one set of godparents and Jay and his wife to be the other set. I asked the pastor one day after church if he would do Lea's christening and he agreed. Then I called Jay to ask him and the missus if they could make it to town for the ceremony and he said, "of course!"

As my last year in law school began, I attended church and was very active when I could be. I was in church plays and even went with the congregation when we visited other churches. I also gave a presentation for Black History Month. I was okay with my limited involvement for the time being because of law school, but I wanted more. I started to hunger for God in my life and any and all that he had for me, but I just didn't have the time, not yet. After my job with the state ended, I went to work in a law office, then it was graduation and bar prep. Maybe that is the point to be made, because I know my God is a jealous God and I should not put anything before Him. So I considered my failing of the bar as a lesson to be learned and another part of my testimony to be told.

The bar is only given twice a year, so I had time to prepare. I went online and ordered my essay questions back so I could see what I did wrong. As soon as I saw them, it dawned on me. "Duh, you can't type! Why didn't you just write it?" I looked at my essay answers and they were horrible. In my haste to type I had typed a bunch of chicken scratch misspelled words. To tell you the truth, I couldn't believe I had gotten this close to passing the bar with some of the stuff I'd typed. It was difficult for me to discern what I meant. This gave me confidence that I would probably make up three points just by clarifying what I tried to say in my typing. Since I still had time to prepare for the next exam period, I decided to retake my bar prep course to refresh and concentrate on doing timed practice tests.

Besides studying for a retake, I was working and going to church every chance I got. Despite failing the bar, I still had so much to be thankful for and if God didn't do another thing for me, He had done enough and I wanted to keep thanking Him.

One Sunday morning in church Elijah, who was seven at the time, told me he wanted to go up to join church and get baptized. I smiled at him as he walk up to the altar and told one of the ministers he wanted to get baptized. Praise God! The minister directed him to sit in the side pews and I went over and sat with him. Tasha cried, as usual, but this time I managed to keep it together-- until the following week.

My son was scheduled to be baptized the next Sunday and our pastor had always stressed that a person can get baptized again, especially if the person was a child and may not have fully understood baptism the first time. That resonated with me since I had gotten baptized at a very young age and had done a lot of dirt in my life that I needed to cleanse away. I texted the pastor and asked him if I could get baptized too. He said that it would be "awesome."

The next morning when we got to church, my son and I went into the dressing room to change. When we came out into the congregation, several of our family members had showed up to see Elijah getting baptized and were unaware I was getting baptized too. I told Elijah to go first after the ladies went so I could see him. Seeing my son getting baptized just filled my heart with the spirit of joy. I was so proud of him and by the time I walked down into the water I was shouting and praising God. They dipped me down in the water and I came up thanking God for allowing me another chance to get it right!

I continued to attend church every week when I began to feel a little stagnated not knowing how to take the next step in my walk with Christ. I talked to the pastor about it and before he could respond I told him I needed to step up my game in seeking the Lord. He said, "You know you telling on yourself, right?" It was this type of self–indictment that directed my path. I knew I could give the Lord more time by reading, studying, and building a relationship with him. We talked for a while and he said that God had laid something on his heart regarding me but he had to pray on it and he would let me know. I told Tasha and she was like, "Oh, Lord, anything but a preacher!" Ironically, my grandmother had said the same thing when my grandfather was called to preach. My grandfather had also dreamed about three robes and believed that three of his descendants would be ministers. Unfortunately, he did not live to see any of us become ministers, and as of this writing, it has not come to pass.

A few months later around Christmas, the pastor told me that he wanted to meet with me. I was very anxious about the meeting. I had come so far with God directing my path and the only things I was scared about were not being obedient and faithful enough and God leaving my side. I came to the meeting with expectations and God filled them. I sat down with the pastor in his office and we joked for a while. Besides being a powerful man of God, my pastor liked to joke, so you had to be on your toes or he would get a good one on you.

Then the conversation turned serious when I told him about my past and all the things God had done for me. I talked about my grandfather and the dreams I had in jail. I think he knew how much I loved God and believed in Him. He told me he knew I had a story to tell but didn't know just how much I had endured. I told him I had to be faithful. He asked me about my wife and my marriage. I still didn't know what God had laid on his heart concerning me, yet. Finally, he asked me to serve as a deacon for the church. I was speechless and brought to tears.

I said, "I am honored you think that much of me and my walk with Christ to ask me to serve." Immediately, the Devil told me I wasn't ready or fit, so I began to doubt myself. I told him I didn't want to embarrass the church and that I still liked to go out and have a few drinks now and then. He told me to not stop drinking because of the position and to not be fake by not doing it in public but going home to do it instead. God sees all regardless.

Then he said he'd asked about my wife and my marriage because my wife and I were one in the church. As I served as a deacon, my wife would be a deaconess. He recommended I go home and talk to Tasha about the position before I gave my answer. By the time I looked at my watch, we had been talking in his office about three hours. Boy, my pastor can talk.

As soon as I got in the car I called my wife and told her. She had her reservations just like I did. She didn't think she was ready and had a lot of questions, so many that I texted the pastor to set up another meeting with both of us. Luckily, he was available to meet with us a couple days later. Similar to when I met with him, Tasha told the pastor that there were some things she was still dealing with in her flesh. He understood and said that he didn't expect us to be perfect. After that, Tasha felt at ease and we accepted our appointments. He told us that it would probably be another month or so before we were installed and he would let us know.

As we walked out he made a joke that Tasha didn't find funny. He said, "I was only a deacon for a year before I started to preach," and laughed. Boy, if you could have seen the look on our faces. Tasha was looking so crazy at me and I know I was looking just as bugged.

A couple of weeks later I was at our monthly men's meeting when the pastor told me I had been unanimously selected by the deacons to join the board. He said, "Get your black and whites together and tell the wife to get her whites for this Sunday!"

That Sunday we were instructed to sit in the front pew and I really couldn't enjoy church because I didn't know in which part of the service he was going to install us. We were seated away from our kids, who were sitting with my wife's mother. The congregation did not know about the installation, but they had to be wondering why we were sitting there. As the service went on, I began to become more and more anxious and then finally the pastor got up and preached the sermon for the day. We had both grown impatient and after he had started his sermon and didn't do it, I figured the Lord had lain on his heart not to do it just yet.

After he concluded his sermon, he said, "You all might be wondering why the couple in front of me isn't sitting in their normal seats." That's when I began to tear up. I couldn't tell you another word he said after that. I could just feel the spirit of the Lord upon us. The only thing I do remember him saying to the congregation was to no longer refer to me as Brother Tony or Brother Duncan and for everyone to refer to me as Deacon Duncan and my wife as Deaconess.

For weeks afterward, the pastor would joke with me and say, "Deacon Duncan, I like the way that sounds!" About a month after I was installed in as a deacon, I had to retake the bar, but this time there were two of us in the fire! And the other one looked like the son of God!

Chapter 20

My Season

The morning of the test I got up, had some coffee, and got my things together. I knew the routine from last time, so I had my transparent Ziploc bag to keep my wallet, pens, and paper. I didn't take my laptop this time because I was going to handwrite the essays. I told Tasha I was leaving and that I would drive myself. The last time she dropped me off I left all my study materials in her car, so I thought if I needed to look at some things at the lunch break I could get in my truck to study. I got in my truck to leave and left the radio off and just prayed all the way downtown during my 15-minute trip from my house.

I arrived downtown and drove around to the convention center where the test was held and saw that it wasn't as crowded as it had been when I took the test in July. It was probably less than half because the majority of the candidates graduated in May and took the bar in July.

When I walked into the convention center, I saw a few faces I recognized from school. I guess I wasn't the only one who didn't get a favorable result on the last exam. I nodded my head at the ones I made eye contact with. The others didn't look my way; I guess they were too embarrassed to speak or just nervous about retaking the exam. I went upstairs and found my seat. The exam proctors started to come around to check names and then the PA announcer told everyone to take their seats. The proctors passed out the exam and at 9am we began. I opened up the test booklet and started on the first 50 multiple choice questions I had taken too long to answer the first time and started to knock them off one by one. I was answering the questions so quickly and effortlessly I thought either they were going to get harder toward the end or I needed to go back and check my answers. I looked at my watch and saw I was way ahead of schedule, so I slowed down and took my time. I finished the 50 questions in 45 minutes and then took another 10 minutes to go over my answers. I proceeded to the morning's three essay questions.

The first essay question was a contract matter like in the July exam, but this time I was ready. I made a short outline and then dug in, scribbling out page after page. I used an erasable pen so my writing wouldn't get dull from using a pencil and so I could still erase mistakes. I finished the final essay with about 15 minutes left, but I'm the type of person who doesn't believe in wasting time. I went back to the other essay questions and started to add details. The PA announcer informed us it was time to stop. The proctors came around and collected the test papers and answers and I went to lunch. I felt great and instead of studying, I called Tasha and then Jay. I knocked out the afternoon session and went home to get ready for the second part.

The next day was the multi-state multiple choice question day, which I had done pretty well on the first time I took the exam, so I only needed to duplicate my past success. Just in case I got tired or drowsy that day, the guy who sat next to me decided he would help keep me awake and alert by not bathing the night before. I mean, I had to keep my head turned away from him during the exam. Every time I forgot and turned in his direction, BAM! I survived and finished the second day of the bar and went home confident, but knowing the waiting game had begun again.

Since less than half of the bar applicants took the bar in February, the process of getting test results was almost cut by two months. My character and fitness evaluation would be in May and the swearing in would be the following month, if my retake was successful. Of course, I experienced the same reruns of people asking me when I would know the test results or if I'd passed. As soon as I was able to settle down and get the test off my mind, someone would ask again. I found comfort through my belief in Christ and my growing relationship with Him. I knew God didn't give us the spirit of fear, so I endured. I continued to serve Him and enthusiastically embraced my position as a deacon.

About a month before the bar results were due to come out, I got a call from the Fourth Department Appellate Division telling me that my bar application wasn't complete. I had listed a legal internship without supplying an affidavit from a person to verify it. As I was calling around and going to see people to get this matter rectified, it dawned on me that no one asked me for this information the first time around and I hadn't sent any new information. It made me think that bar applications were only open to candidates who passed. It made perfect sense because it would save the appellation division from doing extra work by not processing an application of a person who didn't pass. It was a good theory but I didn't know for sure if this was true. I was able to get my situation rectified, which completed my application. By that time, I had gone over the essay questions on the exam about a million times in my head and was very confident I had passed. It was just a matter of getting the notice. Then I started worrying about character and fitness.

A few weeks went by and I decided to go on the NY State Bar Examiners website and see the dates they'd released the results for the February bar for the last five years. According to the dates, the results would be coming out in a few days. I checked the website every day thereafter, and the day I didn't check the website an attorney informed me the results from the tests would be posted the next day. So that meant I would get an email tonight. After work, Tasha and I went over to her brother's house, ate, and had some wine. I didn't tell her about the results coming out because I didn't want her to worry.

That night, I tried to stay up and wait, but was full from over-indulging at my brother-in-law's house. I fell asleep around 11pm without the email results. I woke up around three to use the bathroom and looked on my phone and saw I had an email from the NY State Bar Examiners. This was it! I started to read: "The NY State Bar Examiners would like to notify you that…" It was dark in the room and my eyes were not focusing properly. It looked like the next word was "passed," but I had to re-read the whole sentence. "The NY State bar examiner would like to notify you that you PASSED the NY State Bar…" I had done it! I felt a great weight coming off my shoulders.

I tapped Tasha and woke her up. Instead of just telling her, I said, "Look! Look!" Because she was asleep, it took her a minute. She finally read the email and began to scream and jump on the bed and dance. "Thank God! Thank you Lord!" That part was over, but there was still one more hurdle to get over.

The next day I called Jay on my way to work. He said, "That's what I'm talking about!" Then he asked me why I hadn't called him in the middle of the night after I had gotten the email. He was right to feel somewhat excluded. He had been there for me since day one. After I got off the phone with him and got to work, I marched into my boss's office and sarcastically demanded a pay raise. He looked at me and said, "You must have passed the fuckin' bar."

Because of the time difference, I waited a few hours to call my mother and father in Cali and tell them the good news. They asked me what was next and I told them I had to go in front of the Character and Fitness Committee when I got my notification.

The committee was a group of prominent local lawyers and judges who decide whether an individual is morally fit to practice law. I think my mom sensed I was a little worried and told me God had not brought me this far to abandon me now. I told myself not to worry. Again, I wasn't alone. There were two of us in the fire!

My mother, who was still living in LA at the time, was moving back East after retiring and timed my hopeful swearing in with her moving back so she could attend the ceremony. Since my dad came the previous year for my graduation, I didn't think he would make it back for my swearing in ceremony. He called and asked me if my household could accommodate five extra people. After I said yes, he told me his wife, my brother, and my two sisters were all thinking about coming. He wanted me to ask Tasha first, although I knew she would say yes and that they would be more than welcome. I talked to Tasha about it later and called my dad to tell him it was fine. Of course, with prospective company coming in from out of town, Tasha put on her HGTV gloves and started cleaning, painting, and re-decorating. Not that I was worried, but now I had to get past the committee!

I got my notice in the mail of when and where the Character and Fitness Committee hearing was taking place. Not by coincidence, the men's ministry was having its men only shut-in at my church the night before. We had a great turnout of about 50 men. We were split up into four groups with four facilitators and four different topics to discuss. I was enlightened and uplifted by listening to the struggles of other good Christian men trying to live right and seek Christ. They shared personal stories of forgiveness, which really resonated with me. When I see people in the streets who have wronged me, my family, or someone in my crew back in the day, I still struggle to forgive them. Then, because I am a deacon now, I would try to discount my feelings by saying I have the love of Christ for them. My inability to forgive was hypocritical, as one of the main tenements of the Christian religion is to forgive. How can I expect everyone to see the new me and not judge me for my past when I won't do the same for others? I was a hypocrite!

The other thing I learned that night was that I needed to meditate and let God do the talking sometimes instead of always praying and talking to Him. I needed to do some listening, concentrate on Him, clear my mind, and listen for His voice.

I left the meeting at about 1am and had to be at the hearing at 9 the next morning. I went home and prayed before going to bed. I woke up the next morning and Tasha had already left for work and the kids had spent the night with relatives, so I was home alone. I looked on my phone and Tasha had left a message for me to call her once I was on my way so we could pray before the hearing.

I was on the expressway and about to call Tasha when I thought about last night's meeting and meditating. I turned off the radio and concentrated on God. While I was trying to clear my mind, all kinds of voices and thoughts were going through my mind. God spoke to me and said, *Call your wife and tell her that everything is going to be okay.* I could discern His voice and knew when God talked to me, so I picked up my cell and called Tasha. However, I still felt like I needed to be prepared for questions the committee would likely ask about my past. I had been going over different scenarios and possible questions for weeks that they might ask. I would need to explain every arrest and take full responsibility for my actions and let them know I'd learned from my past indiscretions. I believed I would get through the intense drilling because it was God's will.

I parked my truck and brought out my small pocket-sized Bible to read while I waited. When I walked into the room, there were approximately 70 to 80 people there. The hearing started when a lady walked up to the podium and introduced herself and all of the lawyers and judges on the committee. Each committee member had a stack of applications they would call one by one. I had heard when there's a question regarding your fitness to practice law, you had to go in front of a panel of the committee members, so I knew that my one-on-one meeting wasn't going to be my only interview. Plus, I figured my file would be at the bottom and I would probably be one of the last to be called.

As I sat there, I couldn't help but think that all of my preparation may have been for nothing. My dreams and everything I'd worked for over the past nine years had come down to this day. I knew that even after all I'd gone through to complete all the prerequisite steps in this process that the committee could still squelch my aspiration. That was the chance I took and I'd gladly do it all again. Worst case scenario was they'd say no, but I still had a doctorate of law degree from one of the top law schools in New York.

Along the way, old acquaintances and some family members looked at me like I was crazy and could not believe what I was trying to do. Hell, they didn't even think my goal was obtainable given my prison record. I quit my job of seven years and even had to go to another state and leave my family for a year in pursuit of my goal. I'd had my ups and downs, but I didn't waver in believing I could do it. I was optimistic about things I could control for the most part, but now I was here, and the decision was out of my hands.

I couldn't help but wonder if I had done enough over the past nine years to convince the committee I had changed my life or if I could've done more. I kept going over questions I thought the committee might ask me concerning my past and the way I would answer them. I overheard this white guy behind me tell his friend that he was worried about a disorderly conduct arrest he had gotten during undergrad. His concerns, I thought, were laughable compared to my own.

There were only six people waiting to be called when an attorney came out and said, "TheArthur Duncan." It was showtime! I shook his hand and thanked him for pronouncing my name correctly and we had a little laugh. We went in the room and sat down and he told me I had some very impressive letters and recommendations. He asked me about my pastor and his letter and about the work I did with the state legislature. He told me he called my boss and a few other people and everyone spoke very highly of me.

Then he said, "You know you have a felony and because of it I believe you have to go in front of a panel of the committee automatically."

I thought to myself, *Yeah, here it comes. I was waiting for this. They're gonna grill me.*

I started to go into my spill about taking full responsibility for my past and he stopped me and said, "I've been doing this for a long time and you're a prime example of a person who has turned his life around and what you did was a very long time ago." He continued with, "If I were you, I wouldn't worry about it. I'm recommending that the committee okay your application." He told me to go back into the waiting area and he would call me when a panel of the committee was ready to see me.

I went back into the room and sat there for another five minutes.

The attorney who interviewed me came out and called my name. I got up thinking, *Okay, here we go.* Instead of taking me to where the committee members were, he took me in the nearest room and said, "I thought that it was an automatic hearing because of your felony, but it's not. The committee okayed you, you can go home." I was speechless. I called Tasha as soon as I got on the elevator and told her it was a done deal. Ain't God good?

About two weeks later I got the official invitation for my swear-in held in Rochester. The invitation didn't specify how many people could come, so I did some minor research and didn't find where there was a limit to invitees, so I told the whole family they could come.

My dad had flown in from Cali with his wife and my sisters and brother. It was my stepmother's and siblings' first time in Buffalo, so we introduced them to some of our world famous chicken wings and pizza. On Saturday, we went to Elijah's baseball game and Niagara Falls. The next day we all got up and went to church and out to eat afterward. I went to bed that night thinking, *Finally, my day has come.*

The next morning I got up and I was ready! Rochester is about an hour drive away. We went four carloads deep, about 17 of us, and got to the place before it opened. People were gathered outside waiting. Finally, some individuals from the swearing-in committee opened the door and let everyone in and directed the candidates to sit in the front rows of the auditorium. I sat there in wonderment. I couldn't believe my dream was about to come true. I could hear my daughter Lea up in the balcony acting fussy. All I could think was, *Now I can take care of my family and we can live.*

The ceremony wasn't long at all. An executive clerk introduced all the judges from the Fourth Department Appellate Division and there were two guest speakers. Afterwards, the executive clerk said, "Candidates, rise and raise your right hand and repeat after me." Just like that, it was done. I, TheArthur Anthony Duncan II was sworn in as a licensed counselor and attorney at law in the State of New York.

As I walked toward the back, I saw my family coming down the balcony and I just felt like I was walking on air. I hugged Tasha and began to cry. Then I saw my dad and I just let it all hang out. I hugged my dad and cried and said, "I did it, dad. I did it!" To God be the Glory!

TheArthur Anthony Duncan II, Esq. is an attorney in Buffalo, New York. He was born in Los Angeles, California in 1969 to parents, TheArthur A. Duncan I and Betty Smith. However, TheArthur was primarily raised in Buffalo, New York by his grandparents, Reverend James V. Smith and his wife, Mary Jane. TheArthur's grandfather pastored his own church where, TheArthur was very active at a young age. He attended regularly, sang in the youth choir and even served as a junior deacon. He is affectionately called Tony or Tone by close friends and family, as his father is known as Big Tony.

In grammar school in Buffalo, TheArthur was always the smartest one in his class and topped the honor roll every year. In 1982 when the schools were integrated in Buffalo and he was bussed to a predominately white South Buffalo neighborhood school, he was voted the first black 8th grade class president. TheArthur left Buffalo the following year and moved back to Los Angeles to live with his mother and attend high school.

After graduating from high school in Los Angeles and briefly attending college, TheArthur came back to Buffalo to visit and decided to stay. Thereafter, he began to sell drugs with some childhood friends and was eventually incarcerated for 3 years. Upon his release from prison, he was able to turn his life around; hence the subject of this book. Subsequently, TheArthur graduated from law school at age 43 in 2012 and was sworn into the New York State Bar in 2013.

TheArthur is married to Latisha Duncan and has five children: Frankie, Joi, Isaiah, Lauren and Kimanie. He is also a deacon at First Calvary Missionary Baptist Church and servant leader in the church's "Boys 2 Men" mentoring ministry and marriage ministry. In his spare time, he enjoys spending time with his family, traveling and writing. To God Be the Glory!